ONE CHRISTMAS EVE

SHARI LOW

Boldwood

First published in Great Britain in 2023 by Boldwood Books Ltd.

Copyright © Shari Low, 2023

Cover Design by Alice Moore Design

Cover Photography: Shutterstock and iStock

Every effort has been made to obtain the necessary permissions with reference to copyright material, both illustrative and quoted. We apologise for any omissions in this respect and will be pleased to make the appropriate acknowledgements in any future edition.

A CIP catalogue record for this book is available from the British Library.

Paperback ISBN 978-1-80426-882-7

Large Print ISBN 978-1-80426-881-0

Hardback ISBN 978-1-80426-883-4

Ebook ISBN 978-1-80426-880-3

Kindle ISBN 978-1-80426-879-7

Audio CD ISBN 978-1-80426-888-9

MP3 CD ISBN 978-1-80426-887-2

Digital audio download ISBN 978-1-80426-885-8

Boldwood Books Ltd
23 Bowerdean Street
London SW6 3TN
www.boldwoodbooks.com

To the Murphys, the LeCombers and the Lows,
Who continue to come to us for Christmas every year,
Despite the fact that I haven't managed to cook a decent festive
meal in twenty years.
I love you all.
Shari x

A NOTE FROM SHARI

Dear Reader,

Thank you for choosing *One Christmas Eve*. I can't wait for you to meet Eve, her mother, Helena and her irrepressible gran, Cathy.

Like many of my novels, the action takes place over the course of one day, and in this book, that day is Christmas Eve.

But there's a twist.

The three storylines are set on Christmas Eve in three different decades.

Eve's chapters capture the story of how her day unfolds on Christmas Eve in 2023.

Her mum's chapters follow Helena through the course of Christmas Eve, 1993, when she was about to turn twenty-five years old and starts the day with no idea of the surprises and shocks in store for her before midnight.

And Eve's gran, Cathy's chapters are set on Christmas Eve, 1968, when twenty-year-old Cathy is forced to make a decision that will determine the course of all their lives for generations to come.

From the second I had the idea for this book, I was excited about showing the Christmas Eve of the sixties, the nineties and then the present day and I adored exploring how the decisions made by the women in the past impacted the daughters who came after them.

So thank you again for reading this book and I hope you love visiting three decades, with three generations of women, whose lives were forever changed on One Christmas Eve.

Love,
Shari xx

8 A.M. – 10 A.M.

1

EVE QUINN

24 December 2023

T'was the day before Christmas... and it was absolutely bugger all like the traditional Christmas poem.

Admittedly, Eve Quinn's open-plan kitchen slash living room did bear a slightly disturbing resemblance to the Christmas scene in John Lewis's window. Largely thanks to Gabby, her theatrical flatmate who loved to create dramatic scenes of wonderment, there were silver tinsel strands draped on every wall, fairy light curtains on the windows, and fake snow on every surface. There was also a huge real tree in the lounge that was so big, it blocked half the telly, but they didn't care because it was beautifully bedecked in silver and white balls, and under it lay a pile of perfectly wrapped gifts, courtesy of a night with a bottle of wine, three rolls of wrapping paper, two reels of ribbon and a gift-wrapping tutorial on TikTok. On the radio, Mariah Carey was still demanding that all she wanted for Christmas was a big fat royalty cheque for the most over played festive song of all time.

Yet absolutely none of that mattered to Eve, who was sitting at the kitchen table, staring at her laptop screen again. Staring. Still staring. Just as she'd done for varying amounts of time since the results from the Ancestry DNA test had dropped in the day before.

'You're staring at it again,' Gabby pointed out the obvious, as she passed a skinny soy latte in a reindeer mug to her.

'I know. It's because I still can't quite believe it's true.' Eve took the coffee and, without breaking her gaze on the screen, spooned several sugars from the bowl in the middle of the kitchen table into the mug. She didn't have to look up to know that Gabby would be rolling her eyes at the sugar consumption. Her friend's mission to get her on to a lactose-free, gluten-free, vegan, yoga-bendy, Pilates-crunching, paragon-of-health lifestyle had just fallen at the first hurdle of the day. For the 2007th day in a row. Eve decided she'd be better tomorrow. For the 2007th day in a row. 'I mean, why wouldn't she tell me? Why wouldn't anyone tell me? Merry Christmas, Eve – your gift is a different dad. Hope you love it.'

Gabby sat down on the pine bench on the other side of their kitchen table and pulled the knees of her green and red stripy Grinch pyjamas up to her chest. 'Maybe no one knows. You might be one of those stories that they make Netflix documentaries about – swapped at birth and it's only discovered twenty-nine years later, when the person needs some kind of transplant – and bam!' Gabby's flair for the dramatic was ramping up. 'They find out that the parents aren't a match because they don't share any DNA. Then they reveal there was a mix-up in a maternity ward because a doctor had worked an eighteen-hour shift and was so tired that she confused the wrist tags. I think you need to check if anyone famous had a kid on the same day you were born. I've always thought you bear a weird resemblance to Nicole Kidman. Only shorter and with a greater fondness for calories.'

Eve took a sip of her coffee and waited until her teeth stopped aching from the sweetness of it. She usually only took two sugars. Must have been distracted again. 'Thank you. I think. Although the chances of Nicole Kidman giving birth twenty-nine years ago in a Glasgow hospital are pretty slim, so I'm thinking there's probably a more logical explanation.'

'You're right!' Gabby leaned forward, elbows on the table. 'You were stolen. From the hospital. Your mother, Saint Helena of the Holy Humour Bypass, ramraided a maternity ward and escaped with you in her Prada backpack.'

'Oh no she didn't.'

'Oh yes she did.'

The non-Kidman-like dimples on Eve's cheeks deepened as she smiled. 'I thought we agreed no more panto references.'

Gabby, a half-American, half-Scottish actress, was playing *Cinderella* in the Christmas pantomime in Glasgow's Kings Theatre, her biggest role since moving to Scotland from Los Angeles almost six years before, so the last few weeks had been peppered with the traditional panto hollers of 'He's behind you' and 'oh no, you didn't'. And yes, Eve had pointed out the irony of an aspiring actress moving from Hollywood to Glasgow and landing an acting gig. After growing up in California, Gabby had originally come on an extended trip to spend time with her Scottish dad, who'd returned to his homeland after a holiday romance in the eighties had resulted in a twenty-year marriage, two adult children and an amicable divorce. While Gabby was visiting, she'd made a spontaneous decision to audition for a job in a TV campaign, landed the role and had never left. A few months in, she'd signed with a talent agency in Glasgow, immediately clicked with her booking agent, one Eve Quinn, and shortly afterwards, moved into Eve's spare room.

Five years later, Gabby's résumé now included several commercials, a few plays, a couple of bit parts in Scottish crime shows and – oh yes, she did – four pantos under her belt.

Of course, it had helped that Eve had her finger on the pulse of every acting, singing and extra role north of Carlisle. Gabby immediately became her priority client, a status that arose from both her absolute belief in Gabby's talent, and her absolute requirement to have half the rent paid on their second-floor flat in the Merchant City area of Glasgow's city centre every month.

The wild, messy bun on the top of Gabby's head wobbled as she nodded. 'You're right, we did agree to stop with the panto references. And just to digress from your whole 'who's the daddy' situation' for a second, can I just tell you that I've explained the concept of a panto to my mother every year since I got here, and she still doesn't get it,' she mused, changing the subject as she often did. Gabby's attention span ran at an average of thirty seconds per subject, unless it involved movies, TV shows, job opportunities or Michael B. Jordan.

'What did you go with this year?' Eve asked her, amused to hear Gabby's latest explanation of pantos to her American mum.

Gabby sighed. 'A traditional British family Christmas theatre comedy show, based on fairy tales, that encourages audience participation. Something in my mum's Malibu psyche blocks her from comprehending that it could be fun. She says it sounds like her worst nightmare.'

'It's my worst nightmare too,' Eve replied. 'Well, almost. Apart from, you know... discovering that the man you thought was your dad is most definitely not your dad. Oh, and sorry to debunk your theory but I wasn't stolen, because a couple of people on the list of DNA connections share the same surnames as my great grandparents on my mum's side, so Helena definitely popped me out of her womb. Nicole Kidman will be crushed.'

Eve's gaze went back to the screen. Her paternal situation was there in black and white.

Or rather, it wasn't there.

She'd done the DNA test at the same time as her twenty-two-year-old half-brother, Angus. Or at least, he was her half-brother before this test had proved otherwise. Angus and his twin, Felix, were her dad's sons with Annabel, the woman he'd left her mum for twenty-five years ago, barely four years after Eve was born. Angus had done the test out of curiosity because he was studying genetics at university. Eve had joined in the experiment partly so they could compare results and partly because she'd watched a whole series of *Long Lost Family* and was interested in finding out if she was second cousin twice removed to someone interesting. Maybe royalty. Or a serial killer. Or Delilah, the old lady who lived upstairs and banged on the floor if they spoke in anything louder than a whisper.

When the results had dropped yesterday, she'd fully expected to see Angus Quinn's name at the top of the results, with the highest DNA commonality, but nope, no sign of him. Or any of their cousins on that side of the family. In fact, on the paternal side of the family, there were only a few names and she didn't recognise any of them.

She'd waited for the shock to wear off, then emailed the top one through the message function on the website. Bethany Muldoon. Location, Glasgow. Relationship: second-third cousin, paternal side.

Dear Bethany, I've just received my DNA results and discovered that we're related on my father's side of the family. It's quite a surprise, as I wasn't aware of your branch of the family tree.

Not exactly full disclosure, but she didn't want to scare the woman off with a shouty, all capitals, WHO THE BUGGER ARE YOU??????

No reply yet, but Eve was living in hope, with just a slight touch of trepidation over the potential serial killer link.

Gabby reached for her toast. 'Have you told Angus yet?'

The very thought of that was enough to make Eve want to lie down in a dark room until her twenty-two-year-old brothers were in their thirties. She truly hoped it wouldn't damage her relationship with them. Angus and Felix were really good guys and she loved them dearly. Growing up, the age difference had left them with little in common, but since they'd hit legal drinking age, she'd met up with them at least a couple of times a month for dinner in one of the many student pubs in the West End, usually when they were skint and hungry because they'd blown their monthly allowance on pub crawls. It was worth paying the bill every time, for the laughs and the fact that it gave her warm and bubbly flashbacks to her carefree student days. On the last outing, they'd told her their plans for Christmas. And nope, her dad hadn't invited her to join them.

She hadn't even wrapped her head around how this news would change that dynamic, or her relationship with her father. Or ex-father. Former father. Every cell in her brain groaned at the enormity of that thought. Not that she was a daddy's girl. The stark reality was that they weren't even close. Like her mum, her dad had always been a workaholic, and he'd had little or no interest in parenting her. She'd seen him one Sunday a fortnight when she was growing up, and even then, he'd frequently come up with a reason to cancel. Their relationship had been... perfunctory. Yep, that was the word. At some point in her teens, it occurred to Eve that she should mind, but her grandparents – her mum's parents – had always provided all the love, support and time she could ever want, so it hadn't felt like a huge loss in her life. Still, the very thought of all the family ties that would have to be unravelled filled her with dread.

'No. Angus and Felix are skiing in the South of France with my dad.' For a fleeting second, she'd considered that the lack of genetic connection to her brother's DNA could be due to Bruce not being *the twins'* biological father. Maybe Annabel had a wild fling or was a secret swinger? But no. The answer to that was in any photograph of Bruce with his sons. The boys had his build, his height, his shoulders, and more importantly, younger versions of his face. There was no mistaking the biological link there. Thankfully, the physical side was where the similarities ended. Her brothers were much more fun, more loving and took themselves way less seriously than Bruce. 'Anyway, I feel like I need some answers before I go charging in with truths that'll get me struck off the Christmas card list. Problem is, I'm not sure where I'll find them.'

'Can you really not ask your mum?'

'Gabby, did you not just call her St Helena of the Holy Humour Bypass?' Eve wasn't quite sure when they'd coined that nickname, but it was so apt that it stuck. Her mum was one of the top criminal defence solicitors in the city. It wasn't a role that was typically associated with witty repartee or a barrel full of laughs so Helena's dry, serious personality was perfect for the job. 'She barely admits to having had sex even once, in order to have me. There's no way she'll talk to me about this. And I'm not even going to attempt to broach it, today of all days. She's already miffed because she's having her usual pre-birthday breakfast with me and Gran this morning. I think she assumed she'd get out of it because Gran is moving house today. If I question her, she'll flounce off in a huff and I won't see her until Easter, and even then, Gran will have to negotiate a ceasefire. I just... I just can't believe this. I mean, bits of it, sure. My dad went through three wives before the last one, so he doesn't exactly have a track record of stability, but my mum...? When you told her I had a friends-with-benefits deal with Sonny, she had to have a large sherry and watch back-to-back episodes of *The Good Fight* to calm herself down.'

Gabby's avocado toast halted a few inches from her mouth, 'Again, sorry about that. Forgot my filter that day.'

'You mean that year.'

It was impossible to be mad at Gabby for spilling her relationship secrets, although talking about Sonny had just given Eve yet another reason to sigh. She would see him today when he came to pick up the keys for Gran's old house and deliver the keys for her new home at the same time. He'd been the estate agent who'd sold Gran's home for her and negotiated the purchase of the place she'd bought, so he was doing her a favour by sorting out the key swap. It wasn't usually part of the service – normally the keys for houses that were bought and sold in Scotland were dropped off or collected from estate agents or solicitor's offices – but he'd offered, and Eve was grateful that it gave her one less thing to do. Although, that was before they'd got into a highly contentious discussion about the status of their relationship a few days ago. It had ended with Sonny giving her an ultimatum – and she still wasn't sure what her answer would be.

Eve lifted her mug again, and this time she must have been in the motion sensor zone for their Christmas aviary section, because the family of battery-operated, furry, singing penguins on the kitchen sideboard suddenly burst into life, shaking their feathers while belting out 'We Wish You A Merry Christmas'.

'Why have I never got a catapult when I need one? The World Wildlife Fund would have me cancelled if they knew what I wanted to do to those birds,' Gabby sighed.

'I enjoyed them for the first week, but they're wearing thin,'

Eve murmured, distracted, still staring at the page in front of her – Bethany Muldoon. Location: Glasgow. 'And you can't hurt them. You're a vegan.'

'True. I say we switch them off forever or donate them to your gran. A house-warming present,' Gabby suggested, tossing her wild mane of ebony waves, a gift from her African-American mum and Italian-Scottish dad, over one shoulder. Eve suddenly realised that she was no longer entirely sure of the origin of her own vibrant red, poker straight locks. She clicked open the ethnicity tab at the top of the screen to see a pie chart that explained her heritage was 62 per cent Scottish and 38 per cent Irish. That wasn't much of a surprise or a help. Her gran, Cathy, had Irish relatives and most of the population of the West of Scotland had at least a few ancestors who hailed from the Emerald Isle.

She circled back to Gabby's penguin suggestion and for the first time this morning, Eve smiled. 'Not your worst idea. I'll take them over when I go. Gran loves a penguin. Talking of which,' she checked her watch. 'Time to move my a—'

A ping from the laptop halted her, mid-rise from the chair.

A little notification box had suddenly appeared in the top right-hand corner. Message from Bethany Muldoon.

Eve misjudged her rapid descent back on to her chair, and landed one cheek on, one cheek off, as she rushed to open it.

Hi, it was lovely to get your message, although I'm not sure how helpful I can be. I own Café Croissant in the West End of Glasgow. If you're ever near here, pop by anytime, or if you'd rather talk on the phone, just send me your number. Bethany.

'It's from Bethany,' Eve gushed. 'She says she owns a café which is...' she quickly googled the location. '...just off Byres Road. Not far from Gran's old home and her new one too. I could pop in there if I get a chance today.' She ran the logistics of that through her mind. She was going to be at Gran's new flat for most of the day. She could nip out, maybe buy lunch for them at the café, scope it out, see if there was any sign of familiarity in Bethany Muldoon... 'Or maybe I could just forget the whole thing until after Christmas and worry about nothing more than the gargantuan to-do list that I already have today.' She wasn't sure if that was her sensible head or her cold feet kicking in.

In true form, Gabby was a tad more worried about her own to-do list. 'Dilemma. I feel your pain and empathise like a true friend should.' There was at least a hint of sheepishness, as she pivoted to, 'But can I just check that being the standby to collect Nick from the airport if his flight is delayed is on that list? Dad definitely can't help because he's working today so you're my only available stunt double if I can't make it and he can't get a taxi.' Her brother was due to arrive from Los Angeles, via London Heathrow, at 5 p.m., smack bang between the matinee and the evening showing of the panto. Gabby planned to meet him at the airport and take him to the theatre to watch the second show, but Eve had been put on standby in case his flight was late, throwing all the plans out of the window. Clearly, she didn't have enough to do today without adding someone else's relatives into the mix.

Not that Eve minded doing it for Nick. A few years older than Gabby, he'd clearly absorbed the laid-back, easy-going genes and left the extrovert, chaotic ones for his sister. But their sense of humour and all-round gorgeousness had been an even split and Eve had enjoyed hanging out with him on his last few trips. He was planning to stay at their flat tonight, then the siblings would head off early afternoon to have Christmas dinner at the hotel near Loch Lomond where their dad was head chef. Eve would spend it, as always, with her gran, this time in her brand-new apartment.

Getting back to the point, Eve opened the notes on her phone. Gargantuan To-Do List...

1. Join Mum and Gran for Mum's annual pre-birthday breakfast.
2. While trying not to interrogate Mum as to who impregnated her almost thirty years ago.
3. Oversee the packing of the last odds and ends of the house Gran has lived in for fifty-four years.
4. Be a rock of emotional support (and do not cry, repeat, DO NOT CRY).
5. Take Gran to her new flat.
6. Get her unpacked and settled (armed with brandy and biscuits).
7. Buy Sonny a Christmas present.
8. Try not to interrogate Mum.
9. Be on standby to collect Nick from the airport because you're the best friend ever.
10. Get in the festive spirit (ho ho fricking ho).
11. Still try not to interrogate Mum.
12. Give Sonny an answer to the question he asked last night.
13. Make sure Gran has everything needed for her traditional Christmas Day brunch tomorrow. If not, do a trolley dash around Asda.
14. Crawl into bed having aged years since this morning.

'Yep, right there. Number 9. I'll be at your service should you require me, Cinderella,' Eve answered with a flourish.

She didn't add that on the inside, she really hoped it wouldn't be necessary, so that she could just focus on getting Gran moved today. That was her priority. Even her urgent need to know the truth about her dad came after Gran's happiness. That's why opening a ruddy great big box of secrets and lies should probably join the Keto diet, Couch to 5K and mastering a three-minute plank on the resolutions for January 2024. Or maybe 2025.

'Right,' she announced with resolve, as she closed the laptop, 'Enough of this life changing stuff. I'm late. Mum will be tapping her fingers on the kitchen table, and Gran will be making the removal guys their third cup of tea and trying to force-feed them caramel wafers if I don't get there soon.'

As Eve stood, she closed the laptop and slipped it into her cross-body bag next to the gift-wrapped pressie for her mum. She made a stealth move from the side on the penguins, so she managed to grab them and flick their off switch before they started singing again, then grabbed her bright red puffer jacket from the hook on the back of the door. It matched the scarlet snow boots that she liberated from the shoe chest at the end of her bed whenever there was even a hint of frost or snow. Today there was more than that. A solid two inches had dropped overnight and covered the whole city in a blanket of white. A white Christmas. It was the stuff that romcoms and bookmakers thrived on. Although, today didn't feel like a rom-com, happy ending kind of bloody day.

Eve kissed Gabby on the cheek, and with a hurried, 'See ya, Cinders,' she bolted out the door and took the elevator down to the underground car park, where her old, battered but beloved white Jeep Renegade was waiting. She jumped in, started up the engine and drove towards the electric roller shutter that was so slow there was every chance that cars could run out of petrol waiting for it to rise enough for a safe exit.

Eve drummed her fingers on the steering wheel, weighing up her dilemma. Today was Christmas Eve. It was her mother's pre-birthday celebration. Her gran was moving house. She was on standby to pick up Nick from the airport and deliver him to a panto. And she had to have a relationship-defining conversation with her boyfriend.

And yet the only thing she really, truly wanted to do was go speak to Bethany Muldoon. Because today, Eve desperately wanted to find out if her whole life had been a lie.

2

HELENA MCLEAN

Christmas Eve 1993

'Muesli? For your birthday breakfast. On Christmas Eve.' Helena's mother, Cathy, sighed as she eyed the cereal in Helena's white glossy bowl, on the glossy white kitchen table, in Helena's glossy white kitchen. 'I honestly don't know where I went wrong with you. I mean, would it kill you to have a pancake and a bit of Victoria sponge like normal people?'

Helena didn't dignify the jokey dig with a reply. For about five seconds. Then she cracked and shot back with, 'It must be awful for you. I don't know how you cope with the disappointment.'

A smile played on her mother's lips, but she didn't say any more. Again, for about five seconds. Before she retorted, 'I can't deny it's a burden. Jean McPhee's lassie was arrested last week for swinging her bra at the top of one of the statues in George Square to protest about the lack of women on the city council. I had to admit you hadn't done a single thing wrong in living history. It's mortifying, to tell you the truth. I live for the day that you have a wild blow-out and call me to bail you out of the cells.'

This time, it was Helena who had to curtail a smile, as she scooped up another loaded spoon of her usual breakfast fare. This was how she and her mother communicated. Barbed digs that were dipped in reality, but dressed up in sarcasm and exaggeration. It wasn't perfect, but it was better than the childhood days of her mother trying desperately to coax her out of her shell, the teenage years of conflict over Helena's obsessive dedication to schoolwork above all else, and the university days where she avoided taking her friends home because she never knew what would come out of her mother's mouth. And yes, it still stung that on the few occasions that she did take anyone home, she invariably woke up the next morning to find them howling with laughter with her mother over a bacon roll and a cup of tea, or sharing all their problems for her mother to fix. Which she did, naturally, because all that stuff came so easily to Cathy McLean.

'I'll do my best to find a suitable occasion to swing my Wonderbra around the court next time I'm there. I'm sure it'll go down well with the judge. Anyway, it's not officially my birthday until tomorrow,' Helena stated the obvious. If she was going to protest over anything in life, it would be that her birthday fell on Christmas Day. There should be some kind of law against that. Or a contingency. All people born on the twenty-fifth of December should be given an honorary birthday in the month of their choice, so that they were actually celebrated for themselves, as opposed to their special day being overshadowed by the most celebrated day of the year. Helena had learned from experience that kids didn't give a toss that it was their classmate's birthday, because on Christmas Day they were too amped up on selection boxes and the hope of getting one of those dolls that grew hair and came with scissors, brushes and a full set of rollers.

That was why they had always celebrated her birthday on Christmas Eve – so that she could have a day that was just for her. And it always began with her mum, and sometimes her dad, sharing breakfast. Even though she was now about to turn twenty-five, living in her own flat, a fledgling criminal solicitor with a boyfriend who regularly stayed over, she still wasn't getting off the family rise and shine hook. Her dad was working today, so she'd secretly hoped her mum would skip it this year, but nope, she'd buzzed the intercom at 8 a.m., dressed in a bright red fake fur coat and a silver tinsel boa, clutching a stack of pancakes, a bottle of fizzy wine and a home-made Victoria sponge... that was now missing a Cathy-shaped wedge.

'Excellent. And while you're at it, can you do something about this mausoleum of an apartment? I mean, there isn't a single piece of Christmas tat in here. No twinkly tree. No flashing snowmen. There isn't even a strand of tinsel or an inflatable reindeer,' her mother was still in full tease mode, labouring the point. 'Och, it's a sadness to see how you've turned out, it really is.'

Before she could muster a comeback, they were interrupted.

'Darling, have you seen my... Oh. Hello, Cathy. I heard another voice, but I thought it was on the TV,' Bruce nodded to the screen on the wall behind her, where Gaby Roslin and Chris Evans were speaking to camera on *The Big Breakfast*. The two of them were wearing festive jumpers and the whole studio was decorated with random Christmas tat. Helena was sure Cathy would approve.

Helena swiftly switched the channel and was greeted with the video for that bloody ridiculous Mr Blobby song. It was this year's Christmas Number One hit, knocking Take That off the top spot and it was everywhere, so Helena was already sick of it. Although, at least it was a break from what seemed like a million years of hearing Meatloaf belting out 'I'll Do Anything For Love (But I Won't Do That)' every time she flicked on the radio.

She switched the TV off and turned her attention to her boyfriend. Bruce Quinn. At thirty, he was one of their legal firm's rainmakers, a corporate solicitor who was rumoured to be on the radar for promotion. Not that she paid any attention to rumours. If she had, she'd have stayed well clear of him given that he'd had a reputation as a bit of a playboy when she joined Hutchesons LLP straight out of uni. She'd discovered that the rumour couldn't have been further from the truth. Helena had been seeing him for six months and there hadn't been so much as a whiff of impropriety. In fact, he'd been wonderfully attentive to her since too many cocktails at the company's summer barbeque had ended in a night of passion that had lasted until Cathy, in her position as self-appointed cleaner, had let herself in with her key the next morning and hoovered right up to the bedroom door, where she had, thankfully, taken in the trail of clothes leading from the hallway and stopped before entering. Setting boundaries with her mother was definitely top of Helena's resolutions list for 1994.

'Ah, here they are,' Bruce said, picking up his cufflinks from the breakfast bar, then coming up behind Helena and rubbing her shoulders. 'Hope the depositions go well today, darling. Cathy, I'll see you and Duncan tonight for dinner. I'm looking forward to my first ever birthday-eve dinner to celebrate this amazing woman.'

He emphasised the compliment by kissing Helena on the top of the head. She turned her face up to return the kiss, but he was already on the move, grabbing an apple from the bowl on the white gloss breakfast bar, and the travel mug of coffee that Helena had waiting for him beside it.

At the door, he paused to throw out a, 'Bye darling.' To which, her mother jumped in with a wink and a, 'See you later, sweetheart.'

As he left to the sound of her mother's laughter, Helena's toes curled just a little bit more inside the thick socks she'd pulled on when she woke this morning. She adored her apartment in Dowanhill, in the West End of Glasgow, and had modernised it to within an inch of its white glossy life, but that didn't stop the draughts that came in through the rickety old sash windows she couldn't afford to replace just yet.

'Definitely behind the door when God gave out a sense of humour, that man,' Cathy chuckled.

'Mum! That's not true. He has a brilliant sense of humour. I find him hilarious.' Helena's hackles were rising by the second. She twisted her long dark hair up into a bun and secured it with a scrunchie.

Why did her mother have to be so critical? Not that she gave a toss what Cathy thought. This was her life and Cathy had zero say in what she did, when she did it or who she did it with.

Her mum was already topping up her tea from the pot in the middle of the table. 'How hilarious? Like "marriage and settle down" funny? The happy ever after stuff?'

Helena absent-mindedly pulled off a chunk of pancake and popped it in her mouth, then immediately realised what she'd done. See! This was what her mother drove her to. Calories. Between her early birthday breakfast, dinner tonight and the usual indulgences of Christmas Day tomorrow, her Jane Fonda workout video tape would need an extra outing this week.

Her mother's eyes shifted, and Helena immediately sensed that there was more to that comment than just a casual enquiry. She wasn't the fastest-rising junior solicitor in the company without reason. Not that she'd admit it, but reading people was the one useful skill she'd inherited from her mother, who could pretty accurately sum a person and their actions up in about thirty seconds. It was one of Cathy's superpowers, along with impenetrable brass-neckery and crack interrogation skills. Cathy owned a hairdressing salon in the West end of Glasgow, and she'd spent years drawing out her customers' entire life story before the curls of their perms or the waves of their blow dries left the salon.

Helena's eyes narrowed in suspicion. 'Why do you ask that?'

Cathy put the teapot down as she shook her head, making the curls of her own perm tremble. 'No reason. Just curious about where you see this going. Can't a mother make a casual enquiry about her daughter's relationship?'

'Mother, you don't do casual enquiries. You do pointed questions and invasive curiosity. Come on, spill. What's going on?'

'Nothing,' her mum feigned innocence. But so had the shoplifter Helena had defended last week, despite being caught coming out of a department store with four watches, eight pairs of sunglasses and a kettle stuffed inside his jacket.

Her mother was up to something. Oh God, was she trying to split them up? Had she hatched a plan with one of her mad friends to fix Helena up with one of their loser sons? That was exactly the kind of stunt that her mum would pull, and she'd claim it was for Helena's own good. Well, those days of parental influence were long gone.

'Mum, if you don't tell me what you're up to you can forget dinner tonight. I'm not coming.' She didn't care that she sounded like a petulant teenager. This was how to play Cathy McLean at her own game. Her mum didn't need to know that of course Helena wouldn't miss her pre-birthday, Christmas Eve dinner, especially since it would be the first time all day that she'd see her dad. It was a bummer that he had to work today but he was a conveyancing solicitor and Friday - even the one right before Christmas - was his busiest day of the week because that's when the majority of house sales finalised.

Her dad was the reason that Helena had decided to become a solicitor, albeit in a different field. She adored his cool, calm manner and his attention to detail and order. He couldn't be more different to the spontaneous, gregarious, unpredictable force he'd married. Their relationship had never made sense to Helena until she'd come across the whole 'opposites attract' theory. Not that any of that clichéd stuff applied to her and Bruce. One of the many, many things she adored about her boyfriend was that they were completely on the same wavelength and totally understood each other, both professionally and when they were off the clock too. They could talk for hours about work and then switch off, go to the gym and exercise together, both equally as competitive as the other. Although, it was in bed that they were the most compatible. Just the thought of that gave her a sexy shudder, but her mother was too busy going off on one of her rants to notice.

'For the love of the Victoria sponge, Helena, why do you have to turn everything into a challenge? You know that arguing with the whole world is just supposed to be your job, not your reason for waking up in the morning?'

Helena stared her down in silence, eyebrows raised to signify that she wasn't letting her mum off with deflecting or avoiding whatever was going on here.

Her mum threw her hands up in surrender. 'Fine! Okay. But I want it on record that you prised this out of me, and I want your solemn promise that you will not, under pain of death, grass me up to your boyfriend or your father.'

Helena felt prickles of anxiety spread under her skin. Shit. What now? What could possibly be happening that would involve her dad and Bruce? Another wedge of pancake found its way to her mouth. Jane Fonda was going to show up at her door and thump her with a legwarmer at this rate.

'And I'm only telling you because I don't want you to be shocked in the moment. I need you to think it through. To make an informed decision. To do what's right for you, without any pressure, and knowing that your father and I will support you no matter what.'

'Okay, Mother, I really hope you're just being your usual over-dramatic self, because this is starting to sound mildly terrifying. Spit it out. What's going on?'

The passage of another chunk of carbs would be hindered by the large lump that was now forming in her throat, so she didn't want to chance it. Instead, Helena just continued to stare at her mother in undisguised irritation and anticipation.

'Bruce called your father…'

Helena understood immediately. Bruce must be wanting to jump ship to her dad's company. Her dad was a partner at Miller & Murphy, one of the largest legal firms in the city. It dealt mainly with private domestic clients, but it had a growing corporate side too. Bruce must be trying to get in early and secure a position there and perhaps her dad's recommendation depended on whether she'd be okay with that. After all, it would be a bit awkward at family dinners if her dad had refused to help out her boyfriend.

But why wouldn't Bruce just ask her to vouch for him to her dad? Why go direct to him? Why all the cloak-and-dagger stuff? And what decision would she have to make in that scenario? Whether to endorse her boyfriend for a job at her dad's firm? That was a no-brainer. Of course she would. This was all very confusing. Perhaps her mother should have skipped that large Bucks Fizz.

'And he asked him…'

Yep, she was right. Bruce had asked her dad to recommend him for a job.

Helena took a slug of her wheatgrass. It tasted vile, but her internal organs would thank her for it. Rumour had it that Madonna drank it every day and that was good enough for

Helena. Although, the Material Girl had gone right off the rails with all that sex stuff lately. If that was what over-indulging in wheatgrass did to you, perhaps she should give it a miss before court appearances.

'...For his blessing to propose to you.'

The wheatgrass shot out of her mouth like it was being emitted from a power washer and only Cathy's swift reflexes saved the cake, as she swiped it away from the firing line in the middle of the table.

'He called Dad to ask...' Helena began repeating, but her mum jumped in before she finished the sentence.

'I know! I mean, is that a pathetic, antiquated bow to the patriarchy or what? It should be a mother who is consulted. I mean, what do men know about what makes a good husband? With the exception of yer father, most of them are fairly shite at it.'

The patriarchy was the least of Helena's concerns right now. She continued with her original thought.

'...Because he wants to propose to me? When? How?'

She couldn't quite nail down her emotions, so she settled on shock, wonder, delight, thrills and excitement.

'Tonight. At dinner.'

'That's... that's amazing,' Helena gushed, while mopping up wheatgrass with her evidently non-absorbent two-ply, flowery breakfast napkin. Maybe her mum's conviction that kitchen roll sufficed as napkins would have been apt on this occasion.

'Right then. So I take it from that big grin on your face that you'll be open to this idea?'

'Of course! Mum, he's wonderful. Everything I could want in a husband. I'm just... shocked. I didn't see this happening quite so soon. I thought you were going to say he wanted Dad to recommend him for a job.'

'Yes, well he asked for that too. Apparently, there's some big role coming up in their corporate division and he wants your dad's support for his application.'

Helena was barely listening. Bruce was going to propose. Tonight. This was the most amazing thing ever. She'd never have voiced it, but it had crossed her mind that they might have a future together, and sure, sometimes in her occasional daydreams she'd envisaged them as one of those power couples, like the Shadow Home Secretary, Tony Blair and his barrister wife, Cherie. Only without her dodgy fringe. Or Bruce Willis and Demi Moore. Or Hugh Grant and Liz Hurley. But with a lot more paperwork and two fiercely sharp legal minds.

A thought struck that fiercely sharp legal mind. 'Did Dad say yes to him proposing?'

'He said that whatever you want will have his support. He also told him that he'll put a word in for him on the job front anyway.'

For once, Helena couldn't help but be honest and open with her mother about her feelings. 'This is brilliant. The best Christmas Eve ever.'

'So you're going to say yes then? Don't you want to give it some consideration? Just say the word and I'll head it off at the pass. I could cause a disruption in the restaurant tonight when he's about to ask you and delay the big moment until you've had time to really think it through.'

Helena appreciated that her mum was looking out for her, but her intervention wouldn't be required.

'I don't need to think it through. I'd marry him in a heartbeat.' Helena Quinn QC. Or would she keep her own name? Helena McLean QC. Or perhaps... yep, double-barrel. Helena McLean Quinn. That was it. She'd fit right in with all the other double-named toffs in the legal world. And she'd be able to ponder such technicalities if her mum wasn't still chirping on.

'Yes, but isn't it a bit rushed? You've always been one to consider things thoroughly and analyse all the options.'

A realisation of what was going on here broke through Helena's uncharacteristic bubble of enthusiasm and bliss. 'You don't think I should marry him.' It was a statement, not a question.

Her mum was eyeing her warily now, picking her words. 'I think you've got a whole lifetime in front of you and there's no need to make life-changing decisions at your age. Who we are at twenty-five is someone very different from who we are at thirty-five, forty-five. What's the point of rushing? Especially when you've only been seeing him for, what, six months? How well can you really get to know someone in that time?'

Helena's joy and excitement were sliding down the emotion scale, all the way to pissed off and irritated.

'Talk about a double standard. You're the one who is always preaching about living in the moment. Taking risks. Feeling the bloody fear and doing it anyway.'

Her mum un-pursed her lips to speak. 'I was thinking more of bungee jumps. Or spontaneously jetting to New York for a wild weekend of hedonism. Not tying yourself down to a bloke that wears cufflinks for the rest of your life.'

Helena tossed her half-soggy napkin onto the table, then pushed her chair back. 'I need to go to work. But let me tell you something, Mother. If I'm lucky enough to get a proposal from Bruce Quinn tonight, it'll be the happiest moment of my life when I say yes. And you and all your petty judgements won't stop me. So you'd better get shopping for the big hat and confetti.'

With that, and a set jaw of determination, Helena got up and headed off to the bedroom to change into her work suit. It was her cloak of armour. An outward sign that she'd carved out her independence and the successful career that she'd worked so hard for. It was the nineties and her generation of women knew they could have everything. And that's what Helena McLean was going to have. The high-flying job. The incredible man. A successful, affluent, future ahead of her.

As she fixed the necktie of her silk pussy bow collar blouse in the mirror, she caught sight of her hands and realised that today was the last day of her life that the third finger of her left hand would be bare.

And she couldn't wait until Bruce Quinn, the love of her life, put a ring on it.

3

CATHY (FARMER) MCLEAN

Christmas Eve 1968

Cathy turned down the volume on the radio beside her bed. Bloody hell, that Jim Morrison had the whole brooding sexy thing going on. The first time she'd heard 'Hello, I Love You' on *Top of the Pops* had been back in September, and she'd gone down to the record shop on Byres Road the next day to buy the single but it was already sold out. Last week, she'd popped back there again and managed to get a copy of their album, *Waiting For The Sun*. Actually, not so much 'popped', but waddled. Anyway, the LP was already wrapped and under the tree downstairs as an extra gift for her sister, Loretta.

She'd been awake for half an hour, after a fitful night's sleep, but now she pushed herself up and swung her legs around so that she was sitting on the edge of her bed, then she stretched her hands towards the sky, trying to make her spine slip back into some kind of alignment. Her back was aching, and her head was thudding, thanks to another sleepless night. There had been far too many of those lately and she was pretty sure there wasn't an end in sight.

'Morning, Mum, morning, Dad,' she whispered, as she always did, to the framed photo that sat on the bedside chest of drawers. It was of her parents' wedding day and it had been there, in that spot, her whole life. She remembered coming into this room when she was a kid, climbing into bed with her parents, and picking it up, then telling her mum that she was the prettiest women she'd ever seen. Her mum would come out with that infectious, raucous laugh and say, 'Well, you must have got my pretty genes and a whole bucket of your own, Catherine Farmer, because you're the most beautiful of us all.' Then she'd wrap her arm around Cathy's shoulders and pull her in tight, and they'd listen to Elvis albums on the record player that sat on the dresser on the opposite wall. She'd been the only one of her friends that had a record player in the house and she'd felt like the luckiest girl in the world. That lucky feeling had gone when they'd lost their mum and dad. This was Cathy's room now that her parents had passed, but she still listened to the same songs her mum had played over and over. 'Can't Help Falling In Love', 'Return To Sender', 'Love Me Tender'. Somehow, that made it feel like she was still here.

Cathy chided herself for being sentimental, then sniffed away the tears that were pooling on her bottom lids. What was wrong with her? If her mother could see her now, she'd tell her to dry her eyes and put a smile on her face, and rightly so. They'd never been the kind of family that wallowed in their sadness. Perhaps that's why the universe, or the Gods, or the fates, or whatever higher force was in charge, had given them so much of it, taking her parents from her so long before their time.

Now that the volume was turned down on the wireless, she could hear Loretta singing downstairs in the kitchen. It confused her at first – her younger sister would normally be away to school by now – but then it dawned on her that it was Christmas Eve. No school today. Loretta would be thrilled about that. Despite Cathy's objections, Loretta announced at least daily that she couldn't wait until next summer when she could leave school and she'd made it perfectly clear she was planning to follow in Cathy's footsteps and become a hairdresser.

Cathy adored her job, had loved hairdressing from the very first day as a Saturday girl, when she picked up a brush and began sweeping the floors to now, as a fully qualified stylist, but there was no denying it was tough and hairdressers didn't get the rewards they deserved. She wanted Loretta to find a different path, but it didn't matter how many times Cathy stressed the low wages, the long hours, and the sore feet, Loretta couldn't be dissuaded. She already worked as a junior in the same salon as Cathy every night after school and on a Saturday, and she loved the independence and the wages it gave her. Cathy enjoyed listening to her chattering to the customers or having a giggle with the other juniors in the back shop. And it was great to see her hanging out with the girls after work. It was exactly what a teenager should be doing. It was also what Cathy had missed out on for the last three years. But she didn't want Loretta to spend her whole life in the same shop, in the same city, in the same world she'd grown up in. Cathy's life was mapped out for her now, but Loretta still had the world at her feet and Cathy wanted her to get out there and experience it all. For both of them.

'I'll fill you in on the day later, Mum,' she whispered, as she did every morning, before she pushed herself off the bed and slowly descended the stairs. Everything seemed to be slower these days, even more so when she got closer to the sound that was blaring from the kitchen.

Her mum had always said Loretta's name came from a movie

star who had won an Oscar in the forties, but now it was probably more apt that she had the same moniker as the country
singer, Loretta Lynn, because she sang all day long. Now, she was
doing a pitch perfect rendition of 'Jingle Bell Rock', and it threw
Cathy right back into the past again. Her mum had loved that
song. It was on a Brenda Lee album she had bought a year or
two before she died, and that last Christmas, she'd climbed up
on to a kitchen chair and had them all dancing around her as
she sang it every bit as brilliantly as Brenda. Loretta was doing
the same now, so loudly she didn't even hear Cathy opening the
door, or see her taking a moment to absorb the sight in front
of her.

At Loretta's request, Cathy had cut her sister's light blonde hair
into a chin-length angular bob with a blunt fringe that came
straight from the catwalks of the Mary Quant fashion shows they
saw in magazines. But that wasn't what was capturing Cathy's
attention. Her stare was on her sister's back. From the neck down,
if she wasn't mistaken, Loretta appeared to be encased in a
psychedelic blue, orange, pink, green, yellow, figure-hugging
sleeveless top, with matching bell-bottomed stripy stretchy
trousers. In December.

'Dear God, Loretta, did you make that outfit out of a couple of
spare deckchairs?'

Loretta yelped and dropped the teacup she'd been drying with
a dish towel. Thankfully, it bounced off a bunch of bananas on the
worktop and didn't break. 'Cathy! Don't do that to me! I didn't even
hear you come down the stairs, and let's face it, that's pretty much
a miracle,' she teased, pointedly scanning Cathy from head to toe
with her usual cheeky insolence. This girl was old before her
years, but Cathy didn't blame her for that – she'd coped with so
much more than most girls her age, so it was only to be expected.
'Anyway, do you like it? I bought it with my tips and I've decided

it's my Christmas present from Mum and Dad. They'd have loved it.'

Cathy wasn't a crier, but right now her eyelids seemed to have forgotten that and yet again they were collecting pools of tears. For the second time that morning, she blinked them back. What the hell was going on with her today? Her emotions were all over the place.

She cleared her throat and plonked herself down on a kitchen chair, using the few seconds it took her to do that to get herself together and slap on a smile.

'I think they'd have loved it too,' she agreed, with the best fake cheeriness she could muster. 'Or at least, Mum would have loved it. Dad would have locked you in your room and told you to come out when you were twenty-one.'

The two of them smiled because they both knew she was right. Their mum had always been the more easy-going parent, the one who encouraged them to have fun and told them they could do anything. Their dad was the more sensible, stricter parent, the one who'd sit them down and give them firm but fair warnings about the dangers of the outside world. That was the full-scale, boot-in-the-bollocks, irony of it all. Billy Farmer had told them again and again about the dangers of drinking, the dangers of driving, the dangers of staying out late at night, and yet all three of those things had combined to end his life, and his wife's too, when they'd caught a cab home from a birthday party in the city centre almost three years before, and their speeding taxi driver had jumped a red light and ploughed their car into an ambulance coming from the other direction, red lights flashing and siren blaring.

Even the medics on board hadn't been able to save them. Both dead at the scene. The taxi driver too. It came out later that he was drunk, but then, half the drivers on the roads were probably the same. Drink-driving laws had come into force in 1967, two years after the accident and too late for their parents. Not that people were taking much notice of them. Most folks still thought nothing of having a few pints or knocking back a few vodkas, then driving home. Old habits died hard. Cathy was pretty sure that a fair number of people who read about the accident in the *Evening Times* would probably have gone right out and downed a few pints before driving home the following weekend. Maybe they'd have reconsidered if they'd been there when the police had knocked their door that night and told them that their parents were dead.

She still had that edition of the paper somewhere. Not that she'd read past the headline.

FATAL CRASH LEAVES TWO TEENAGE GIRLS ORPHANED

She didn't need to. She knew the rest. The only positive thing to come out of it was that she was already seventeen and working in the salon, so she'd been granted automatic guardianship of thirteen-year-old Loretta. The same Loretta who was now sporting a shiny psychedelic catsuit.

'So go on, educate me. Is this look inspired by the Beatles, Stones or The Doors?' Cathy prompted, listing Loretta's favourite singers.

'The Stones. Mick was wearing this style of trousers when he sang on the David Frost show. I'm over mini-skirts. If one more old lech on the building site at the end of the road shouts something at me he'll be going home with no teeth. Anyway, if Mick wears stuff like this, it's good enough for me. I found this outfit in that weird shop that's opened across from the salon. Sells all sorts of fashions I've never seen before. Feels strange though. This fabric is so clingy, it's not half making me sweat. There's rivers running under this top already.' She pulled the front of it away from her body, then let it ping back into shape with a soggy slap that made Cathy wince.

Loretta giggled as she spooned tea leaves into the teapot in front of her and then poured in boiling water from the kettle. She swirled it for a few moments then filled a waiting cup, using a strainer to catch any stray leaves. Next, she added some milk from the bottle on the worktop, before bringing it over to the table and sliding it in front of Cathy. Until a month or so ago, they'd only ever used loose tea in the house, but a client who owned a local food distribution warehouse had given Cathy a box of teabags. They were keeping them for special occasions.

'There you go, fatty. You're welcome.'

'I'll ping the arse of those trousers so hard you won't be able to sit down for a week, any more of your cheek,' Cathy warned, but it was impossible to hide her amusement. Her sister was everything a sixteen-year-old should be. Cathy remembered being like that once. Sometimes it seemed like a million years ago. Before her parents died. Before her heart was broken. Before she made the decisions that had fast-forwarded her life by years.

'Are you going into the salon today?' Loretta asked, and Cathy shook her head.

'No, I finished up yesterday. Don't think I could have spent another day on my feet and today would have been too busy. I'm going to take this tea and go back to bed, and then I'm going to curl up under the duvet with a good book until I need to get up and start preparing everything for tomorrow's Christmas dinner.'

Even without their parents, or perhaps especially now that they didn't have their parents, Cathy tried to make Christmas Day exactly the way it used to be when they were still a whole family. Presents under the tree that was already up next door in the living room, in front of the window. All the food her mum would make.

Top of the Pops in the afternoon, then whatever movie was on the BBC. Some of Loretta's friends might pop round in the evening to keep her company too. Since the accident, they'd been great about looking out for her and making plans to help the hard days become a little bit easier. Cathy wished her friends had been the same, but they'd drifted off after her parents died and other than going to work, she'd become a bit of a hermit as she adjusted to taking care of Loretta. Now, well, her situation wasn't exactly ideal for hanging out with pals late at night or going to concerts or dances.

Loretta retreated back to man the toaster, catching two slices as they popped up. 'I can't believe I'm going to be an auntie in two weeks' time.'

The thought gave Cathy a swift kick of trepidation. Two weeks. Sometimes she was scared that she wasn't ready for this. For motherhood. For the responsibility. For the pain of getting this beach ball of a baby out of her lady bits. She suppressed a shudder, determined not to show anything but calm positivity to her sister. With a bit of teasing thrown in to keep things normal. 'Yup. You've got fourteen days to become a good influence on this baby. I'm thinking it might take a bit longer than that.'

Loretta seemed to wear that as a badge of honour. 'No way. I'm going to be a brilliant aunt. Wait and see. I'm going to teach him or her all the smartest things. And it'll have the best clothes in the street. We'll be like twins.'

'God help us,' Cathy groaned, feigning horror. 'This poor baby might be better staying where it is right now.' They both knew she was joking. Much as she was terrified, there was also a bigger part of her that was desperate to meet her baby. He or she would be someone else to love, they'd be her family, and Cathy couldn't wait to take care of them.

'Do you want this toast or not?' Loretta shot back, gesturing to the plate with two thick slices of freshly buttered toast on the counter in front of her.

'I do.'

'Okay, well, be nice or the birds are getting it,' she gestured to the back door. But she couldn't keep up the stern act for long before her ever-present sense of humour kicked back in, and she slipped the toast in front of Cathy, next to her tea. 'There you go. I can't have a starving preggers woman on my conscience. Or three wise men showing up at the door. We haven't got enough bread to feed them.'

Cathy had to try really hard to keep her bladder under control when she giggled. 'Anyway,' Loretta went on, 'I need to go soon. I said I'd go into the salon for a few hours and help out. Christmas Eve – the tips will make it worth it.'

This girl would go far. She definitely wasn't afraid to graft or to hustle, but that wasn't what Cathy wanted for her. Their mum had reluctantly accepted Cathy's decision to leave school at sixteen and go full time at the salon, but she'd always said she hoped that Loretta would stay on at school, maybe even be the first one in the family to go to college. Just because Cathy's carefree teenage years had then been cut short by tragedy, didn't mean Loretta's should be too.

Loretta was still chattering away. 'And just think about how much I'd make if I worked there full time,' she said pointedly.

Cathy sighed, preparing for their regular debate. 'Shall we have the argument about you leaving school in the summer now, or can I save it until after my toast?'

Before Loretta could reply, the doorbell rang and Cathy was suddenly aware that she was sitting in her white nightdress, her long blonde hair a distant stranger to a brush. Didn't matter. It was probably just the postman with a card that was too big for the letter box.

Loretta went out into the hall to answer it while Cathy took a generous bite of her toast. She was still chewing it when Loretta came back in, and Cathy immediately saw that every shred of her sister's happy disposition had been sucked right out of her. There was a paleness to her skin that hadn't been there before, a fear in her eyes, or maybe it was worry, and she was biting her bottom lip, which had been the sure-fire sign that she was nervous ever since she was a kid. And she wasn't carrying anything. Not the postman then.

'Erm, Cathy, it's for you,' she murmured, and there was no mistaking the trepidation.

Cathy's body flooded with anxiety. This wasn't good. Bailiffs? Had she forgotten to pay the electricity bill. Police? Had something happened to someone she loved? No. Not again. She wasn't even going to consider that.

She didn't have to, because Loretta stood to one side and Cathy gasped at the sight of the man behind her. He was tanned. His hair was much longer than it had been when she'd last seen him. He was wearing jeans and a jacket that looked like they'd been slept in. And yet he was still the most breath-taking, heart-stopping, handsome guy she'd ever seen in her life. Richie Clark. Her Richie. Her love. The one she'd said goodbye to when he'd landed an apprenticeship, working alongside his uncle in the engine rooms of cargo ships that sailed from England to countries all over the world. He'd begged her to come, said they'd find her a job on the ships too, but she couldn't leave Loretta, so she'd insisted he go without her. She'd kissed him goodbye at Glasgow Central Train Station and they'd both cried.

'Go and have the best time,' she'd told him.

'I'll be back,' he'd promised.

He hadn't said when and she hadn't asked, too broken with grief, too heartsore from yet another loss of someone she loved.

There had been no expectation. No deadline. But as the months passed, her hopes faded until there were none left at all.

Now, here he was. There had been no letters because he was travelling, so she had no address to send them to. No conversations, because neither of them could afford an international phone call and even if they could, they wouldn't know how, because the ships didn't take incoming calls and Cathy didn't have a phone. The only time she ever rang someone was from the phone box at the end of the next road.

When he'd left, they'd both agreed that they'd live their lives, both do their own thing, because they'd had no other choice. Even though the thought of that broke her heart, she hadn't shown it because she'd known that letting him go was the right thing to do. Holding him back, keeping him here with her would only be selfish. She'd loved him too much for that.

In the beginning, she'd wait for him to come back every night. Then every week. Then every month until it became clear to her that he wasn't coming. One day she'd finally decided to stop waiting and get on with her life, figuring that he'd forgotten about her. Maybe even met someone else on the ship and wiped her from his mind.

'Hey, Cath,' he greeted her with that grin that used to make her go weak at the knees. She stayed seated, because she didn't want to test the theory. And also because...

A frown on his face. Confusion. As she followed his gaze, she realised that it came straight to the hand that had flown to her face when she'd seen him. Her left hand. And now he was staring at the two gold rings that were there. One was her mum's. The other was her own, placed there by someone else, just a few months ago.

'I don't understand...?' he said, still staring.

'I'm married, Richie,' she forced out, then cleared her throat and prayed that her voice would hold up under the utter devastation of seeing him there.

'You're what?' He knew exactly what she'd said, so she didn't repeat it. No point. It wasn't going to change. 'No, Cathy. No. How could...?' His words drifted off because they both understood the answer.

She could, because he'd left her over eighteen months ago. Yes, he'd promised he'd come back, but as time passed Cathy had needed something more tangible than promises. That was only one side of the story, though. She didn't have the words to tell him the other reason for the wedding, so instead she slowly stood up, revealing the part of her that had been concealed by the table.

'Oh bugger,' Loretta blurted, to no one in particular.

Cathy didn't react, her gaze still locked on Richie's, her legs almost buckling when she saw the pain on his face as he took in the outline of her body, the curve of her stomach.

Today was the day that the love of her life would find out she was married to another man. And about to give birth to her husband's child.

10 A.M. – 12 NOON

4

EVE

Christmas Eve 2023

It was a minute after 10 a.m. when Eve's trusty Jeep finally exited her city centre building's underground car park, and set off for the West End. Rush-hour traffic would usually have subsided by now, but not today. The slushy December streets of the Merchant City, home to Ralph Lauren, Emporio Armani, Mulberry and many other high-end stores, were already packed with people sporting one of two expressions – firm determination to get the last minute Christmas shopping done or blatant panic that they might have left it too late.

Eve cut down past George Square, one of Glasgow's most famous landmarks, where the annual Christmas market was just waking up around the ice rink and under the kaleidoscope of lights and decorations that appeared there in the festive season. Eve remembered her mum and gran bringing her here every year on the first Saturday in December. It was a tradition. Just like celebrating Mum's birthday the day before the actual event. Or having Christmas Eve hot chocolate after nightfall in a beautiful little, fairy-lit park not far from Gran's home in the West End.

There were no traditions with her dad. At least, not that she could remember. Her memories only stretched back to when she was eight or nine, and by then her parents were already divorced and they'd all settled into a routine that never changed. Christmas Day was always spent at Gran and Grandad's house with her mum, Great Aunt Loretta and whatever partner she'd brought along. There would be a late-morning brunch, then games and TV, and then dinner at night, with Mum's birthday cake for pudding. Then Aunt Loretta would start singing (always kicking off with something by The Stones or The Doors) and they'd work their way through every song they all knew the words to, and even Mum, Saint Helena of the Holy Humour Bypass, would join in if she'd had a few glasses of wine. One night Aunt Loretta got Mum wasted on tequila she'd brought back from a trip to Mexico and they'd ended up doing a duet to 'Relight My Fire' – the Lulu and Take That version. Loretta did a brilliant Lulu, but if Gary Barlow had heard Mum singing his part, he'd probably have sued. After the singalong, the blankets would come out and they'd all crash on sofas and watch a movie, usually Grandad's choice, but he'd pick one he knew they'd love, and Gran would lie on the couch beside him, her head on his shoulder, and the whole world would be perfect.

That little bubble of bliss would be well and truly burst on Boxing Day, when she'd be dropped off to spend the day with her dad and his new family, although that had an interchangeable cast of characters. There was Annabel, the fellow solicitor who'd worked with Dad at Grandad's company until their affair was discovered and they'd both left under a scandalous cloud. That was all the info Eve had managed to find out, and even then it had come from Annabel when she was in her early teens, because Mum and Gran both point blank refused to discuss it or bad-mouth her philandering father. That relationship had produced her twin brothers, Angus and Felix, before her dad had hot-tailed it off with Clarissa when the boys were about six or seven. That union had lasted around five years or so and they hadn't had kids, which was probably a good thing, given that he wasn't particularly dedicated to the three he already had. It was just as well that the hotshot firm he'd joined after leaving Grandad's company had a family law division, because he needed the staff discount again six years later when he traded Clarissa in for Millie, a twenty-nine-year-old cosmetic nurse who now kept his sixty-year-old face and body in peak physical shape with the combination of a strenuous exercise and Botox. And no, it would never feel normal that her latest step-mother was the same age as her, but at least it meant they could relate to each other's lives. If conversation dried up at dinner, they could always pass the time comparing their favourite One Direction song.

Question after question about her parentage flipped through Eve's mind.

Were there clues that he wasn't her dad? Was that why he was fairly indifferent to her? No. He was fairly indifferent to Angus and Felix too, and they were both younger clones of Bruce Quinn.

Did he know that she wasn't his? No. There was no way that he would have maintained their relationship for all these years if she wasn't his kid, so clearly he was unaware. But that meant Helena must have cheated on him before they got married. No. Not even an option. Never. Helena McLean was the most straightforward, no-nonsense, honest woman of integrity that Eve had ever known. She didn't break the rules. She would never cheat. Impregnation by aliens was beginning to look like the most plausible explanation.

The uncertainties were like tiny volcanos erupting in her mind all the way across town. Thankfully, as soon as she cleared the city centre, the roads became quieter, and as she drove under grey skies down Great Western Road in the West End, the traffic was lighter, and the only challenge was navigating the endless sets of traffic lights on that stretch of road. She thought about diverting to Café Croissant to ambush Bethany Muldoon and get some answers, but again decided against it. Today wasn't the day and she had no time for it. No matter how much it was killing her to put it off.

Twenty-five minutes after Eve had left her building, she was pulling into the driveway of the home her gran had lived in for fifty-four years. Two Luton vans were there, the back of one of them wide open, revealing a space that was crammed with furniture and boxes. Most of the stuff had been packed up yesterday and stored overnight in the vans in the removal company's warehouse, so this was the last of it, ready to be taken to the new house, just ten minutes away, and unpacked this afternoon.

Taking a deep breath, Eve steeled herself for what was ahead. Today was going to be a tough day for her gran, leaving the place she'd called home for over five decades, where there were memories in every inch of every room. It would be heart-breaking for their matriarch. Emotionally draining. Not even a whole colony of singing penguins was going to take the sting out of this one. Eve decided to leave the bird family in the back seat for now, planning to take them into Gran's new home later, so she just grabbed her bag, and her mum's birthday present. The scarf and hat set didn't seem particularly personal or apt for the moment. If she'd had more warning, she could have researched the best place to buy a polygraph machine.

Her red boots crunched on the icy smattering of slush as she approached the semi-detached stone house. Deep breath.

Gran. Soothing her heartache. Giving her comfort. That was Eve's priority.

Cathy greeted her by throwing the door open before she'd even rung the bell. 'Hello, my love,' she chirped, cheery as could be. 'Come on in and join the party.'

Erm, perhaps she was just doing a really good job of hiding the heartache.

Eve opened her arms and wrapped them around her gran.

'Happy Christmas Eve and happy moving day. How are you holding up, Gran? This can't be easy for you.'

'I'd be a lot more chipper if your mother would let me have a Buck's Fizz for breakfast, but she's insisting I can't have a cocktail until after lunch. I don't know where I went wrong with that woman.' Gran said it all with a familiar twinkle in her eye, and Eve felt her tension lower a few points on the 'stressed out' scale. Gran had been lamenting her mum's good behaviour for as long as she could remember, so it was reassuring to see that nothing had changed today. Maybe she wasn't wallowing in devastation about uprooting her whole life after all.

It was strange walking down the empty hall, past imprints on the wall where pictures used to hang, spaces on the floor where there had been a beautiful old sideboard, an umbrella stand, a console table packed with framed photos. As she walked past the glass door to the living room, she saw that it was empty too. A whole lifetime packed up.

When they reached the kitchen, Eve saw that wasn't quite true. A whole lifetime, apart from a white plastic patio set consisting of a table and four chairs, that Gran always kept in the shed for when she needed extra seats at one of her many garden parties and barbeques. Now, these were the only pieces of furniture in the middle of the kitchen, and her mother was sitting on one of the chairs, sporting her peeved face. Or maybe it was her standard pre-birthday, 'can't be arsed with this' face. Eve was pretty sure it wasn't her 'Sweetheart, I've been carrying a secret – your dad is not your dad' face.

Eve bit her tongue. Now wasn't the time. Not yet. Not when Gran was facing a life-changing day and her first Christmas in a new home. This was time to play nice and keep the peace. She could pull the pin out of the grenade and explode her life next week.

'Happy birthday-eve, Mum,' she said, leaning down to kiss her mother's upturned cheek, taking in the huge Victoria sponge in the middle of the table, and the plate piled high with pancakes next to it. This was what Gran made every year for Mum's pre-birthday breakfast, and every year, Mum pulled a box of muesli out of her bag and ignored the rest. Case in point, the bowl of cereal sitting in front of Helena right now.

'Thank you, darling. Tuck in. I just got here myself and your grandmother informs me that we've got less than an hour before Sonny will be here to close this place up and collect the keys.'

Every year, she'd watched her mother try to rush this breakfast so that she could go do something, anything, else. Now she finally had an actual reason to cut it short and Eve knew she'd take it. It was an eternal mystery to Eve how her gran, the most loving, gregarious woman, could have raised someone so serious and lacking in joy. The happy genes must have skipped a generation somewhere. Or perhaps they were just lying dormant, and her mother would hit fifty-five tomorrow, jack in her role as a high-flying legal eagle and spend her retirement going to raves in Ibiza and shagging her way around Europe. Eve could only hope.

'Not working today, Mum?' she asked as she pulled out a plastic chair.

'Going to the office straight from here. I'm prepping for an important case that kicks off in the new year and I just want to check on the progress.'

Maybe it was because Mum had such an important, high-pressure job as one of Scotland's top criminal Solicitor Advocates. Maybe it was because she'd had – as far as Eve knew – no other significant relationships since her marriage ended and Dad... Bruce... what should she call him now? Fake dad. Yep, that would do it. But back to the point. Perhaps Helena was so damn miserable because she hadn't loved anyone since fake dad had upped and left her for another woman. Yep, Eve could see how that could put someone as rigid and proud as Helena off the romantic stuff for life.

Her gran plonked two mugs down and filled them from the teapot in the middle of the table, sliding one to Eve and keeping the other for herself. Sometimes she still made tea the old way, with loose leaves and a strainer, but today there was an open packet of Tetley teabags on the counter. Her mother only ever drank wheatgrass with breakfast. She said she'd been doing that since she was in her twenties, and it was obviously agreeing with her because she regularly dropped into the conversation that her figure hadn't changed in three decades. Her hair had some blonde highlights in it now to cover the grey, but a committed skincare regime, daily facial exercises and regular laser treatments in expensive salons ensured she still had the cheekbones and skin of a woman a decade younger.

Eve fished her gift out of her bag. 'Happy Birthday, Mum,' she said with a heartfelt smile and a barely reciprocated hug. 'I hope you like this. If not, I've tucked the receipt in the wrapping paper, so you can take it back to the shop. It's a gorgeous little boutique in Princes Square that does bespoke accessories.' She hoped that was good enough to pass her mum's designer criteria. Helena's body didn't leave the house unless it was encased in an Armani or Tom

Ford suit, or maybe a Vivienne Westwood outfit if the occasion called for evening wear. Her briefcase was Mulberry, her handbag Chanel and her shoes had red soles. She was impeccable and clearly expensive.

Eve took a pancake and slathered it in maple syrup. Life was too short for wheatgrass when she could have her gran's home-made pancakes in the morning.

'You didn't answer me earlier, Gran – how are you feeling about the move? Does it feel weird that you won't sleep in this house tonight?'

Her gran sat down and pulled her mug towards her, thinking through her answer before she said it. 'You know, in some ways it does, but I'm ready to go. We moved here from the house I grew up in when your mum was barely a year old and it's only the second home I've ever lived in. This house is nothing but memories and I'm grateful for all the smashing ones. I used to dance with your grandad over by the window while I was waiting for my potatoes to boil. And our Loretta once split the seams of her trousers doing a handstand against that door.'

There were no tears. That wasn't her gran's way. Even when grandad had died the year before, she'd held it together, said she was grateful for the years they'd had, but that he wouldn't want her to spend the rest of her life grieving. Cathy McLean was of that stoic generation whose leg could be hanging off and they'd say it was nothing a crepe bandage, a couple of painkillers and a seat wouldn't solve. Her gran was the most resilient woman she'd ever known, and Eve had always wondered if losing her parents so young had made her even stronger. How could it not? That said, Eve could hear the sadness in her voice today, see the pain in her smile, and it stung. This last year had been brutal, yet she was still whipping up pancakes and insisting she was fine.

'But, at the same time, I don't want to live surrounded by

memories. I'm seventy-five, I'm not dead. And now that I'm on my own, what do I need all this space for? Or the astronomical heating bills for a house that's way too big for me? I could have bought a small island with what I've paid in gas and electricity in the last year. Robbing bastards. Don't get me started...'

Helena rolled her eyes and spoke into her muesli. 'Oh God, here she goes. The MP for social justice.'

'Mum!' Eve chided her. 'Gran's right. It's been terrible. Gran, you should run to be a councillor. You're younger than the president of America. I'd vote for you.'

'Aye, that's what I'll do,' her gran got in on the joke. 'I reckon I've got a whole manifesto. Affordable energy. Set the retirement age at sixty and pay a decent pension. And make it law that women can take their bras off at six o'clock every night and let it all hang where nature intended. Oh, and free tickets to Tom Jones concerts for anyone who knows all the words to 'It's Not Unusual'.'

Eve immediately burst into song, rhyming off the whole first verse, before her gran joined in on the chorus.

'I don't know how I can be related to you two, I really don't,' her mum murmured, but the edges of her mouth were twitching. There was a sense of humour in there somewhere.

They finished with jazz hands and laughter, and Eve finally got the first bite of her pancake. 'Right, Mum, what's your birthday resolutions for this year then?'

Eve was pretty sure that 'discuss your paternity and tell you why I've lied all these years' wasn't one of them, but she didn't say that out loud.

Helena shrugged. 'Same as every year. Find a better work/life balance and travel more. Oh, and conquer this bloody menopause. It's making me so irritable and short-tempered.'

Eve ignored the swift kick her gran delivered under the table. She knew what Gran was thinking. Mum had been irritable and short-tempered since the beginning of time. The menopause was just taking the rap for it now.

Her gran piped up with a suggestion to help her mum's work/life woes. 'Helena, I think you and me should get on that Winder. I mean, what do we have to lose? Most of my pals are dead and you haven't been out on the town since the nineties, so maybe it's time we made an effort to expand our social lives.'

'Winder?' her mum muttered, confused.

Rock. Hard place. Eve knew what her gran meant but didn't want to say it in case it set her mum off. She resisted the urge to put her head on the table. This was exactly the kind of ribbing that Gran thought was hilarious, and her mother definitely did not. A United Nations peacekeeping force was required for these two.

'It's Tinder, Gran,' she murmured, ripping off the Band Aid. 'Tinder.'

'That's what I meant. Is there an elderly section?'

Eve sucked in her cheeks to stop herself from laughing. 'If there isn't, you can introduce it when you're the MP for the Over Seventies.'

'I'll add it to my manifesto. What do you say, Helena? Up for it?'

Her mum's sneer answered the question, even before she replied. 'I'd rather chew my own arm off. Why would I want someone else in my life? No thank you. Been there, done that, learned the lesson. I'll stick to running my own life, thanks very much.'

Pretty much the irritated rant that was expected. However, Eve saw an opportunity and went for it before she could think better of the idea.

'Did you ever fall in love with anyone else, Mum? I mean, apart from my dad?'

Fake dad. Fake dad. Fake dad.

Helena dropped her spoon back into her bowl, clearly uncomfortable talking about her personal life.

Eve watched her face closely, searching for something. Just a hint of a mystery. Of a story untold. But nope, her mum wasn't the best criminal defence advocate in Glasgow by accident. The woman had a poker face that didn't budge.

'No, once was enough.'

Bugger. So it wasn't some wild, random love affair that had resulted in her existence. What was it? And when?

'I can see why that one would put you off men, right enough,' her gran interjected. 'I always thought Bruce was a smarmy big chancer. When he announced to your dad that he wanted to propose, I was horrified, but when I told you about it... well, you were thrilled. And that was on your birthday too. Your last one as a single woman. Now what year would that have been...'

'1993,' Helena answered.

'That's right. Christmas Eve, 1993. Feels like yesterday. I wish I could go back in time, so I could warn you that he was going to be a cheating big tit years later. No, I take that back, because then I wouldn't have you here with me,' her gran threw Eve a wink, 'so I'll stick to the present day and just be old and knackered with the best granddaughter a woman could have.'

Eve could feel her face smiling at the compliment, but inside, her brain was cranking and firing out numbers on an internal calculator.

If Bruce 'fake dad' Quinn and her mum were madly in love, and he was planning to propose on Christmas Eve, 1993, and then Eve was born in September 1994, approximately nine and a half months later, then who the hell was her father?

And how was she going to get through today without asking?

5

HELENA

Christmas Eve 1993

The chambers in the Sheriff Court had the heating turned up way too high to compensate for the cold outside, and Helena could feel her body temperature rising under the silk of her blouse. Just as well she'd put on extra deodorant this morning. Not that there was a danger of anyone seeing her with something so ghastly as sweat marks. The beautifully cut navy-blue suit jacket she wore over her blouse would be staying on even if they got to sauna temperatures. It was all about professionalism. And while she couldn't yet afford the designer labels that some of her colleagues wore with nonchalant confidence, Helena McLean never let her standards drop for a second. Not even on Christmas Eve. And definitely not inside the courthouse.

She'd arrived at court bang on 10 a.m., for a case that was due to be called at 11 a.m., and she'd been waiting around ever since. It was all part of the job. Only a month after completing her statutory two-year training period, she could finally call herself a solicitor, but the truth was, she knew, that she'd been demonstrating her skills since the day she'd started at Hutchesons LLP. Everyone had expected her to join the same company as her father, Miller & Murphy, but she'd decided, with her dad's blessing, that she should establish her own identity and earn her success without any snide claims of nepotism. She'd also spent years interning at Miller & Murphy during summers and in any other spare time, and she didn't want to work somewhere that everyone knew her as the sixteen year old who'd franked the mail every night, or the eighteen year old who'd got tipsy the first time she'd been persuaded to go out after work with the girls from the typing pool. Looking back, she could see that they were just sucking up to her because she was one of the partner's daughters, but that had spectacularly backfired when they'd had to call her dad to collect her, and she'd thrown up on his shoes. Tough lesson and drunken night outs with the admin staff had never happened again.

For most of her training period since leaving uni and joining Hutchesons, she'd worked with lead counsel, and her closest friend in the firm, Bree Halston. Actually maybe, technically speaking, not close friend. It wasn't like they went for long lunches or met up at the weekend, unless they were preparing an important brief, but Helena felt they were definitely more than colleagues. Bree was five or six years ahead of her in both age and experience, but they'd clicked on Helena's first day on the job, and had formed a formidable team, with Helena doing all the background research, and contributing to case preparation and strategy, and then working together in court on any cases that required a second chair.

Helena was more than happy to learn from someone she considered one of the best and their success rate backed that up. They'd defended everything from drugs charges, to theft, to serious assault, and in the two years that Helena had been Bree's right-hand woman, they'd only lost a handful of times, and only then because the evidence made it a slam dunk. The rest of their clients were, of course, innocent.

At least, that's what Helena told herself. It had been one of the ethical dilemmas that had been much discussed during her law studies – how was it possible to defend someone if you were sure that they were guilty? For Helena, the separation of crime and client wasn't difficult. It was her job to give the best defence and it was a sheriff or jury's decision whether to convict. As long as she gave the case her best efforts, she had no problem sleeping at night. Apart from that one time a drug dealer from a notorious Glasgow crime gang got three years for smuggling crack up from down south and was so furious he promised to track Bree and Helena down when he got out. Bree dismissed it as part of the job, but Helena had made a note to keep an eye on his incarceration and tighten up the security at her flat before his release date.

Today's case didn't carry the same level of danger, given that this bloke was less of a drug mule, and more likely to get busted nicking Versace mules from their store in the Merchant City.

Bree had disappeared to speak to the clerk of court, so Helena went through the motions of checking her notes. What she should have been seeing there was a rundown of their client's actions on the day he stole over £1000 worth of fake-fur coats and jewellery from the St Enoch Shopping Centre, then assaulted a security guard with an ostrich feather muff. However, what she was actually seeing was just a blurred sheet because her eyes had glazed over and her mind had been hijacked by one thought. *He's going to propose.* Bruce Quinn was actually going to ask her to marry him. And it was intoxicating. Thrilling.

Before she'd met Bruce, she'd had a few casual relationships and a few one-night stands when she just wanted some physical fun, but nothing more because her studies and training took priority. Now, it was like she'd gone from zero to the stars, landing such a smart, sexy, utterly brilliant man. The prospect of marrying him appealed on so many levels. Physically. Professionally. Logistically. And it saved a whole lot of messing around with guys who weren't good enough. If this was the tombola at the fair, she was walking off with the best thing on the stall at the first attempt.

'What are you thinking about? You're in another world there,' Bree said with a friendly nudge to her shoulder. Not that Helena actually felt it. Between Bree's shoulder and hers, there was a whole load of power-dressing upholstery to cushion the blow. The sharp, shoulder-padded suit may have been an eighties fashion staple, but Helena and Bree had made a pact to never let it go.

For a second, Helena was tempted to answer the question truthfully, but she clamped her mouth shut. Probably best to wait until Bruce actually asked her before sharing it with the world. Or, more importantly, with anyone at the firm. They'd kept their relationship strictly secret because neither of them wanted to be the subject of gossip or rumours, especially with her being a junior and him being far more senior.

That would change now though. This wasn't some trifling little office fling – she was going to be Mrs Helena McLean Quinn. She was going to have to get her business cards changed and she'd only just got them. Maybe she'd just keep her maiden name for now. She'd never wanted to be accused of riding her dad's coattails, and she certainly wasn't going to let anyone attribute her advancement or success to her future husband.

Bree was still waiting for an answer, so she went with, 'Christmas! Just thinking about the things I've still got to organise before tomorrow. A few odds and ends to pick up.' She desperately wanted to add, 'Socks for Dad. Perfume for Mum. A fiancé for me,' but again, she clamped her jaw shut. Not yet. It would be so much sweeter to announce it with a rock on her finger. Bruce was always impeccably organised, so she knew he must have bought the ring already. On her way to work, she'd been pondering what it would look like. Impressive but elegant. A solitaire was her guess. Big but not flashy. Platinum.

Bree's grin preceded the second good news moment of the day. 'Well, I'm about to give you the best Christmas present, because the sheriff has adjourned the case. I explained our client was held up...'

'Is he?' Helena wondered if she'd missed something.

Bree pushed back her long poker-straight auburn hair and fastened her jacket. 'No idea. I was just stalling for time and living in hope, but the sheriff was having none of it. Adjourned until January, although he's agreed, in the spirit of Christmas, not to issue a warrant for his arrest for non-attendance today. Win-win. No harm to our waste-of-space client and we get to go home early on Christmas Eve.'

Today was just getting better and better.

'Look,' Bree went on. 'I'd really like to go join a friend for lunch, so would you mind going back to the office and filing this paperwork and then chasing down our client before you call it a day?'

Helena shook her head. 'Of course not. I'll take care of it. My sad obsession with doing everything in a timely manner would only spoil the rest of the day if I bunked off anyway.'

'Sad but true,' Bree agreed and Helena noticed how perfect her teeth were. Flawless. Like the rest of her. This was definitely veering between friendship and a bit of a girl crush. She wanted to be exactly like Bree Halston when she grew up.

They made their way out onto the street and Bree whistled for a taxi. One stopped almost immediately. 'Jump in and I'll drop you at the office,' Bree offered.

'No, it's fine, I can walk.' Even as she was saying it, Helena could feel the hot sweat being rapidly replaced with a pervasive chill that was seeping straight into her bones. Bloody hell, it must be about minus four degrees right now. Glasgow in December required more than a smart suit and heels.

'Don't be crazy – it would freeze your feet off out here and the whole city centre will be bedlam with Christmas shoppers. It'll take ages to navigate the crush.'

Helena didn't refuse a second time. Instead, she climbed into the black Hackney cab and took the flip-down seat opposite Bree. They chatted about their plans for New Year during the ten-minute ride back to the office, and when they got there, Bree stretched over and hugged her.

'Okay, well, I'll leave you here. Have a lovely Christmas and a fab birthday tomorrow, and I'll see you in January. Make sure you get every bit of enjoyment you can over the next couple of weeks, because I plan to keep that brilliant brain of yours busy next year.'

'Can't wait,' Helena said, returning the hug, clambering out and turning to wave as the taxi drove off. Her body temperature had finally regulated and now she just felt the warm glow of someone who was loving her life. Her cheeks were starting to hurt with smiling and that wasn't a familiar sensation on Planet Helena. She was much more comfortable at the focused and serious end of the emotional spectrum. Or as her mother called it, the 'face like a wet weekend' side of the scale. What her mother didn't understand was that the law and her own ambitions to succeed gave her much more pleasure than half a dozen Pina Coladas and a sing-song on a Saturday night lock-in at the salon. Her mum chose that life. The soon-to-be Helena McLean Quinn chose this one.

There were only a couple of secretaries and die-hard assistants still in the office, as the rest of her fellow solicitors had already bunked off for Christmas. They deserved it. All year long, they worked ninety-hour weeks, especially in the junior ranks, so no one could blame them for cutting short the work day on Christmas Eve. As soon as she was sure all tasks were completed, and her desk was clear, she had every intention of doing the same thing.

The white fairy lights on the eight-foot real tree in the hallway were twinkling, and there were cards on display on a few desks, but those – and the deserted rooms – were the only nods to the time of year.

In the office she shared with two others, both nowhere to be seen, Helena quickly filed the paperwork and updated the computer systems with the situation regarding this morning's case. Next, she called every phone number she had for their errant client – his own, his girlfriend's, his mum's – but they all went unanswered. She refused to judge herself for thinking they were probably all out partying on the profits of his latest ramraid, his mother sporting a natty new fake fur boa and a tiara from one of his more successful shoplifting sprees.

Everything done, she was about to head home when she noticed that Darleen, the secretary for the corporate team, was still at her desk. Maybe Bruce was still in the office too? She shouldn't ask in case it aroused suspicion. There was no professional reason for Helena and Bruce to communicate during work hours because they had completely different specialities – but sod it. Darleen wouldn't have a chance to spread gossip because the office was almost deserted, there were only a few working hours left in the day, and by the time they all came back to work in January, they'd be officially engaged anyway.

'Darleen, is Bruce Quinn still here?' Helena asked casually, loving the tiny flip of excitement that saying his name gave her.

This was crazy. She had never been this giddy over anything in her life, much less a man.

Darleen's right eyebrow rose in question, but she managed not to transfer the query to her mouth.

'No, he's already gone for the day. I think he said he was going out for lunch at the Rogano, then home.'

Damn. She'd missed him.

'Was it something I could help with?' Darleen fished.

Helena's smile was wide and only a tiny bit condescending. 'No, just had a quick question about something pertaining to a case I'm working on.' If Darleen knew she was lying, she didn't give anything away. 'Thanks, Darleen. Have a lovely Christmas.'

'You too, Helena.'

If the secretary's gaze was following her out the door, she might have noticed an extra little swagger in Helena's step.

Outside, the cold hit her instantly. What she wouldn't give for an ostrich feather muff right now. She checked her watch and did a quick analysis of the situation. It was almost noon. It would take her about twenty-five minutes to get home on foot, or she could jump in a taxi and be home in ten. Or... she replayed Darleen's words. Bruce was having lunch at the Rogano. It was his favourite eatery, a stunning art deco seafood restaurant just off Royal Exchange Square. Bruce dined there every day that he was free – sometimes with colleagues or clients, but quite happily alone too. He had a standing reservation for his favourite table, the last walnut burr booth in the back corner of the beautiful room. It was a spot that gave him privacy for confidential conversations, but still allowed him to soak in the atmosphere of the venue. It was close to the office too, only about ten minutes' walk from where she was now.

The decision was instant. She would discreetly pop in and see if he was with colleagues. If so, she'd back out without interrupting, or feign surprise and claim it was a chance meeting. However, if he was alone, she could join him and start their Christmas and her birthday celebrations early. Win-win.

Anticipation and the crowds in the streets kept her warm until she turned into Exchange Place, just off Buchanan Street, and saw the Rogano straight ahead, under a breathtakingly beautiful blanket of fairy lights that were strung between the buildings.

Her cheeks were starting to ache from smiling again, as she pulled open the heavy door, and was immediately greeted by the maître d'. Behind him, she could see that the restaurant was already packed with its usual early lunchtime trade, complemented by groups of Christmas shoppers, bags emblazoned with the names of the upmarket stores in the nearby Princes Square shopping centre piled at their feet.

'Good afternoon,' the maître d' welcomed her. 'Table for one?'

Helena stretched up to peer over his left shoulder at the row of booths on the right side of the wall. 'No, I'm actually just looking for a friend.'

Her gaze went from the front of the room to the back and, yep, there Bruce was, sitting on a leather banquette in the very last booth. His square jaw was set and his brow was furrowed, as if he was listening intently. He clearly wasn't alone, but the partition between his booth and the one before it blocked her view, so she couldn't see who was with him. Whatever they were discussing looked serious, so it was probably a client. Ah well, that settled it. She wouldn't disturb a work lunch, so best to just leave it and catch up with him at home later.

Just as that thought made her begin to turn, she caught a movement, as his elbows went onto the table and one hand moved forward. Turn aborted. Instead, bypassing the maître d', she took a few steps forward, her eyes locked on the table as a hand from the anonymous figure in the other side of the booth came down and settled on his.

Another few steps.

He leaned forward, as if reaching over to stroke someone's face.

Another few steps.

The person opposite him began to come into view. A flash of auburn hair.

A few more steps.

Bruce's hand. Touching alabaster skin. Tenderly. His thumb caressing a cheek.

Helena froze.

This was the man who was supposed to be planning to propose to her tonight.

So what the fuck was he doing stroking Bree Halston's face?

6

CATHY

Christmas Eve 1968

The last half hour had been the most awkward of Cathy's life. Richie had frozen for at least ten seconds while his brain had tried to absorb the enormity of the situation, before Loretta had broken in with, 'Richie, I think you should sit down, before you fall down. Because if you knock yourself unconscious, me and chubby over there are never going to be able to lift you.'

For once, Cathy had been grateful for Loretta's interruption and her unfailing habit of saying exactly what she thought at all times.

'No, I think I should go. It's fine. Sorry.' He'd started to back out, but Cathy had finally found her voice.

'No, don't. Please. Sit down. Have some tea. I know it won't help, but I'd like to talk to you.'

His hesitation had told her that the only thing he wanted to do was run. Behind him, Loretta had taken a small step to the side, so that she was blocking the door, making it more of a hostage situation than a social visit, but Richie hadn't seemed to register that. Instead, after a momentary pause, he'd come forward and pulled out the chair at the opposite side of Mum's old oak table, so that they were facing each other, only a couple of feet apart.

'I'll make more tea,' Loretta had offered. 'And I'll chat nonsense while I'm doing it and then I'll leave, so save anything you don't need me to hear until after I'm gone. Richie, have you heard that Captain Kirk bloke from Star Trek has done his own version of 'Lucy In The Sky With Diamonds'? Honest to God, it would have been a mercy if the Starship Enterprise had left him behind in space. If he ever meets the Beatles in a dark alley it would be even more awkward than you two sitting there,' she'd wittered, with such a knowing look and perfect timing that, if this had been any other occasion, with any other person across from her at this table, Cathy would have laughed until she needed another of her thousand daily visits to the loo. This baby was clearly very comfy right on top of her bladder.

As it was, she just sat in silence as Richie had replied, 'Nope, but I heard the Rolling Stones new song. Something about the devil. I mean, it's weird, but it's got a great tune.'

Grabbing the kettle, Loretta had been on the way to the sink when she'd shot back, 'Right? That's exactly what I think. I love them. I mean, I'll always love The Doors and maybe even The Beatles more, but...' And on she went, dissecting the current music scene as only a sixteen-year-old could. Filling the kettle and waiting for it to boil was accompanied by a monologue on John Lennon's brilliance. Emptying the teapot and popping in fresh leaves invoked an enthusiastic review of Mick Jagger's fashion choices. Pouring the newly boiled water in the teapot and getting the cups ready came with a couple of verses of Marvin Gaye's 'I Heard It Through The Grapevine'. And finally, pouring the tea through the strainer, adding two sugars to each cup and delivering it to the table was fuelled by the declaration that she really wanted The Doors new album for Christmas. It had been the only positive since the minute Richie had walked in the door.

She'd put the cups down with a flourish, kissed Cathy on the cheek, and announced that she was going off to work for a few hours and would check in on her later.

'She's changed a bit,' Richie had said, with a fond smile when the door banged behind her.

'It's been a while. She turned sixteen last month.' The tension and nervousness Cathy had been feeling gave the comment an edge that made it sound like a dig and she had immediately wanted to take it back. Instead, she'd followed it right up with, 'Tell me about your job. Was it as good as you hoped?'

That had at least got him talking, allowing her to just listen and try to take in the sight in front of her. Richie's unseasonal tan looked great on him and so did the longer hair. They'd started going out together in the third year of high school, where Richie had played for the football team, and that tall, athletic frame was still there, but his shoulders were wider, his arms thicker.

He'd explained that he'd been on board the same ship for pretty much the whole time he'd been away, learning his craft as an engineer and...

She'd tuned out. Now, his mouth was still moving, sometimes hers did too, but she felt nothing except confusion and heard nothing but blood rushing in her ears, until thirty minutes of surface conversation, internal turmoil and awkwardness had gone by and she suddenly blurted out, 'I'm sorry.'

Richie halted his jittery, nervous story and lifted his eyes to settle on her for the first time since he'd sat down. Goosebumps were making Cathy shiver, and the tension was making her sweat, so she wasn't sure whether to pull on a jumper or open a window.

Either way, she knew that any kind of anxiety wasn't good for the baby, so she made an effort to slow her breathing and gave her stomach a gentle rub.

For a moment, neither of them spoke, until Richie cleared his throat. 'You've got nothing to apologise for. I think I should be saying sorry to you. None of this is the way I thought it would be and that's my fault. I left.'

'You did,' Cathy stated the obvious, keeping her voice tender this time so that it didn't sound petty.

Richie Clark had been her boyfriend since they were thirteen years old, when he'd slipped her a note in maths asking if she wanted to go to Crossmyloof Ice Rink with him that weekend. It was on the other side of Glasgow, and it took two buses to get there, but it was a favourite hangout because they played music on a Friday night and there was a chippy nearby so they could get a fish supper for the buses on the way home.

She'd gone that night, and that had been it. He was the first boy she ever dated. Her boyfriend for the next five and a bit years. And the first person she'd ever slept with. Just once. On the night before he'd left to take up his new job eighteen months ago.

It had been her decision to go all the way with him. She'd been trying to hide the fact that she was distraught that he was leaving, devastated that she was losing someone else, and so, so tired of being strong and taking care of everything. Just once, she'd wanted a bit of fun. A bit of escape. It had been amazing and she'd never regretted it, not even for a second, not even when he got on a train the next day and she'd swallowed back aching sobs as she waved him away.

A sad smile crossed Cathy's face. 'But I made you go. I talked you into it.'

He didn't argue, because they both knew it was true. That was a day she didn't ever want to revisit.

'How long are you home for?' she asked him. Not that it mattered now. For the first few months after he left, if he'd turned up on her doorstep, she'd have considered it the happiest day of her life. Now? Each circle of the minute hand on the kitchen clock chipped another tiny fragment off her heart.

'Just until the day after Boxing Day. The ship docked yesterday, and I came up on the sleeper train. Got into Glasgow an hour ago.'

He'd come straight here. That wasn't lost on her. His first port of call.

Struggling to fill yet another pause, Richie took a sip of his tea and then grimaced.

Despite the situation, Cathy laughed. 'Loretta still makes terrible tea. Not that I could ever tell her that. Couldn't bear to hurt her feelings.'

He sat back in his chair, a tiny bit more relaxed in his body language. 'It's my fault for letting it go cold.' Cathy almost bought his stoic defence of Loretta's tea until he added an amused, 'But it's always been truly miraculous that she can go that wrong with just water, milk, sugar and tea.'

It was the icebreaker they both needed. The little anchor of familiarity that made them recognise each other again.

'I know I need to ask you who you married, but I'm terrified in case it's Billy from chemistry, with the cabbage in his lunch box and the bad breath.'

It was as if he was becoming more himself with every exchange in the conversation. This was more like the Richie she knew. Funny. Always with a joke. Always making her laugh. Never taking himself seriously.

She feigned astonishment. 'It is! I just banned the cabbage and the bad breath disappeared. I can't believe you guessed it was him.'

Now it was his turn to for astonishment. 'You're kidding!'

She managed to keep a straight face for a solid five seconds before she crumbled. 'Of course, I'm kidding. It's not Billy. Although, I might put up with the bad breath now because his granny just won ten thousand pounds on the Premium Bonds a few months ago and bought him a brand-new Ford Cortina.'

'Bloody hell. I might marry him for that.'

Another silence, but not so awkward this time. Just sore on the heart to have to reply to what he was asking. 'His name is Duncan. Duncan McLean. He's not anyone you know. I met him when he came into the shop because the barber next door was fully booked. We got chatting while I was cutting his hair and...'

She let that trail off. Telling him about how they got together seemed too personal, felt like it would be disloyal to Duncan. Or maybe too hurtful to Richie.

A thought must have struck him, because he suddenly scanned the room. 'Does your husband live here?'

Cathy understood. He was thinking that nothing had noticeably changed since the last time he was here. The same walls, painted yellow, except the one behind the kitchen units, which Mum had wallpapered with special stuff that you could wipe clean. It was white, had pretend tile squares on it and lemons in the middle of every third square. The same white cupboards still lined the walls. They had the same cooker, the same undercounter fridge with the tiny icebox at the top, and the space next to the back door where they kept the twin tub washing machine. Everything on the brown fake wood worktops was exactly the same, in exactly the same place. This table hadn't changed and neither had the wooden chairs with the flowery pads on the seats. Mum had made those herself and she'd been so proud of them, declaring that it was like sitting on clouds. There was, Cathy realised, not a single sign that someone new lived here with them.

'He does, but only at weekends. It's a long story.'

'I've got all day. My plans have been cancelled. I was going to see my girlfriend and spend time with her, but it seems like she got a better offer while I was gone.'

Ouch. 'Richie don't...'

His face flushed. 'I'm sorry. That made me sound like an idiot. I just... I just don't know what to say. Help me out here, Cath.'

Reaching over, she put her hand over his and the jolt of electricity was so sharp, she almost pulled it back. How she had loved this boy. And yep, that's what he had been. Just a boy. And she'd been a carefree teenager too when they'd got together. Now that seemed like a lifetime ago and she felt older, wearier.

'Okay, I'm just going to say it and tell me if you want me to stop.' She took a breath. 'It was a few days before Christmas last year when Duncan and I met...'

'I was supposed to come home last Christmas.'

'You were?'

We got back to shore the week before, but there was a fire in the engine room, so we had to stay on to deal with it and get it ready for the next sailing. I'd been planning to surprise you then too. Now I wish I had.'

Neither of them even wanted to consider the implications of that or how it could have changed the situation they were in now. Cathy pushed a whole chorus of 'What If's' away by carrying on with her answer.

'Duncan was in Glasgow visiting some pals. He's from Edinburgh originally. Went to university in St Andrews and then moved back to Edinburgh to finish his training.'

'Training for what?'

'He's a solicitor.'

Richie just nodded and Cathy wondered what he was thinking. None of their friends had become solicitors. Most of his pals took up apprenticeships and were electricians, plumbers, or they worked in the shipyards like both their dads. And most of hers became hairdressers like her, secretaries like her mum or worked as receptionists in the big offices in the city centre. Except Janine McLay, who was a model in one of the posh dress shops on Bath Street, but she had legs like lamp posts and a face like Sophia Loren, so it wasn't surprising.

'He still works in Edinburgh during the week, and he'll do that until he finishes his training next month, then he'll move here full time. He comes home here at the weekends, so he'll be back later on tonight. Anyway, we started seeing each other and...'

Her face flushed at the thought of telling him what happened next, but there was no way round it. 'Around May, I realised that this little one was on the way. We got married three weeks later in the registry office in Martha Street. Loretta was our bridesmaid and Duncan's brother was our best man. His family came too, but they live in Edinburgh, so we don't see them much. It all happened so fast...'

Richie's shoulders seemed to slump with every new fact in the story and she could see that he understood the situation. She'd been dealt a massive blow when her parents were killed and she had been left to bring up Loretta. They'd scraped by, but it wasn't easy. When she'd found herself pregnant, she'd known that adding a baby into that equation would have been so much more difficult. Impossible, really. How could she have worked? How would she have supported them? And that was before she had to deal with other people's nonsense and judgements. Her friends would all stand by her, of course, and so would the girls in the salon, but she'd seen how people treated single mothers, the gossip and the nudges and the terrible things that were said. Bloody hypocrites. No such rotten things said about the dads that ditched the women as soon as they got in the family way, right enough. Oh no. Off they went without even a look over their shoulder.

But not Duncan. As soon as he'd found out, he'd asked her to marry him, and he'd stuck by her and Loretta. During the week, when he was in Edinburgh, he stayed with his parents, so that gave him the finances to take over the costs of running this house. She hadn't even had to ask him. He'd just stepped up, and done the right thing by them all. The memory of that made her smile. 'Cathy, I've wanted to marry you since the first time I saw you,' he'd said. 'This just makes it all happen a bit quicker and I'm okay with that if you are.'

What was she going to say to that? He was such a decent man. A catch. Any girl would be so lucky to have him. And what choice did she have? Richie was long gone and even if he wasn't, wel—

His voice snapped her back to her kitchen.

'I wish I'd known.'

'There was nothing you could have done. It was too late.'

'Was it though?' He leaned forward in the chair again. 'Too late because of the baby, or too late because you love this other guy?'

'It doesn't matter,' she snapped, refusing to go down the path that led to any other option than the one she was on now. She'd been out of choices back then. She'd done the only thing that was right for them all.

'It does. Do you love him? The way you loved me?'

Her reply stuck in her throat. Yes, she loved Duncan for what he'd done for them, for the man that he'd shown himself to be. Was she *in* love with him? Was it the crazy, heart-thudding way she'd felt about Richie? No. But she wasn't going to disrespect Duncan by admitting that.

'Yes.' She held his gaze with defiance, daring him to call her a liar even though they both knew that she was. 'You left, Richie. He didn't.'

'No, you don't get to do that. I left because we had a deal—'

'Well, I guess I broke it. I hadn't heard from you for six months when I went out that first night with Duncan, and it's just as well I didn't wait, because now it's been a year and a half. What did you expect, Richie? That I'd wait for you forever?' The truth was, that if Duncan hadn't walked into the salon that day and caught her in a weak moment, she probably would have. He was the only other man she'd ever touched, ever kissed, and Cathy was sure in her heart that there would never be another.

The vehemence in her reply made Richie fall silent again. The Cathy she'd been when her parents were still alive would never have stuck up for herself like that, but the last three years had made her stronger than she ever thought she could be and she damn well wasn't going to let him guilt her for doing the right thing. The *only* thing.

Eventually, he found his words. 'If I'd been here, would I have been able to change your mind. Would you have chosen me?'

Her heart said she would. Her brain and her mouth lied again, 'No. I'd have chosen Duncan.'

Richie gently dropped her hand and stood up. 'Then I'll go. For what it's worth, I'm sorry, Cathy. I really am. I hope you have a great life.'

She couldn't look at him any more, so she stared into her cup as he walked across the room, down the hall and out of the front door.

With every step, another tear dropped into her cold tea.

She had no idea how long she'd been sitting there when the doorbell rang. It crossed her mind to ignore it, but Mrs Copeland next door had taken to handing in a pie or a casserole every few days, and Cathy didn't want the lovely old dear standing out there in the cold holding a heavy dish. Or maybe it was the postman with Christmas cards or notification that she'd won enough on the

Premium Bonds to buy a Ford Cortina too. Chance would be a fine thing.

With a groan, she pushed herself up, and gingerly, hand pressing on the ache in her lower back, made her way down the hall and opened the door.

It wasn't the postman or a kind neighbour with a home made pie.

It was Richie. And he spoke before she could say a word. 'Spend the day with me. Please. I just want to talk. To make things okay with us. You're my best friend, Cath. There's no-one else I want to see. I promise I won't try to change your mind about who you should be with.'

Cathy wasn't sure he would have to try very hard, because she saw the pain on his gorgeous face, felt the tug of love that was twisting her gut, and realised with absolute devastation that he could walk away right now and she'd never see him again.

Spending the day with him was a terrible idea. Awful. The worst decision she could make.

Yet she didn't seem to be able to stop herself taking a step back and holding the door wide open so he could come back in.

12 NOON – 2 P.M.

7

EVE

Christmas Eve 2023

The doorbell rang and her mum used the interruption to announce that she was off to the office. Eve tried not to show her surprise.

'Don't you want to stay with Gran until she's ready to go?' she hissed to her mother, making sure her gran, who was on her way to the door, didn't overhear.

Her mum slipped Eve's woolly hat and scarf birthday pressie into her Chanel bag (no doubt to languish in the back of a drawer until the end of time), picked up her Hermès silk scarf and grabbed a coat that probably cost more than Eve's car. With a career that paid an exorbitant salary, and only herself to spend it on, Helena made no apology for indulging herself in the finer things in life. Eve couldn't ever remember a time when her mother wasn't impeccably groomed. As a child, she'd watch her mum pull her perfect glossy bob back into a chignon at the nape of her neck, step into an expensive suit, apply her trademark red lipstick and she'd wonder at how beautiful and smart she looked. Even in adulthood, Eve still couldn't pull off that level of aesthetic perfection. There would be creases in her shirt, perhaps the odd coffee splash on her suit, and her make-up free complexion would probably be a shiny shade of Santa's suit with the anxiety of the day.

'Darling, what is there to say? The place is empty. Time to move on. Gran will be fine. If I get done sharpish, I'll pop over to the new place tonight to make sure she's settled in.'

Eve noted the 'if I get done sharpish'. Her mother had worked obscene hours all her life, staying in the office or bringing work home and sitting at her desk until late at night. It didn't surprise her that Christmas Eve was included in that too.

As far back as Eve could remember, she'd always spent Christmas Eve with her gran. They had created their own traditions. If it was any day other than a Sunday, she'd spend the afternoon in Gran's salon, sitting in the staffroom with a pile of books or passing out Christmas crackers at reception, wrapped up in the excitement as everyone shared their plans over blaring festive songs and clinking glasses of fizzy wine. Then she'd walk home with Gran, and they always stopped at a little park, not far from the house, that was all lit up with fairy lights and looked magical. They'd sit on a bench there and they'd both make a wish, but they would never reveal what it was, because then Gran said it wouldn't come true.

Just thinking about that now made Eve smile, as did the memory of Grandad, who usually arrived home just after them. They'd all have a dance in the kitchen and watch movies in front of the fire, eating fish and chips out of the paper. Before she went to bed, Eve would hang their stockings, and leave out carrots for Rudolph and milk and chocolate digestives for Santa. When she was twelve and wiser to the realities of the man in the red suit, she'd asked if she could stop it and been given a firm reprimand from her granny. Apparently, it was a non-negotiable part of their Christmas preparations. Turned out that after she was asleep, her gran would immediately pop the carrots into the soup she was making for the following day, and her grandad had the milk and biscuits as his midnight snack and wasn't for giving it up.

Every year, they did the same thing and Eve treasured every moment. It was just a shame that her mum had never been a part of that, no matter how many times she'd been invited to join them over the years. When Eve was growing up, Helena always arrived late Christmas Eve, after she was in bed at her gran's, or first thing on Christmas morning, before Eve was awake. Either way, she always made it so that she was there to open presents. Eve had always put her mum's Christmas Eve absence down to Helena having pre-birthday plans with her friends, and it had honestly never bothered her back then. Probably because she didn't know any different and because she adored her traditions with Gran and Grandad. Today, her mum was making it clear that her other option was work, yet she was still choosing that instead of spending time with them. Now, with the perspective of adulthood, it irritated the life out of her. What the hell was her mother's problem? Why did she refuse to just relax and enjoy Christmas Eve with people she loved? Was she so devoid of warmth and affection that she couldn't even do that? Eve reckoned that was probably the case. There was no helping this woman.

Her mum's clipped words made her seethe inside, but again, today wasn't the day to say anything. She didn't want Gran's last memory here being of Eve telling her mother she was a heartless cow who could stick her Louboutin boots up her Armani-clad arse.

Breathe. Breathe. And breathe.

Her mother's heels clicked across the tile floor to the doorway, where she met Gran coming the other way. 'I'm off, Mum. Thank you for the birthday brunch and I'll maybe see you later. If not, I'll be over tomorrow morning.'

Eve half expected her to say, 'Unless I get a better offer,' but instead, she kissed Cathy on each cheek, swerved around her like a pro, and was off.

Her gran flashed Eve a knowing smile as the front door closed. 'Why do you let her press your buttons? You know what she's like. She doesn't mean anything by it – it's just who she is.' For years, her gran had been going with that motion for the defence, and much as Eve knew she was right, it didn't always help. Especially today, when she had a huge bloody great elephant-shaped, genetic, who's-my-daddy, grievance in the room.

'I know, I know, you're right. Who was at the door?'

She didn't need to wait for an answer, because Sonny appeared right behind her gran, dangling a set of keys in his hand. 'Here we go, Cathy! The keys to the new place.' Her gran hugged him. 'Honestly, son, if I were forty years younger and you liked bingo, we'd be perfect together.'

Eve shook her head, laughing at her gran's incessant cheekiness.

Sonny returned the hug. 'I know. It's one of the great travesties of my life. That and the fact that your granddaughter doesn't want to fall in love with me.'

'Try diamonds, son. I'm not saying she can be bought, because I don't fancy your chances, but if she doesn't like the jewellery, maybe she can flog it and get a new car. That one she's got is a hazard. It makes my false teeth rattle.'

'I'm having nothing to do with either of you,' Eve quipped, taking the keys from Sonny, and throwing him a side eye of amusement.

Sonny West. One of four flatmates when she was in her final

year at Glasgow College of Art – the other three being an aspiring engineer, a trainee nurse and a plumber. They'd lived in a tenement flat just off Sauchiehall Street and it had been a carefree time of drunken late-night occasional hook-ups with Sonny.

After graduation, she'd gone on to land a job as a booker in a talent agency, kicking off with Gabby as her very first client, and Sonny had gone to work for a city centre estate agency. Back then, she'd envisaged that they might all lose touch, but nope, something had stuck with her and Sonny. Over the eight years since then, their casual, no-strings sex, had been interrupted by a few monogamous ill-fated relationships on both sides, all of which invariably ended with the two of them having drinks in a bar, proclamations of 'relationships are for fools' and the resumption of a friends-with-benefits arrangement – until the next time one of them met someone they wanted to be faithful to, and they'd go through the whole cycle again.

Eve had been under the impression that suited them both, until a few nights ago – yep, it was a week for emotional bombshells – when they'd had an intimate moment over a thin crust Hawaiian at Pizza Express. At least, as intimate as they could be with East 17 warbling about staying another day on the sound system. And while sitting next to a Christmas night out that seemed to comprise of twelve elderly ladies telling raucous jokes and singing Christmas songs while demolishing deep pan turkey pizzas. If she wasn't with Sonny, Eve would definitely have wanted to join them.

Sonny had been in jeans and a jacket, looking smart and slick, while she was trying and failing to pull off day-to-night office chic that the magazines always heralded like it was some magical transformation. Eve could confirm that adding a big pair of hoops from Accessorize and swapping her Converse for a pair of heels, hadn't in fact, transformed her from 'every day office wear' to a

Kardashian at a cocktail bar. Not that she cared. All the mattered was the wine, the food and the chat with her favourite bloke. She'd been relaying a story about how she'd been packing up old photos at Cathy's house, and came across one of her gran, aged about fifteen and beyond beautiful, ice skating in a tiny Biba dress with backcombed hair that added a solid six inches to her height, when he'd suddenly blurted, 'Have you ever thought that maybe we should give it a try?'

Her ham and pineapple slice of goodness had frozen, midway to her mouth. 'What? Ice skating? I don't think I've got the balance for it. I'd end up in accident and emergency.'

'No, us. You and me.'

'Give what a try?' It just wasn't sinking in.

'A relationship. A proper one. Drop the whole casual thing and give it a proper go, just us.'

'As in, be together? All the time?'

Sonny had laughed as he'd picked up the next slice of pizza. 'Well, no I need Wednesday night off for football, but apart from that...'

Eve was still staring at him, chin dropped, baffled. It wasn't that she didn't want to. Sonny was a catch. Solvent. Attractive. On the downside, he probably spent too much time in workout shorts and occasionally wore a baseball cap backwards at the weekend, but if he didn't do those things, she'd have nothing to tease him about. It was more that... well, she'd never given it any real thought before because she liked their arrangement the way it was. She had no desire to be in something serious. No desperate need for commitment. And what if it didn't work out? Then one of her closest friends would be nothing but a memory? She wasn't ready for that.

'I don't know. Can I think about it?'

Sonny had feigned devastation. 'You mean you're not going to faint with gratitude and tell me you've been dreaming about me saying all that for years?'

'No. Fainting would be a criminal waste of this pizza. What's brought this on, Sonny?' she'd asked, turning serious. 'I thought you had an aversion to commitment.'

'True. You're not wrong. And I know what I'm about to say goes right against all those bollocks stereotypes, but I was thirty this year and I'm thinking maybe it's time to stop messing around and get my life together. You know, do the grown up stuff. Marriage. Kids.'

A sharp inhalation of shock had forced a chunk of pineapple to get lodged in Eve's throat, and after a couple of seconds of airless choking, a sharp cough had sent it firing across the table.

'Okay, I'd rather not kill you in the process of this discussion, so I'll just leave it with you. I'd like us to try full commitment. Maybe move in together. See if it works.'

Luckily, she wasn't consuming pineapple at the 'moving in together' part.

She was scared to ask the obvious question, but she did it anyway. 'And if I don't think that's right for me?'

'Then maybe we need to call this quits, Eve. It's too easy. Too comfortable. If we don't change something now, then what? Much as I like the thought of the naked bits, I don't want us to still be single and meeting a couple of times a week for a shag when we're fifty.'

It was a fair point, but her intention to give it serious thought had been derailed by the minor blip of the DNA results that questioned her very existence. Now, in her gran's kitchen, as he came over to hug her, she could see that there were positives to his suggestion. Her gargantuan to-do list was being replaced by a gargantuan 'Sonny's Plus Points' list. She was attracted to him. They had great sex. He was one of her favourite people to hang out with. He made her laugh. And it wasn't like there were any deep dark secrets between them. They'd been mates for so long, she knew everything there was to know about him.

Before she could add anything else, the bulging frame of Harry, the head guy in the removal company, filled the doorway. Harry and his lads had totally saved the day for her gran. None of the removal companies that they'd contacted had been available, but Sonny had explained the predicament to the developer who'd built the flats Gran was moving into, and they'd pulled some strings and sorted everything out for them. Apparently, the developer also owned a removals firm, so he'd sent his own people to do the job. According to Gran, Harry usually worked on the construction side, but he'd volunteered to do some grafting today because the team was short-staffed over Christmas.

'Right, Mrs McLean, that's us all done. The cleaners have finished up upstairs too and just need to give the kitchen another quick going over, so we're good to go and get out of their way.'

Sonny had organised everything else for the move, using the cleaning team that worked for his agency, so it had been as seamless as it could possibly be. Eve added 'Resourcefulness' and 'Kindness' to Sonny's list.

'Latisha came with me,' he said, referring to his highly efficient and capable assistant at the branch, 'and she is going to take the keys for here back to the office as soon as the cleaners are done. I'll come with you to the new place and make sure it's perfect, then I'll just hop in a cab back to the office.'

The list was back out and Eve added, 'Caring. Considerate. Organised.'

'Right, Harry and I will rally the troops and get the rest of this stuff lifted,' Sonny gestured to the patio table and chairs.

'We're not taking any of this with us, so it can just go back into the shed for the next folks who live here.'

Sonny nodded. 'Even better. We'll get that sorted and then we'll wait outside and let you have a minute to wander around here and say goodbye.'

'Emotionally intelligent'. Tick.

Eve held out her hand. 'Come on, Gran. Let's do one last tour.'

Cathy took her hand and followed her into the hall and upstairs, Eve moving slower than normal so that her gran didn't get winded on the stairs.

It was so strange to see the house empty. Taking the contents of a large old Victorian, three-bedroom home that had been lived in by the same people for over half a century and fitting it into a two-bedroom flat would have been an impossible, chaotic task, so as soon as her gran had signed the contracts to sell, Eve had gone around the house with her, pinpointing exactly what her gran wanted to take to the new place and ruthlessly editing out everything else. Eve had never seen a clear-out like it. It had been a two-month project – clearing every drawer, every cupboard, and every nook and cranny of the house. They'd found four Christmas trees, a million toys, six suitcases and ten year's worth of old birthday cards in the loft alone.

Anything that couldn't be repurposed was taken to the landfill, but everything else was distributed wisely. Her gran whittled her clothes down to a capsule wardrobe and every other well-preserved garment in the house (including boxes of clothes that were Eve's when she was a kid) was taken to the local refugee centre or to the nearest charity shop. All the extra furniture, crockery, cutlery and kitchen items were donated to a women's aid centre, to help furnish flats for women moving on after escaping from domestic violence. The end result was the two packed Luton vans sitting in the drive, and a house full of empty rooms.

On the top landing, they stopped at the room that had been her mother's first, then Eve's when she stayed here, which was almost every weekend and all summer growing up. They were alone. In a special place. This could be a moment to ask about the whole 'who's my dad' thing, but again, Eve didn't want to take this time away from her gran, so she clamped her mouth shut.

'I loved every single night that I would come in here and see your sleeping face,' her gran said, nodding to the other wall of the empty room, by the window, where they'd pushed Eve's bed when she was five because she wanted to see the stars when she was falling asleep. It had stayed there until yesterday, when Harry's guys had loaded up the first van.

'I loved every single night that I was here,' Eve said, the words catching in her throat. Wow. Gran was holding up, but she was feeling this right in the heart.

Gran squeezed her hand, and they made their way to the next room, the one Gran and Grandad had slept in for fifty-four years. Her gran blew a soft kiss into the room. 'Goodnight, Duncan. Sleep tight, my love. And thank you for our lives together.'

Oh, dear lord. The lump in Eve's throat got even bigger. Her grandad had been a lovely man. Kind. Quiet. Maybe a little serious. However, he had the razor-sharp legal mind that her mum had inherited, with none of the superior abrasiveness. He couldn't have been more different from her gran, but they'd always seemed happy. Content. Yep, that was the word.

Eve deliberately stayed silent, wanting to let her gran have the moment, but they were still holding hands when they took a couple of steps into the doorway of the third and final room. That's when it all got too much for her gran.

'Oh, Loretta,' she whispered into the void, huge fat tears sliding down her face now. 'I miss you so much. It still feels like half my heart is gone.'

Eve put her arm around Cathy's shoulders. 'Gran, it's okay.'

'I just...' Gran pulled a tissue out from the cuff of her pink cardigan and dabbed at her eyes. 'I just feel like a part of me is missing.'

Eve had a fleeting thought that she should perhaps be miffed that her childhood memories hadn't evoked this kind of emotion, and for that matter, neither had her dearly departed grandad, but she chided herself for the uncharitable thought.

'Gran, you'll see her again one day...'

'Will I though?'

There was a pause, as Eve tried to work out what to say, to frame it gently, to show that she had compassion, empathy. Then she decided that was a waste of time and went for a firm dose of reality.

'Yes! Gran, she's just doing a cabaret in Benidorm, she's not dead!'

Cathy blew her nose so loudly it was a wonder the windows didn't rattle. Aunt Loretta, the family superstar since she was discovered singing her heart out while she was doing a music agent's blow-dry in a Glasgow hairdressing salon back in 1968. Her heyday was long gone, and she was over seventy now, but she was still a much-revered, iconic blast from the past who packed them in at holiday resorts across Europe. Glasgow's answer to Cher had been on a one-year residency at a five-star hotel on the Costa Blanca since May.

'Right, let's go, Gran. We can call Aunt Loretta when we get to your new place.'

'On your FaceTime thingy? I want to see her.'

'Yep, on the FaceTime thingy.' Eve tried and failed to hold back a chuckle. Her gran stubbornly refused to embrace modern technology except when it suited her, then she demanded a FaceTime call or a double caramel cappuccino from the coffee machine Eve bought her for her birthday.

Back downstairs, Sonny was waiting at the front door for them.

He spotted Eve's red eyes and shot her a quizzical look. 'Everything okay?'

Eve glanced at her gran, who, by some magical restorative powers, had gone from full-scale tears and snot to fresh as a daisy, the second she'd tucked her hanky back up her sleeve. Great. Cathy was ready to embrace the rest of the day, and Eve was already so drained she needed a lie-down. There was definitely some kind of generational swap going on here.

'Everything's fine. Right, Gran, grab your coat. My car is in the drive.'

After picking up her parka and her bag, Cathy sashayed past them, to a waiting Harry, who took her hand and steered her towards his van.

'No thanks, lovely. Harry said I could ride in his cab. I've always wanted to be a trucker. And besides, I'm not going in that claptrap of yours. I've made it to seventy-five, and I'd quite like to get to seventy-six in one piece.'

With that, the poor, devastated woman who'd been breaking her heart just moments ago blew her a kiss and climbed up into the passenger side of Harry's vehicle like a twenty-five-year-old hitchhiker going off on an adventure.

Sonny watched her go, laughing. 'I really hope you're like that at her age.'

'Nope, she'll have been the death of me by then. *Here lies Eve McLean, worn out and exhausted trying to keep up with her granny.* Come on. And don't say a bloody word about my car.'

They climbed into her old, and admittedly weathered Jeep Renegade, and she gave the dashboard a pat, just in case the car had some kind of sentient powers and had been listening. A hundred and twenty thousand miles and it was still going. That was the very definition of a survivor.

After a couple of shaky starts, Eve pulled out of the driveway and fell in behind Harry's van, riding in convoy with the second van containing all the stuff that had been packed up yesterday. Now, Gran's entire worldly goods were being driven along Great Western Road, on a crunchy blanket of snow.

'Fairytale of New York' was belting from the speakers of the car, and the Christmas lights were already on and dangling from the lamp posts. For the first time today, a wave of Christmas spirit made Eve smile.

'Tell me,' Sonny asked her. 'Are you grinning like that because your gran is a legend and that wasn't too painful, or because you've decided you're madly in love with me and we should definitely make this a real thing.'

Damn. She'd been hoping he'd at least let Kirsty MacColl and Shane MacGowan sort out their differences before he brought that up.

'It is already a real thing to me.' Crap answer, but she didn't have the brainpower for this right now. There were only so many major things she could handle in one day.

Sonny attempted a clarification. 'I mean a more permanent th—'

'My dad isn't my dad,' she blurted out, cutting him off.

He eyed her quizzically. 'I don't get it. Is that the name of a TV show or is it a song request? Or do we need to take you to a hospital?'

'Sonny, I'm serious. Remember the DNA kit thing I did a few weeks ago?'

He shook his head. 'I don't think you told me about that. But I was still seeing Anoushka then, so maybe we just didn't have the chance to discuss it.'

Anoushka. Eve remembered her. Ballet dancer. She was part of the *corps de ballet* in the nightly performances of *The Nutcracker* at the Theatre Royal. Spoke with a very sexy Spanish accent. Extremely flexible. And Sonny had been besotted with her for about a month and a half, until he got bored with her rigid diet and not being able to see her every night, called it a day and they'd resumed 'friends with benefits' status. Eve had been perfectly happy to reinstate their former, uncomplicated, highly enjoyable arrangement, because it suited her. Suited them both. At least, it used to. Apparently, Sonny no longer agreed.

'Ah, maybe... Anyway, I did a DNA test, because Angus did one too and I thought it would be a fun thing to have, and turns out I'm no relation to Angus at all. So either I was swapped at birth, or my mother shagged someone else.'

Diverted from his original question and now fully committing to her story, Sonny whistled. 'I'm not sure your mother even had sex in order to conceive you.'

'Exactly! I was definitely swapped at birth. Gabby thinks Nicole Kidman could be my mother. I think she's just living in hope that she'll get a ten-part series produced by Miss Kidman and Reese Witherspoon out of it.'

'Of all the ways I thought our conversation about our relationship was going to play out today, this didn't even hit the right stratosphere.' He shook his head, but there was a hint of a grin there, so she knew he didn't mind too much.

'I know. I'm sorry.' She felt slightly ashamed for just blurting it all out, but in her own, admittedly clumsy way, she was trying to explain why his ultimatum hadn't been her emotional priority this week. 'It's been a lot to process. You know, the "whole life has been a lie" thing.'

'No, no! Don't apologise. I totally get it. Shit. This is the maddest thing I ever heard. Total mindfuck.'

He turned the radio down and adjusted his seat belt, giving him room to twist his body so he was almost facing her. 'Okay, I'm getting on board and into supportive pal mode. So what's the plan?'

This was why they made great friends. With or without the benefits. He was always ready to listen and genuinely interested in what was happening to her. 'I don't know. According to the DNA test, there's a woman in Glasgow who is my aunt. I contacted her and she owns Café Croissant on Byres Road.'

'I know that place. Their apple Danish rocks. Sorry. I realise that wasn't the most important factor in that exchange.'

She tried to feign exasperation, but crumbled into amusement. 'It's okay. I realise that your tastebuds are the most important factor in any exchange. Anyway, I contacted her, and she said she'd be happy to speak to me so I'm going to do that first. I want pieces in the jigsaw before I talk to my mum.'

In front of them, she saw Harry's brake lights turn red, then his hazards begin to flash, and realised he'd pulled over. Eve scanned the street, a majestic boulevard full of beautiful Georgian detached mansions. Bloody hell, they were at their destination already. A major personal crisis apparently made the time pass quicker.

'Listen, can we talk later about the other stuff?'

Sonny unclipped his seat belt. 'Sure. The boss is taking us out for Christmas drinks when we finish this afternoon, but I'll give you a call tonight, see where you are and if I'm in any kind of respectable state, I might stop by. I'm promising nothing. Last time we went out, I woke up at Glasgow Airport with a flight ticket for Amsterdam on my phone.'

'I remember. You left a McDonalds McMuffin in my car after I came to rescue you and you insisted we detour for a drive through breakfast.' It was impossible not to laugh. The night in question had been around Sonny's birthday, and a few of his drunken colleagues had the idea to fly to Amsterdam first thing in the morning and return that night. They'd booked it after many beers and gone straight to the airport from the bar they'd been partying in. There had been several highly pissed off partners collecting half his office from the airport the following morning. Eve had thought it was hilarious, because she was his friend. Would she have been quite so entertained if she was his girlfriend. Or, steady now, his wife?

The very thought made her head hurt, so she chose to block it out as Sonny added, 'But if you need me, I could cancel.'

'Don't be daft,' she waved that suggestion off. She had enough on her plate today without having this discussion again tonight. 'Just go and enjoy yourself.'

He leaned over and kissed her cheek, but curiosity got the better of her and Eve turned her face, caught him on the lips. It felt... good. Nice. Did she want to do it again? Did she want him to be the only man in her life? The one that she'd have to stay with for the foreseeable future, because if she went into this, it felt like it would have to be a long-term, maybe even permanent thing? Urgh, nothing inside was giving her a definite 'yes' answer. But it wasn't a 'no' either. Her buttocks would end up with skelfs if she sat on this fence for much longer.

In her mind, there were two potential options. Make a go of it, and potentially fail and lose his friendship for ever. Or say no, and then create an awkwardness that could also result in losing his friendship forever.

Before she could examine that thought any further, her gran battered on the window.

Eve switched the car off and they both got out.

'Sorry to interrupt love's young dream, but you've got the keys for this place,' her gran reminded her.

'Sorry, Gran, I completely forgot.' She fished the keys out of her pocket. 'Right, let's go.'

They made their way into the old Georgian building, originally built as a home for a wealthy city merchant in the 1800s, then later transformed into a very posh boutique hotel, then offices and finally converted into retirement flats only a few months ago. As soon as she'd seen that the new homes had been released for sale, Cathy had signed on the dotted line. Eve understood why. They were ten minutes away from her gran's old home, in an area she felt safe in. It was a gorgeous building with a caretaker on site twenty-four/seven if she needed anything. And the ground floor had been transformed into a fitness studio and a lovely residents' lounge with a tea and coffee bar, where Gran could meet friends to play cards or have a drink or watch a movie. The fact that Sonny's company was the estate agency that was handling the sales just made it seem even more like it was meant to be.

The three of them trooped in, letting Eve lead the way, while Harry and his men opened the back door of the vans and began loading up the tailgates, ready to get the first lot of stuff moving.

The advance party went up in the lift to the first floor, and as Eve opened the door of the flat, she immediately got a whiff of fresh paint, of new carpet and of something else... A fresh start. Optimism. Comfort. The high ceilings and the huge windows facing on to Great Western Road made the view look like a work of art on this snowy, December day.

She'd been here once before, when her gran came to view it, but it looked different now, probably because it was no longer just a newly remodelled empty flat, it was Gran's home. Although, Eve still thought leaving the move until January would have been a better plan, but even though it was going to be chaotic, her gran had insisted it had to be today. 'I don't care if I'm sitting on boxes and sleeping on a mattress on the floor, love. I just want to be in there for Christmas. I don't know how many I've got left and I want to spend every one of them in my new home.'

And now they were here. 'Oh Gran, it's wonderful. You're going to be so happy here.'

'I hope so, my love. Because life's too short to live somewhere that doesn't bring you joy.'

Before Eve could comment on the profound statement, Sonny interjected. 'We should make that the new slogan for our company. I'll tell them I thought of it and take the credit.'

That made her gran hoot. 'Fine by me, son. Just pay me in brandy.'

'Deal. Right then, are you definitely happy with everything here? Is it all as you wanted?'

'Couldn't wish for anything more,' her gran beamed.

'Okay, I'll be off then. Happy New Home, Mrs M.' He gave her gran a hug, then kissed Eve again. It stayed on the cheek this time. 'I'll buzz you later.'

At that moment, Harry and his lads came through the door with a sofa.

'Right, Cathy, tell me where this is going. You're getting the express, Christmas Eve service today. We've got four hours to make this perfect for you and then get home before Lenny here's missus gives him a divorce for Christmas.'

At the other end of the sofa, Lenny's amused smile suggested he didn't actually mind that idea. Nevertheless, her gran was having none of it. 'Don't you worry, gents. Eve and I will direct operations and you lot provide the muscle. We'll have this done in no time. There will be no relationship break-ups on my watch. Not today.'

As Eve watched Sonny say his goodbyes to the lads and head out she realised she wasn't sure whether her gran's declaration would turn out to be true.

8

HELENA

Christmas Eve 1993

Helena felt like her feet might be about to detach themselves from her body. Actually, maybe they already had, because she couldn't feel anything below her ankles. She'd been standing in the doorway on the opposite side of the pedestrian street from the Rogano for so long, the homeless guy in the next doorway along had offered to share his soup. She was so cold, she'd considered accepting it.

After she'd spotted Bruce canoodling with Bree fucking Halston, she'd thought about charging over there and demanding answers, but that kind of emotional outburst wasn't her style at all. That was the sort of thing her mum would do. And for once in her life, she'd do anything to have Cathy here with her, and to watch all five foot two inches of Glaswegian mother march in there and drag the esteemed Bruce Quinn out by the ear, kicking his arse with every step. But that would mean sharing this shame with her mother and she'd never do that either.

Next option was to walk away. Go home. Lock the door. Wait until Bruce contacted her and then read him the riot act, get answers, then eviscerate him for doing this to her. But something about that plan didn't sit well with her either. She was a solicitor. She liked to be in full possession of the facts before making any decision. She also knew that people lied under pressure, or for their own ends, and she wanted to get to the truth of exactly what the hell was going on. Bruce was an even better solicitor than her, with far more experience, and she suspected that he'd be able to outmanoeuvre her if she showed her hand too quickly.

As always, her brain had kicked in, analysing, calculating, playing scenarios through to their conclusion, until she had a semblance of an idea as to how she was going to handle this. First step of the plan? Try not to die of frostbite while attempting to implement the strategy. And in her wool skirt and jacket, with the silk pussy bow shirt and sensible navy pumps, staying outside would be the equivalent of trying to conquer Everest in flip-flops. The counter? She'd made a dignified retreat from the restaurant, then run to the department store, House of Fraser, only fifty yards or so round the corner on Buchanan Street and straight up to the women's wear floor, where she'd purchased a snow jacket she couldn't afford and fur-lined suede winter boots that she could afford even less.

She'd pulled the jacket on over her suit, slipped on the boots, shoved her own shoes in the boot box and been back at the Rogano in half an hour, stomach churning, as she went inside. Thankfully, the previous maître d' was no longer there, so there had been no awkward questions when she'd told the stunning young woman with jet-black hair, dark skin and huge brown eyes at the reception podium that she was just looking for a friend.

The restaurant had been absolutely packed, every table full and two deep at the bar, festive music on the sound system and a tangible air of Christmas bonhomie. Helena wasn't feeling it. In fact, if she'd had a catapult she'd have taken out the speakers that were playing an orchestral version of Jingle fricking Bells in the background.

For the second time, she'd scanned the room, and yep, there he was. Still there. The bastard. She'd gingerly taken a few steps further, trying her best to avoid being spotted, until she saw... yep, the auburn hair was still there too. She'd clenched her teeth, biting back down the fury, as she'd retreated, then flipped a switch and uttered a smiley, 'No, I don't see my friend anywhere,' to the new gatekeeper at the door.

'Ah, sorry, I hope you track her down. Merry Christmas.'

'Merry Christmas to you to,' Helena had managed. All those years of training to keep a poker face in interactions with witnesses were paying off. On the outside: sunny, calm niceness. On the inside: seething, vitriolic rage and devastation.

Back out on the street, she'd searched for a suitable waiting spot, and that's when she'd noticed the doorway about twenty yards further along. It gave her a clear view of the Rogano doors, but the angle and the crowds would stop her being spotted by Bruce and Bree if they ever stopped all the romantic shit and actually came outside.

For the first half hour or so, fury had warmed her from the inside out. For roughly the next twenty minutes, the snow jacket and the furry boots had done their jobs. But now, the slush underfoot, the bitter cold and the lack of movement were combining to let the chill seep into every bone and sinew of her body, starting at the feet and working its way up. If they came out right now, she wasn't sure that her body would even follow commands to walk, talk or scream.

The worst part of it all was that it just didn't make sense. Why would Bruce ask her father for his blessing to propose, and then mess around with another woman? It wasn't as if Helena had been demanding commitment or prying into his life or his intentions for the future. The truth was that she was just grateful to be in his orbit, to be noticed by him, loved by him. She hadn't expected or asked for any more than that, so why sign up for a commitment that he clearly didn't want?

Even as she was thinking that, an answer was twinkling in the icicles that were forming in her brain. The job with her father's company? She wasn't being stupid or naïve, but surely that couldn't be it. If he'd told her that he was interested in the position, she would have asked her dad to recommend him, no strings attached.

Ironic that the one part of her body that wasn't yet frozen solid was her gut, and right now it was churning. There was nothing worse for Helena than being out of control. She was a fixer. A doer. Someone who took no shit, fought her corner every time and always won. So why the fuck was she in a situation that was leaving her open to some serious damage?

'Are ye sure you don't want any of this soup, hen?' the homeless man a few feet away asked for the second time. 'It's tomato. Someone wi' a sense of humour said he bought me that one in case I was a vegetarian. "Aye, son," I said. "I regularly refuse a feed because it contravenes ma policies on the ethics of eating meat." I swear some o' these bams don't have the sense they were born with. Grateful for the soup tho.'

In any other situation, in any other place, Helena would have ignored this man and just kept walking. Unshaven and dishevelled, he was lying in the next doorway, on top of a pile of newspapers, wearing two sleeping bags and what looked like at least two woolly hats on his head. But this was the humbling reality check of a lifetime and she was grateful to him for the kindness. 'That's okay, you keep it, but thank you.'

'Nae bother. Are you, like, a spy or something? Or a private investigator?'

'Something like that.'

'I knew it. Once before, had a woman standing there all night – turns out her man was in there with another woman.' He nodded to the restaurant. 'She battered the two of them when they came out. Never seen a left hook like it.'

Before she could answer, Helena saw the doors of the restaurant open and a crowd of laughing, buzzed-up customers exit the building. Nope, no Bruce. She was about to resume her conversation with her new friend when a flash of auburn caught her eye once again. Bree Halston was at the back of the crowd, clearly alone, and coming straight towards her. The only blessing was that her head was down, so she couldn't see that Helena was in front of her. Just to be on the safe side though, Helena turned her back and began rummaging in her bag, her face hidden from passers-by.

As soon as she reckoned Bree had passed her, Helena turned to check. Yep, there she was, a couple of yards ahead, following the route Helena had taken earlier on to the pedestrian area of Buchanan Street. Her frozen body instantly thawed and she began to move, but not before her fingers retrieved twenty quid from her purse, which she handed to her new friend as she passed. 'Thank you for offering to share your soup. Merry Christmas.'

'Ya dancer! Merry Christmas to you too, hen. I'm always here if ye want some soup and a blether,' he called out, laughing, as she sped off.

It was the first time she'd ever given money away and it would probably be the last, but in the moment, it had felt like the right thing to do.

Turning back, her peripheral vision checked again if there was any sign of Bruce. None. He must still be inside. Okay, that made this easier.

Helena sped up, using the Christmas crowds to conceal her as she cut down the same pedestrian street as Bree, on the opposite side, hustling much faster. This was the woman that she'd respected. Whom she thought of as a friend. Whom she wanted to be just like. Yet now Helena was seething and chasing her down through the Glasgow streets. A couple of times she thought she'd lost her, but then she'd spot her again over the heads of the teeming throng of shoppers. The next bit had to be timed to perfection. When she was far enough in front of Bree, she began to cut across the street, circumventing a band of drummers and pipers busking their hearts out, zigzagging through the pedestrians, earning a few shoves and a few choice words along the way.

Almost there. Almost there. Almost there...

She reached the spot, right in front of her target, at exactly the right moment, turned and blocked her way. 'Bree!'

The other woman lifted her head, startled, and Helena could see that it took her a moment to process what had just happened.

'Helena!'

'What a small world,' Helena chirped back, with her friendliest smile. 'I get to see you twice in one day. I was just in Fraser's, picking a few things up' – she held up the bag that contained her shoes – 'and... Oh... are you okay?' Helena peered closer at her colleague's face, and she could see the red cheeks, the swollen pink eyelids, the bloodshot eyes. 'Bree, have you been crying? What's wrong?'

Being concerned and doing the whole overly friendly thing didn't come easily to Helena, but once again, she could turn on any technique to get the most out of the witness, the victim or the perpetrator of a crime. She still wasn't sure which category Bree was in.

'Nothing, I'm fine. I'm just... just...' No more words came. Instead, to Helena's complete and utter shock, Bree Halston, arse-kicking, ball-breaking, phenomenal legal brain burst into tears in the middle of Buchanan Street.

'Oh my goodness, Bree! What's happened?' She didn't even wait for a reply before she jumped in with, 'Look, it doesn't matter. Let's get you inside out of the cold, and get you a drink. I could do with one too. Come on, Princes Square is right there and at least it'll be bloody warm.'

She slipped her arm around Bree's elbow, clad in what was obviously a very expensive cream cashmere coat. For a moment, Helena thought the other woman was going to refuse, or pull away, or find an excuse not to speak to her, but no. Bree Halston allowed herself to be steered back across the road and up to the heaving entrance to Princes Square, a former merchants' square built in Victorian times and now converted into a chic, cosmopolitan emporium of fashion, bars and restaurants.

Predictably, for lunchtime on Christmas Eve, the whole centre was packed with wall-to-wall people. The stunning decorations dangling from the four-storey glass atrium, the fifty-foot tree that rose up past the brass and glass balconies, and the musical back-drop of a choir, singing in the rotunda on the ground floor, made it as close to Christmas perfection as a shopping centre could be. And neither a stressed Helena or a distraught Bree noticed or gave a damn.

They took the escalators up to the top level, where bars strad-dled each side of the majestic atrium. Helena immediately started to panic as she scanned the area and didn't see a single free table. Bugger. She couldn't lose the moment now. She needed to sit Bree down and speak to her properly. This wasn't the kind of conversa-tion that was to be had standing in a corner getting jostled by irate shoppers.

She was about to hatch a new plan when, by some Christmas miracle, two women in fake-fur white coats, matching fur hats and scarlet manicured nails sitting at a nearby table, stood and began gathering their bags. Helena was in one of their seats before their posteriors had even left the area. She unapologetically pushed their glasses to one corner and cleared a space for Bree.

Ignoring the harrumphs of the two women who were irate at the enforced speed of the departure, Helena pulled her damp hair back from her sweating neck, took a breath, then leaned forward so her hands were almost touching Bree's red leather gloves.

'Oh, Bree,' she said, in her very best sympathetic voice. 'Start at the beginning. Tell me what has happened to upset you.'

9

CATHY

Christmas Eve 1968

Richie was in the kitchen, his head stuck in the fridge, while Cathy sat at the table, sipping yet another cup of tea. No wonder she was getting heartburn. Sally, the head stylist in the salon, had four kids, and she'd told Cathy to limit tea to one cup in the morning, but today, Cathy had downed at least three out of sheer desperation for a distraction from the reality of Richie Clark being here. Richie. Her Richie.

After she'd answered the door and let him back in, they'd gone into the kitchen and he'd sat down in the same chair he'd been in before. She'd bought time by nipping upstairs to change out of her nightdress and into a flowing red smock that she'd worn to death over the last month. Back downstairs, he watched her take her seat, and she cut off any questions before he could ask them.

'Look, I don't think I can talk to you about Duncan. It feels wrong. He's my husband now...' A flip of her stomach as she said that. Her husband. As a teenager, if she'd ever thought about who her husband would be in the future, the first and only candidate would be this guy right in front of her. Oh, and she didn't think for a second that she'd ever have a husband at the age of twenty. Most of her classmates and friends were already married or engaged, but Cathy had always planned to buck the trend. Even after Mum and Dad passed, she was going to work really hard, save what she could, and one day find a way to open her own salon. That was the plan. Past tense.

Richie held up his hands. 'I get it. Husband off limits. How about I just bore you to death all day talking about football?'

'That was most of my teenage years,' Cathy teased him. Wow, how easy that still came to her. Making fun of each other had been their favourite sport and she'd just slipped straight back into it.

He obviously felt the same because he immediately returned fire, his cheeky grin back in full force. 'Yeah, well, it was a bit more interesting than talking about the Beatles all day. I mean, Paul McCartney isn't exactly God's gift. Have you seen him lately? He's like an old man with that whole beard thing and the long hair.'

Gasping dramatically, she played along. 'Shut your mouth right now. Loretta would do you an injury if she heard you say that in this house.'

'You're right. If I ever disappear, I'm probably tied up in your coal cellar.'

'You did disappear.' The short, sharp rebuke was out before she could stop it. And her tone made it obvious that she wasn't playing any more.

He reeled back as if she'd slapped him, leaving a handprint of hurt all over his gorgeous face. 'Cathy, I'm sorry. You know that wasn't how it—'

'Stop! I'm sorry. I shouldn't have said that. I don't mean it.'

'Cath, you know I wanted to stay...'

'I know. It's fine. Really. I'm sorry.' She couldn't do this right now. Needed to think. Supressing a groan, she pushed up on to her feet, feeling like she'd gained ten stones since this morning. 'I just need to go to the loo.'

Leaving him at the table, she passed him by, the urgency of needing to pee surpassed by the urgency of getting out of there before she burst into tears. This crying stuff was getting out of control. She couldn't help herself.

Sally at the salon, the oracle of all knowledge when it came to pregnancy and motherhood (and also hairdressing, council regulations, a television show called *Bonanza*, and Cliff Richard), had told her there were things called hormones that you got when you were pregnant and they could affect your emotions, making you more sad, happy, upset, worried or short-tempered than usual. Cathy had thought she was just saying that as an excuse because the last time Sally was pregnant, she'd lost the plot and thrown all her husband's clothes out the window, but now she wasn't so sure. Whatever those hormone things were, she must have a load of them, because she didn't know if she was happy, sad or ready to cry a river.

In the loo, she sat down, and leaned her head forward so that it rested on the green sink. This bathroom had been put in just a couple of months before her parents died and it had been her mum's pride and joy. She swore she'd seen in a magazine that Cilla Black had one just like it. Cathy wasn't quite sure that Cilla had a whole bathroom that was a dull shade of frog, but weirdly, the fact that her mum had picked it gave her some kind of sense of calm. Made her feel like a bit of her mum was still here.

Eyes squeezed shut to stop the tears, she let the cold porcelain of the sink cool her down. Cruel comments didn't come naturally to her and she had no idea why she'd blurted that out to Richie.

They both knew that the truth was, he hadn't wanted to take

the job. She'd forced him. She'd never blamed him, because since the moment he'd packed his case and left, Cathy had known that she shared the responsibility for it. It was the biggest mistake that she'd ever made – even worse because he didn't know the reason that she'd told him to go.

When they'd finished school, she'd got the job in the salon and Richie had gone to work in the shipyards, just like his dad and his grandad before him. Her dad had worked there too, but he'd been in the offices, not out on the ships. That was usually how the young lads got work there – if they had a relative or a friend who was already in the yard, then they were a shoo-in for the jobs. Richie was young, fit and strong, so he'd been sent to the boiler room, where he shovelled coal into the fires that the metal workers used to fabricate the panels. He did that for ten hours every single day until his hands bled, his back ached, and he hated every second of it.

He'd tried everything to get moved to another job in the yard, but he'd hit a brick wall. He had to pay his dues like everyone else and it wasn't like there were a ton of better positions for someone who'd left school with a few O levels to his name. Cathy had watched him sink lower and lower, and it had broken her heart – a heart that was already fractured by the loss of her parents a couple of years before. So when Richie's mum had knocked on her door one tea time, she'd taken in the desperation on the woman's face, and the pain in her eyes as she'd let her in. Mrs Clark still had on an apron over her dress, and her hair was in a scarf, with two rollers sticking out at the front, so Cathy guessed she was on the way back from the steamie – a stone building at the back of the tenements in the next street, where the women went to wash their family's clothes. Her mum had stopped going there when they got their shiny new twin tub and she'd said it was the best day of her life.

'My Richie doesn't know I'm here and I'd like to keep it that way,' she'd announced straight away. His mum had always struggled with her nerves and it gave her a jittery way about her. Cathy saw that her hands were trembling as she sat down.

'That's okay, Mrs Clark. I won't say anything. Do you want a cup of tea?'

Richie's mum had shaken her head. 'No, hen. Listen... I'm not quite sure how to say this, but I'm just going to have to come right out with it.'

Cathy could feel her stomach start to clench. What was wrong? Was Richie in trouble? Was he hurt? This wasn't making sense.

'You know how miserable my lad has been since he started in the yards.' Richie was eighteen, but mothers around here referred to their sons as their lads until they were about forty-five. 'Cathy, I've been heartsore worried about him.'

This wasn't news. 'I know. I've been worried too, Mrs Clark.'

'The thing is... Oh hen, this makes me sick to my stomach to say this to you. But my brother, Ken, has managed to get him a job working with him.'

Cathy had been confused. She couldn't remember meeting Richie's Uncle Ken, but if he'd got him a new job, that had to be a good thing. Great, actually. So why weren't they celebrating?

'That's smashing, Mrs Clark.'

'Aye hen, but the thing is...'

Cathy had seen she was close to tears now and she was starting to feel sick. What was she missing here?

'He works on the ships. Not the ones at the yard. The cargo ships that sail in and out of Southampton to America and Africa and all the far-away places. Richie would have to go down there and I'm just going to be honest with you, he'd be away for months at a time. Maybe longer.'

Cathy's stomach had felt like it had dropped out of her body. No. He couldn't go. She couldn't lose anyone else.

'He's saying that he's not going...' she went on, and Cathy had felt a wave of relief. 'Because he won't leave you.'

In that instant, the relief had vanished as Cathy realised exactly what was happening. This was a mum who was about to ask her to let her son go.

''Cathy, pet, I know what you've been through, and och, it's a heartbreak. You know how much we thought of your mum and dad. They were damn good people. But I would be no kind of mother if I didn't try to do my best for ma boy. It's a great job. Our Ken makes smashing money and he sees the world. Richie would learn a trade – he'd be an engineer at the end of it – and it would set him up for the rest of his life. So I'm begging you, Cathy. Give him a chance. Let him make a great life for himself, at least for a few years, and then, if you two are still sweet on each other, you can get back together and you'd have a man that was happy, with a good job and a different life from the one you'll have if he stays in the yards.'

Cathy couldn't find the words to reply, so she'd said nothing as Mrs Clark got up and went to the door.

'I'll never tell him that we had this conversation, but I hope you'll do what's best for him, Cathy. If you love him as much as I do, I know you will.'

Three months later, after Cathy had spent weeks persuading him that it was the right thing to do, that she'd wait for him, that if they were meant to be together, then it would work out somehow, Richie Clark got on the train from Glasgow to Southampton, and the next time Cathy had heard his voice or seen his face was almost a year and a half later, when he'd walked through her door this morning.

And still, even now, she knew she'd never tell him about the conversation with his mum because that had been the deal she'd made. Tell him to go. Don't tell him why. If she loved him, that's what she'd do. But if she'd known how things would turn out, would she do it again? She couldn't bring herself to answer that. Not now. Maybe not ever. Instead, she dried her eyes, flushed the loo, washed her face and went back out there.

Richie was where she'd left him and she hoped he wouldn't spot she'd been crying.

'I'm sorry. I didn't mean to upset you,' he said, as soon as she sat down and he saw her face. So much for hiding her feelings.

'It's okay, it wasn't you. It's these things called hormones that come when you're pregnant. Sally at the salon told me about them.'

'Has she left her husband for Cliff Richard yet?' he asked, grinning as he moved the conversation on to old familiar territory.

'Not yet, but she's living in hope.'

That was the thing. They knew all the same people, all the same things, had this shared history. Duncan couldn't compete with that and she shouldn't expect him to.

For the next two cups of tea, they kept to neutral subjects, chatting about anything that didn't come too close to being personal – his family, her job, the people he worked with and the places he'd been. It started to feel easier, more comfortable. As long as they stayed on neutral ground and avoided discussing their relationship past, present or future, it felt fine. More than fine. It felt like having someone she loved in her kitchen. She just couldn't let herself think any deeper than that.

Richie suggested making them lunch, although the very thought of that made her laugh. In all the years that she'd known him, she'd never seen him prepare anything more than cheese on toast or a sandwich involving jam.

He opened the fridge and bent in to see what treats it held

inside. 'Okay, so there's cheese. And butter. And' – he stretched back up and opened the breadbin on the counter above the fridge – 'we have bread and long strange stick things,' he said, pulling a packet of spaghetti out of the breadbin. Cathy had no idea why it was kept there – probably because the box had fallen out of the cupboard above it a few times and the strands had gone scattering all over the floor.

'That's spaghetti. Pasta. Duncan likes to cook a thing called spaghetti bolognaise. It has that spaghetti in it and fancy mince. It tastes really good. Much better than the mince we used to eat out of the tin.'

Duncan had first made his spaghetti bolognaise for them after they'd been dating for a few weeks.

Cathy still remembered every single detail of that night, as vivid as if it happened yesterday. They had planned to go into town for dinner and then go to the cinema, but Loretta had gone down with the flu, and Cathy didn't want to leave her. 'I'll come to your house then and I'll cook dinner. I'll bring the ingredients with me,' Duncan had suggested.

Cathy had blushed to the very insides of her face. 'No, don't be daft.' Her father had never cooked a meal in his life, and she just couldn't picture a man throwing together dinner in their kitchen. 'We could just get fish and chips. Or I could make us some ham and eggs.'

Duncan had given her a big grin as he shook his head. It made him look handsome when he did that. He wasn't her usual type of man. Not that she had a type, given that she'd only ever been with Richie Clark. For a start, he wasn't tall like Richie, who had been over six foot since they were about fourteen. She was five foot two and Duncan was maybe five inches taller. He had dark curly hair, with brown eyes that crinkled when he smiled. Which, Cathy had discovered, he did a lot. He could be quite serious sometimes though – always had his head stuck in a book and seemed to know about all different things.

His family went abroad every year on holiday. France. Spain. Italy. Cathy had only been out of Glasgow a handful of times in her life, and she'd certainly never been on an aeroplane. One of the highlights of her summers used to be a day trip with her mum and dad to Renfrew, a town about twenty miles away, and they'd go back and forth on the Renfrew Ferry a few times, a car and foot passenger vessel that crossed the couple of hundred yards stretch of the Clyde between Renfrew and Yoker. After that, they'd go for a walk around the Robertson Park and then they'd pick up some ice cream and go up to the airport at Abbotsinch to watch the planes taking off and landing. Now she knew that Duncan might even have been on one of those planes. So yep, there was no getting away from the fact that he was definitely posher than her, but, strangely, it didn't make her feel uncomfortable or disinterested, because he had such a lovely way about him. His kindness and thoughtfulness was obvious just from meeting him.

That was why she'd gone out with him in the first place, but she wasn't sure what the attraction was on his side. She was decent-looking, although she didn't believe her mother's claims that she was beautiful, and she'd left school at sixteen with barely a qualification. Yet, he'd seemed to think she was gorgeous, and they never ran out of things to talk about or things to laugh about either. Cathy hadn't tried too hard to understand it. After months of working, looking after Loretta and not much else, it had been nice to have someone to spend time with and do fun things again – like eat the spaghetti bolognaise he'd rustled up for them that first night in her kitchen. She'd never even heard of it before then, but now it was a weekly favourite.

A clatter from the kitchen cupboard snapped her out of the memory and back to the present, and she saw that two tins of tomato soup had liberated themselves from the top cupboard of the kitchen and only a swift duck had saved Richie from a possible concussion.

'Why don't we go down to the café at the end of the road?' he suggested, and Cathy experienced her first flutter of anxiety since he'd come back in the door.

The café. They'd spent a thousand days there when they were at school, bunking off at lunchtime and sitting there in the afternoons, passing the time with each other and their gang of pals amidst the heady aroma of sausage rolls. After they'd left school, they mostly went at weekends, after Cathy had been paid at the salon and Richie had his hard-earned wages from the shipyard.

The place had memories. Lots of wonderful ones. And a few, at the end, that had broken her heart.

Despite the trepidation, she pushed herself up from the chair. 'Sure. I'll just get my jacket and put my boots on.'

Maybe she could pretend, just for today, that this was her perfect life. Christmas. With Richie by her side. Making her heart flutter and her laugh. A baby on the way. The happy ever after that she'd always thought she'd have with him.

She just had to remember that this wasn't reality.

She belonged to someone else. And no matter what Richie Clark said or did, he couldn't change that.

2 P.M. – 4 P.M.

10

EVE

Christmas Eve 2023

'It's official, Gran,' Eve said, glancing around the living room. 'Harry and his guys are miracle workers. Or maybe superheroes. Either way, they are bloody marvellous.'

Two hours ago, it had been an empty space, but already the sofas were in and correctly placed in the middle of the room, opposite each other, on a huge cream rug, with Gran's beautiful old walnut coffee table in the middle. At the end of each sofa, there was also a matching side table with Gran's beloved Tiffany lamps on each one. Eve knew that she liked to lie on the sofa at night, her favourite cushion under her head, her fleecy throw over her legs, and read while having a cup of tea or a glass of wine within reach. Sonny had prearranged with the developers that there would be a TV fitted to the wall, above a real-flame, inset fire, and it looked stunning. On the opposite wall, Gran's ancient but meticulously preserved burr sideboard sat, with a record player from the sixties on top that would now be considered a vintage treasure. A floor lamp in one corner, a gold art deco bar trolley in the other, and an armchair and footstool by the window completed the room.

The only sign of the move was a brown box in the corner, containing all Cathy's ornaments, framed photos and art for the walls, and they were slowly but surely emptying that and placing things in the spots they belonged in.

Eve picked out a photo of her gran's wedding day and put it in place on the sideboard, feeling a tug on her heartstrings as she looked at the face of the man who had been so much more of a father to her than her dad ever had. Her grandad was pure kindness. Measured. Someone who would think before he spoke. The type of person that made you feel safe and a little bit smarter just by being in the room. And he couldn't have been more different from her wild, raucous, irreverent gran, yet he'd adored her. He once told Eve that he was like a planet and her gran was the sun, and life was brighter when he was near her. It had been one of his rare moments of poetic romance, but Eve had never forgotten it.

She wished he was still with them, but he'd passed in his sleep, an aneurism, and her gran had found him like that in the morning. For a while Eve had wondered if Cathy would ever get her spark back, and it had taken about a year, but now, here she was, starting a new chapter of her life, aided by a moving team that was getting on with transforming this from a house to her gran's home.

The first thing Eve and her gran had done was unpack all the food and drink they'd brought with them into the fridge, freezer and kitchen cupboards. Even if they had nothing else, that gave them everything they needed for dinner and drinks tonight, for endless teas and coffees, and for Cathy's annual Christmas brunch tomorrow. Meanwhile, after placing all the big items in the lounge, Harry's team had moved into the bedrooms and they were unloading all the furniture piece by piece. Gran's stuff was all from the fifties, sixties and seventies – not a flat-pack item in sight. The irony was, it was now all classed as 'mid-century modern' and bang on trend again.

'I think you'll find,' Cathy replied archly, 'that their muscle was aided by the planning genius that is you and me.'

Eve nodded with mock solemnity. 'You're right. We're brilliant. And modest.'

There was a grain of truth in there. It helped that the move had been meticulously planned so that it would be as swift and smooth as possible. The end result of the clear out was that every single thing left in Gran's house was coming here, to a pre-determined spot, and that's what was making the move so seamless. That, and Harry and his five burly helpers. They'd even refused Eve's offer of tea when they'd arrived and got straight to work instead.

Her gran was busy taking cushions out of a huge net bag that Harry had dropped by the door and arranging them on the sofas, when Eve pulled the next photo frame out of the box. The gilt frame had a black and white photo in it, of her mum holding Eve, who must have only been a few days old. Something triggered in Eve's memory. She'd seen that before. Years ago. But somehow it looked different, smaller...

'Gran, did you cut my dad out of this picture?' she blurted, trying not to laugh. It was classic Cathy behaviour. God help anyone who messed with someone she loved.

There may have been a slight sheepishness in her first reaction. 'Maybe.'

Eve was tempted to just blurt out, 'Ah, no worries, he's not my dad anyway,' but stopped herself. *Not today*, she repeated in her head for the hundredth time.

Her gran's mind was going in another direction – from vague denial to guilty as charged.

'Och, okay, I did,' Cathy fessed up. 'Sorry, love, I know he's your dad, but I didn't want to look at that smarmy face for a single second after how he treated your mum.'

'So when did you cut him out?'

Cathy pursed her lips, and looked heavenward as she worked it out. 'Erm, about 1998. Right when he ditched your mother for that tart he worked with.'

None of those details were news to Eve. Her dad leaving when she was four was a fact of life and she barely remembered a time when he was living under the same roof. It was her norm and over the years she'd hardly given a thought as to how it had happened or the effect it must have had on her life, because she'd never known any different. Until now. Now it mattered, because maybe there was something in the story that would give her a clue as to how she now found herself to be a grown woman who bought fathers' day cards for the wrong man every year.

'Was I upset when he left?'

Cathy stopped fixing cushions, picked up her tea, and plonked herself down on the couch.

'Honestly? Not especially. He was a workaholic. Never home. In fact, they were both as bad as each other on that front, so that's why you spent so much time living with us. I don't think there was ever really a moment when you realised what had happened. Our lives all just carried on, exactly as they were before. Except for your mum's, of course, and she just carried on drowning herself in work to get past it. Nothing's changed, really, has it?'

Eve decided to continue along the 'seemingly innocent probing' trail.

'You know what Mum was saying earlier? About never being in

love with anyone else? Do you think that means she had no other men in her life? Or maybe she was just saying that?'

Her gran took a sip of tea and unwrapped a caramel wafer while she pondered that. 'I honestly don't know. Your mum has always been one to keep her cards close to her chest. She's never been a talker like us. I adore the bones of her... What is it you young folk say? Unconditionally. Aye, that's it. But I always thought, to be honest, that she was a difficult combination of me and your grandad. She's got my sharp opinions and avoidance of vulnerability, combined with your grandad's love for solitude. Means she never has a chance to have a good old rant, or get things off her mind by talking problems or feelings over with her pals. That must be tough.'

It amazed Eve that, despite her mum's general disdain and lack of interest in her family, her gran still sought to understand and have compassion for the way she behaved. And she couldn't even put it down to some sort of inherent parental devotion in their family genes, because that had definitely skipped a generation with Helena. No, it was just down to Gran being wise and thoughtful and the kind of person who saw the best in the people she loved and tried to make everyone's lives better.

A bite of her caramel wafer got Gran back on track with the question.

'If she's had boyfriends since the divorce, she's certainly not brought them to meet us. Although, they say it's the quiet ones you've got to watch. Maybe she's one of those mad swingers you read about. Or a dominatrix. Oh, dear God, the damage that one could do with a whip. I watched that *Fifty Shades Of Grey* and ma toes were curling.'

'Eeeeew, Gran, don't do that to me. That's my mother! I don't need that mental picture in my head. Although I'll be checking her wardrobe for steel spiked stilettos next time I'm over there.'

'I'd need to do all that business in my slippers,' Cathy cackled. 'My bunions couldn't take the heels.'

Eve pulled another photo out of the box. One of her this time. Maybe about two or three. Grinning at the camera. Her red hair in bunches, her green eyes huge, above her chubby cheeks. Why hadn't she thought before about how there was not one feature on her face that resembled Bruce's dark eyes and chiselled jaw? Or her mother's rich chocolate hair and sallow skin, for that matter. Who did she look like? Anyone?

'What about before my dad. Was there anyone else? Any other boyfriends?'

If her gran thought her questions were odd or excessive, she didn't say. But then, Cathy was seventy-five years old and still endlessly curious about life and people, so this wouldn't be a stretch for her.

'Maybe some when she was in university. She went off to live in a flat in Glasgow and we barely saw her after that, but every now and then I'd paid her a surprise visit...'

Eve spluttered. 'Oh, I bet she loved that.'

'Aye, I'm pretty sure she wasn't for letting me in, but your grandad was usually with me and she could never say no to him, so she'd open the door. It was great fun. Every time, the look on her face could have curdled milk. Anyway, once or twice there were men there, but I don't think there was anything serious. And then, of course, when she went to work for her firm, she met your dad and that was it. I think they were together for about six months before he popped the question.'

Eve tried to make sense of what she'd learned so far. Her mother was with her fake dad for six months before she was conceived, and then she went on to marry him a few months later. So how? Where? When? Who the hell was her father?

This was all making her head hurt.

Her gran was back up on her feet now, break over, and pulling Christmas cards out of her handbag and putting them on the sideboard. Eve had to laugh. They were just moving in. They hadn't even found the tin opener and the removal guys were just cracking open the garment packing boxes and putting her clothes in the newly situated wardrobe, but her gran had her Christmas cards up.

'Do you see him much now? Your dad, I mean?' Gran asked, putting a nativity scene next to a card that had a flashing Santa. Cathy was nothing if not accepting of all faiths and feelings.

'Maybe once every couple of months or so. Birthdays. Weddings. Funerals. To be honest, it suits me fine. Even when I was a kid and I'd go over at weekends, I'd mostly be left with whatever wife he was with at the time, because he was working or in his study, or doing a hundred other things rather than just being a dad. It's strange though. I've never felt that I was missing anything in my life, probably because I never knew any different really.'

'I don't condone violence...' Her gran began, which invariably meant she was about to declare that someone should be kneecapped. 'But I could rattle that man round the ears, I really could. I'd need to stand on a box, right enough. But, you know, Eve, it's his bloody loss. He missed out on a wonderful life with you and that's on him. Sod him.'

Eve had the distinct feeling that when her gran found out the truth, she'd organise a celebration involving bunting, a brass band and a choir singing the Hallelujah Chorus. It was something she hadn't quite given any thought to though – how would Bruce feel when he found out? Not that Eve was going to be rushing round to tell him, especially if she couldn't track down her real dad. No. That was a conversation her mum could have with her ex-husband, because Eve wasn't taking that one on. She was pretty sure he'd be conflicted. On one hand, he would probably be relieved that he had one less offspring in the world to consider or dedicate even meagre time to. On the other hand, he'd be pissed though, because he'd been forced to acknowledge and partially support her throughout her childhood. The big-shot, legal titan Bruce Quinn wasn't a man who would take well to being played.

'Anyway, talking about boyfriends, I'm about to pry and overstep my boundaries, so you might want to buckle up there,' her gran warned her. She was back in her Tardis of a handbag again, pulling out a string of fairy lights and heading to the window with them.

'I swear, Gran, if you pull a Christmas tree out of that handbag, I wouldn't even be shocked. But on you go, overstep away.' There was no way to derail the Cathy McLean opinion train. It would come on down the tracks at some point, so she may as well board it now.

'Sonny. He's a lovely lad, that one. What's the story then?' Gran asked, while concentrating on draping the lights on the locks halfway down the double sash windows. The result was simple but gorgeous.

'It's complicated,' Eve said, as she discarded the empty box and pulled a new one into the room from the doorway. She opened it to see her gran's record collection and slid it over to the sideboard. 'We've been... friends... with... with...' She hesitated to say it, even though she'd never been shy about discussing sex with her gran.

'Oh, for God's sake, spit it out. I was around in the sixties. Your Aunt Loretta once had a threesome.'

'No way!' Eve felt a weird sense of admiration.

'Yes indeed,' her gran said with a solemn nod. 'And I'm not saying it was with anyone famous, but she'd just been to a David Bowie concert and I'll leave it there. My lips are sealed.'

Eve almost pulled a muscle laughing. 'Okay, well there were no threesomes with Sonny, just a casual arrangement that we are friends who are sometimes more than friends, whenever we are both single.' That was the most diplomatic way she could think of framing it, so that her gran would understand.

Her gran interjected. 'Friends with benefits, that's called. I saw it on *Grey's Anatomy*. I can't remember who was doing it. They're all forever changing partners in that show. I flipping love it.'

And welcome to the craziness of my life, Eve thought, thoroughly amused. *I'm a twenty-nine-year old-woman who is being schooled in sex slang by my seventy-five-year-old grandmother.*'

'Ten out of ten for terminology there, Gran, and yep, that sums it up. Anyway, that's the way it's been since we were in college and now he's told me that he'd like to make it something more.'

'And what do you think?'

As Eve thought about it, she slid the albums one by one into the cupboard in the sideboard, exactly where they'd lived in Gran's old house. When she came across one of Gran's favourites, she put it up on top of the record player so it would be easy to find later. Her gran rarely went a night without singing along to the Temptations belting out 'My Girl'. When Eve was growing up, having a dance to it in the living room had been part of her standard bedtime routine when she was staying at her gran's house.

'I think we make great friends. I think we could maybe make a great couple too. But I'm just not sure I want to dive in. I don't know why. Terrified, probably. Worried I'll make a mess of it. Or it'll be the wrong thing to do. Argh, who knows...' She threw up her hands. 'Sometimes I think life would be a lot easier if I just met the perfect man first time round, and spent a whole lifetime with him, just like you and Grandad.'

At first, Eve wondered if her gran was having a funny turn when she froze, as if her whole body was suspended in time, then slowly shook her head.

'No, love, that wasn't how it happened. I loved your grandad very much, but he wasn't the only one for me. Before him, there was someone else, someone I loved...'

Eve was so stunned, she didn't register the sound of her phone ringing, until her gran broke off what might have been the single most shocking revelation of Eve's life – DNA test excluded – with a casual, 'Are you going to answer that?'

Snapped back into action, Eve grabbed her phone out of her pocket.

'It's Aunt Loretta.' They had buzzed her earlier, but Loretta hadn't answered. Now her aunt's smiling face was flashing up to signal an incoming FaceTime call.

Her gran beamed. 'Och, smashing. Make sure you ask her about that threesome.'

11

HELENA

Christmas Eve 1993

Helena was struggling to maintain her expression of care and concern as she waited for Bree to speak. There had been two false starts already, which ended in another round of sobbing before any information could be delivered, followed by an interruption from a waiter, who'd cleared away the last customers' glasses, then spent an inordinate amount of time noting down their order. How long did it take to write two glasses of bloody Chardonnay?

And then, just when she'd leaned over the table to encourage Bree to go on again, a menagerie of kids wearing red jumpers and gold tinsel halos had appeared at the entrance to the restaurant, right next to their table, and – on the instructions of a teacher who took himself way too seriously – broke into a choral version of *Frosty the fucking Snowman*. Without the *fucking* bit, obviously.

Helena had felt her internal impatience scale ramp up to borderline explosive when they got to the last line of the song, pulled little cloth bags out of their pockets, then spread through the restaurant like locusts, hitting up all the customers for cash donations.

She had put a fiver in one of the snotty little kid's bags and waved him away. Bloody hell. Twenty-five quid down today so far on good Samaritan shit, and she was still having the worst day of her life. Karma could piss right off.

She was just about to reignite the conversation, when the waiter came back with their drinks and, without even looking at the receipt on his tray, she pulled out another tenner and handed it over, figuring that would cover the drinks and if there was anything left for a tip, he could have it. She was going to have to get a part-time job at this rate. Maybe their AWOL shoplifting client from this morning could set her up as a getaway driver on his next ramraid.

Finally, *finally,* the waiter retreated and it was just Helena and Bree again, with absolutely no reason not to have the conversational exchange that would determine whether Bruce Quinn was a cheating prick who was about to ruin her life.

'I'm sorry. This is deeply mortifying,' Bree said, taking the festive red drinks napkin the waiter had brought with their wine and blowing her nose with it. 'I'm so embarrassed.'

Helena reached over and patted her arm. 'Please don't be. Bree, I know we're colleagues, but we're friends too. I'm here to help if I can, so please, tell me what's happened. Start at the beginning.'

Was it the masochist in her that wanted Bree to share every single detail of every single way Bruce Quinn, Helena's boyfriend of the last six months, had betrayed her?

Bree took a deep breath and shook her head.

For a horrible moment, Helena thought she was about to change her mind and brush the whole thing off. In which case, she was going to go and find that brats' choir and force them to sing 'Jingle Bells' in Bree's ear until she cracked and spilled everything.

Bree took yet another glug of wine. Damn, she was dragging this out. Come on lady, speed it up.

Bree inhaled. Exhaled. Managed not to cry again. 'Okay, but everything I tell you today must be kept purely between us. Do you promise? Because, honestly, if this got out it could cost me everything.'

Helena rearranged her face to something she hoped said 'earnest and truthful'.

'Of course, I promise.' She definitely didn't.

'Well, the thing is, I've been seeing someone. For a while, actually.'

Helena felt her temperature begin to rise again and she shrugged off her snow jacket. If Bree noticed the tag dangling from the inside, she didn't mention it. Helena wasn't going to remove it, because she'd already decided that the jacket was going back to the shop on Boxing Day. It had been a purchase made of necessity and she wasn't having something in her wardrobe that would remind her of this day every single time she looked at it. Not to mention it had cost the equivalent of a week's wages and if she was spending that kind of money, she wanted it to involve a life-changing experience or a weekend somewhere really, really posh.

Helena went for mild surprise. 'Oh right. You never mentioned that. I always thought you were single, like me.'

Bree's shoulders slumped. 'I know, but that's because, well, the man I'm seeing asked me to keep it quiet. I'm really sorry, but I can't tell you who he is.'

'Oh, I love a mystery,' Helena teased. 'Is it because he's famous? If he's one of the guys out of Simple Minds, I'll faint.'

Keeping this pretence up was killing her, but she knew she had to act as if she was unaware of the situation and any potential pitfalls. It was the technique she always used when interviewing a client for the first time. Tease the story out of them, don't jump to conclusions, let them speak. Going in too hard would just make them shut down and Helena hadn't spent hours freezing her tits off to come away with nothing.

'No, no, nothing like that. It's just... Look, I'm sorry, I can't say. But anyway, I've been seeing him for a while...'

'For how long?'

'About a year, actually. We started dating last January.'

Helena wanted to punch a wall. So Bruce had been with Bree the whole time they were together? The secrecy and the fact that he insisted on spending half the week at his own flat was all starting to make sense. The bastard. Why hadn't she seen the signs? She thought back to the work barbeque where they had first got together and flipped through images of that night in her mind. Nope, nope, nope, nope, no Bree. Why not? It took a moment to recall, but then it came back to her. On the Monday following the party, she'd been scheduled to assist Bree defending two blokes who'd gone into a city-centre jeweller's, smashed the cases with a hammer and made off with thousands of pounds worth of rings. She specifically remembered that she'd been excited about it because the press were covering the story, but on the Monday morning word came in that Bree had chickenpox. There wasn't enough time to bring in a new senior solicitor, so the case had been postponed and by the time it was retried, Helena had been assigned to something else and she'd missed the whole thing.

A new wave of fury distracted her from the fact that Bree was still talking.

'He'd asked me to meet him for lunch today. Said there was something important he wanted to talk to me about. I thought... I thought he wanted us to maybe move in together. Or at least, go public with our relationship and make it official. Anyway, I said I'd make it if I could – I had a hunch our case would be adjourned today – so when we finished early, I headed straight to the restaurant. It's not far from here. He has lunch there every day, so I knew he'd be there.'

'Definitely not Simple Minds then. They'd get swarmed in any restaurant in Glasgow.'

Helena was trying desperately to come off as the funny, supportive friend, but it wasn't her field of expertise. Except when Bree was dating the man Helena had been in a relationship with for the last six months.

Bree obviously thought the same and acted like she hadn't even heard her. 'I thought it would be the most wonderful surprise, and that he'd be thrilled to see me, but instead he seemed... perturbed. Yes, that's the word. Definitely perturbed. I didn't understand it at all and put it down to perhaps a work issue.'

'Oh Bree, that must have been awful.' She put her hand over her faux friend's, and that was the first time she noticed that Bree was wearing a Patek Philippe watch. She had no idea how much they cost, but she knew they were expensive. She compared it to her own Citizen one, a gift from her mother when she started work, and the contrast burned her cheeks. Her gaze then went to the Gucci bag by Bree's side. This woman was only a few years older than her and already she looked so much more... expensive. Together. Like the kind of person who had money and status. Helena decided right there and then that the refund for the snow jacket was going towards a new watch. And every spare penny for the next few months would be spent on upgrading her work suits, her bag, her briefcase. From now on, she was going to look the part. She was going to go full-scale Bree Halston and beat her at her own classy, designer-clad game.

'Anyway, we had lunch and he seemed to relax, so I thought I must have been imagining something was wrong. He ordered a glass of wine for me and a beer for him and I never drink during the day but... it's Christmas.'

'Well, this time it's medicinal.' She slid Bree's glass of wine closer to her and urged her to carry on the drinking theme. Bree took a slug.

'Anyway, so then...' A sob caught in her throat, heralding fresh tears, and it took her a moment to recover. 'I don't know if I can say it.'

'Of course, you can,' Helena prompted. Including these drinks, she was thirty-five quid, a snow jacket and a pair of boots down and she wasn't going home without the truth, the whole truth and nothing but the truth.

'He told me how much he loved me. How much our time together had meant to him. And then...'

Teeth grinding, Helena literally slid to the edge of her seat.

'Then he said that he has to let me go.'

A spark of hope, of joy, began to take root in Helena's gut as she sought clarification. 'To let you go... where?'

'Anywhere,' Bree said, looking slightly bewildered. 'He told me that we're over.'

In one respect, Helena wanted to punch the air in victory, but the jubilation came with a harsh dose of reality. Bruce Quinn had been dating both of them for the last six months. He'd been telling Helena he loved her, while telling Bree the same thing at the same time. The feminist in her wanted to link arms with Bree and go over to his house right now to set fire to his collection of bespoke tailored suits and his Porsche. But the realist in her, the one who understood that every situation must be clearly assessed before action was taken, knew that wasn't the right thing to do. Bree hadn't coughed up the name of the person she was seeing, so right now this was a purely anonymous conversation. Helena decided to leave it that way, at least until a few more facts were gathered.

'Oh Bree, that's awful. The absolutely stupid bastard. Any man who doesn't realise how incredible you are doesn't deserve you.' That sounded like the kind of thing they espoused in *Cosmopolitan* magazine. 'Did he say why?'

'That's the worst bit... he says that he's met someone else. Someone who is better for him. Argh, I'm so fucking furious. I should have seen this coming. I mean, I knew he had a reputation, but I thought...'

'You thought he'd change for you?' That was a depressingly familiar concept.

'Exactly!'

Bree's tears had subsided now, leaving anger in their place. And thirst.

'Excuse me!' she summoned the waiter, who was delivering drinks to a nearby table. 'Can we have two more Chardonnays please?'

When he nodded and said he'd bring them right over, Bree leant in towards Helena. 'Would you mind getting these too? I forgot my purse this morning, so I don't have a penny on me.'

'No problem at all. I'd be happy to.' Helena's face was beginning to hurt with the effort of smiling when she was furious on the inside. Niceness and sympathy didn't sit well on her.

'I'm puzzled though. How could someone else be better for him than you?'

This morning, this woman had been one of her heroes. And Helena had considered herself to be a pretty switched on chick who could suss out any situation. How could they let themselves get played like this? Torching his Porsche was becoming more appealing by the minute. She was pretty sure the serial arsonist they'd defended a few months ago would do it just for fun.

But that said, if this was a battle between her and her mentor, Helena had won. Bruce had chosen her.

That filled her with satisfaction until Bree replied, 'Apparently she's got great connections that would be good for his career.'

The noise in her head was like a record player needle going right across that damn song her mother played every night before bed.

Her connections. It was for the job. He wanted to marry her, not because she was the most incredible woman he'd ever met, but because her father could help him secure the job he desperately wanted in another firm. And because being related to Duncan McLean would bring him serious clout and contacts.

The lying, cheating, bastard. Sod it, Bree could bloody well have him.

Helena couldn't even speak, so she welcomed the waiter with the next round of drinks. Fishing in her purse, she saw that she was down to her last ten pounds. She could have used her credit card, but she couldn't even contemplate all the faffing with the machine right now. She kissed her last tenner goodbye and the waiter toddled off. This time, she was the first one to drink, gulping back almost half the glass in one go. Bree's eyes widened.

'Sorry. Got a sudden thirst. Must be the heat in here.'

'Me too. Definitely the heat.' With that, Bree knocked back half of hers too.

Helena was starting to feel slightly giddy and she didn't care in the least. If she was going to get through the rest of this conversation, she was probably going to have to do it drunk.

'Do you know what the worst thing is?' Bree said, and Helena could hear a slight slur in her voice.

'You want to torch his car?' Helena suggested.

'Yes! Definitely. But that's not it. The worst thing is that I'd take him back. I would. I love him. I thought we were going to have this amazing future together.'

That was the most depressing thing Helena had ever heard, and yet, on some level, she understood it. In the legal world, Bruce Quinn was someone, and out of court, he was the kind of guy that made you feel like you were the only person in the universe. That was an addictive, intoxicating place to be.

Helena heard words coming out of her mouth but she wasn't sure if they were powered by jealousy, sisterly solidarity or alcohol. 'Don't take him back, Bree. You're better than that. You really are.'

Bree was nose deep in the wine again so Helena had to wait until she put the glass down before she replied, 'I know. That's the thing – I do know that. And tomorrow I'll probably know that even more. But right now, I just want to drink and feel sorry for myself.'

Helena was having the opposite reaction. She felt an irrepressible and immediate need to get out of there. She knew the whole story. Had all the facts. She had to be somewhere that she could process the information and think it through, the way she did with every single situation in her life. Or maybe, just this time, she'd skip the strategic analysis and go straight to Bruce Quinn and annihilate the bastard.

'Bree, I'd love to stay, but I need to go home. My parents have plans for this evening and I'm joining them.'

Even without her adding, *because I'm supposed to be getting engaged to the prick who just dumped you,* Bree's face fell.

'Okay. I suppose I should really go home too. My family is coming for Christmas lunch tomorrow and I haven't even picked up the turkey yet.'

Helena had a feeling Bree's family would be having turkey, roast potatoes, veg and a serving of woe tomorrow.

She picked up her glass. 'Bree, I'm so sorry this has happened to you. You deserve so much better. Forget about him. Fuck him. I mean, not literally, obviously.'

Bree picked up her glass and clinked it against Helena's, suddenly all puffed up chest and full of resolve. 'You're right. Fuck him.'

They clinked again, then both downed the rest of the wine.

An hour and what felt like a lifetime after they'd gone into the grotto of festive fabulousness, the two of them, arms linked, made it back out onto Buchanan Street.

'How are you getting home, Bree?' Helena asked, suddenly fearing that the answer would involve her finding somewhere to take out cash and paying for that too. This was turning into the most expensive day ever, and all she had to show for it was raised blood pressure, a cracked heart and an urge to strangle her boyfriend.

Smiling, Bree pulled ten pounds out of her pocket. 'Look what I found! My trusty stash. I always keep ten pounds in my pocket in case of emergencies. I think this is officially an emergency.'

'I think you're right. Come on, let's find you a taxi.'

They crossed over Buchanan Street, and made it to the rank on Gordon Street, outside Central Station. The red mist and the white wine had receded just enough to let Helena think coherently. It was some consolation that at least Bruce had ditched Bree before proposing, but that didn't excuse the fact that he'd been shagging them both at the same time. She was going to put Bree in the cab and then go and track down Bruce fucking Quinn and get answers. Had the relationship with Bree been as serious as she made it sound? Was he really just proposing for her connections? Or was that just something he said to Bree to smooth their break-up and explain why he was choosing someone else over her? Did he even love her? And how could she trust a single word that came out of the cheating bastard's mouth now anyway?

As the next taxi pulled up, she watched as it sprayed slush all over Bree's white coat, but missed Helena completely. Maybe her karma was kicking in after all. However, she wasn't leaving the fates to deal with Bruce's betrayal. Helena was going to take care of that one all by herself.

12

CATHY

Christmas Eve 1968

The café was usually busy in the early afternoon, mostly with kids from the high school who'd bunked off early, just as Cathy and Richie had done a couple of days a week during their last two years of education. This place had been their constant. Close enough to Cathy's home that she could nip back there early if her mum and dad were at work, but far enough away that she didn't worry about her mother walking past and catching them.

Today, though, it only had a couple of old dears at the table in the window, probably because the rest of the world was working, shopping, or preparing for the Big day tomorrow.

'I'm closing early, today. About half past three,' the woman behind the counter told them with a smile.

'That's fine. We're just in for some chips,' Richie replied with that smile that won over everyone he met.

Cathy was still staring at the woman, and not just because she had the biggest beehive she'd ever seen. What got her attention was the chain of multicoloured paper hoops around her neck, and when Cathy looked up, she saw where they'd come from. The jolt of recognition was fierce. Every year, when her mum was alive, she'd come home with strips of pastel-coloured paper, with stamp-like glue at one end. On the first of December, Mum, Cathy and Loretta would put Nat King Cole's *The Magic of Christmas* album on the record player, and they'd sing along as they made what felt like miles of paper chains. Curl, lick, close. Then put the next strip through the first one and curl, lick, close. On and on, until they had enough to drape chains from the top of the wall in each corner of the living room, into the ceiling rose in the middle. Then they'd add another few chains in the middle of each wall too, so that the ceiling was a kaleidoscope of colour.

This year and last, she'd remembered to do all of the other things her mum loved. The Christmas tree had gone up, covered in tinsel, with every ornament the girls had ever made in school dangling from the ends of the branches. They'd played their mum's favourite songs. They'd displayed all their cards on the sideboard. But they'd forgotten the paper chains and now the memory gave Cathy an almost physical pain in her heart.

Of course, Richie knew her so well, he spotted her reaction straight away and pulled out a chair for her to sit on. 'Are you okay? Is it the baby?'

She smiled, waved off the suggestion. 'No, the baby's fine. I was just thinking I hadn't been in here for such a long time,' she said, trying her best to keep things light. The way she'd been bursting into tears all day, she didn't want to talk about anything sad in case she ended up sobbing into her chips in the middle of the café.

He waited until she'd sat down, then checked what she wanted. Her response was automatic. A glass of milk and some chips. Their staple lunchtime diet for most of their teenage years.

He went over to the counter to order it and Cathy watched him go, almost felled by a sudden wish that she could turn back time to any of the hundreds of other days they'd sat in here, back when life was so straightforward and easy. Richie loved her. She loved Richie. Her mum and dad were alive and well and the biggest problem they had was that Loretta had cracked the kitchen window twice playing rounders with her friends in the garden.

Right on cue, the tears welled up again and Cathy furiously blinked them back.

'Are you sure you feel okay?' Richie asked as he came back to the table.

'I'm sure. I was just thinking about my mum and dad. I miss them.'

He reached for her hand and she let him hold it, not caring that everyone else in the room had probably clocked her wedding ring and would be thinking they were a married couple having a heart-to-heart.

All intentions of keeping it light went out the fake-snow covered window. She wiped away her tears with the cuff of her jacket. 'I don't think it ever gets easier. Sometimes I think I miss them more as the days go by instead of less.'

Richie stroked the top of her hand with his thumb. 'I should never have left you to take care of everything on your own. I should have stayed in the shipyards and stuck it out here. I'm so sorry. I was just... stupid. I listened to everyone else, and somehow convinced myself that going away was the right thing to do.'

'I convinced you of that too, so don't beat yourself up about it. I didn't give you much choice.' That was true. How could she leave him languishing in the shipyards in a job he hated, when he'd had an incredible opportunity to see the world, learn a trade, improve his life. She'd loved him too much to hold him back. Persuading him to leave her had been the right thing for him, even if it had been oh so wrong for her.

'Two plates of chips and two glasses of milk,' the waitress chirped as she put their lunch down, snapping Cathy out of her memories.

'I'll leave some sauce here in case you or your husband want it. There's salt, pepper and vinegar on the table there.'

Her husband.

Richie was staring at her, watching her reaction. He didn't speak until the waitress was out of earshot. 'I wish I was. Your husband.'

Cathy's anxieties reared right back up again and caused another sharp stab of heartburn in her chest.

No. Enough. She pulled her hand away.

'Richie, I can't. You promised, just friends, no pressure or any of that serious stuff. I can't do it. I really can't. It hurts too much.'

The flare of panic in his eyes told her that he was worried she'd get up and walk out, as did his immediate apology. 'I know. I'm sorry. I can't help it, it's just that...' He must have registered her pained expression because he immediately changed tack. 'Nothing. Sorry. Okay. No more soppy stuff, I promise. Just friends. And chips.'

She picked up her first one and popped it in her mouth. 'Promise?'

'Promise.'

She almost believed him, until the record on the jukebox changed and the opening bars of a familiar song flooded the room.

Even Richie groaned. 'I swear that wasn't me. I swear it. You've been able to see me the whole time. I didn't go near the jukebox.'

She knew he was telling the truth, but still... even the bloody gods of music were conspiring to give her more heartburn now.

The Temptations were singing about sunshine, and cloudy

days, and the month of May and my girl. 'My Girl'. Their song. The one that Richie had played almost every time they came in here. For her. His girl. Except she wasn't his any more.

They ate the rest of their chips in silence, and Cathy was on her last one when Richie suddenly blurted out, 'Shit. Shit. Shit.'

'What?' She realised his stare was on the door and whipped her head around to see the problem. It was unmistakable. His sister had just stopped outside the door and pushed it open, and now she was walking in towards the counter, oblivious to his presence, until some sixth sense must have intervened and she stopped, turned...

'Richie? Oh Jesus, Richie!' Betty threw her arms wide and Richie immediately jumped up and returned his sister's embrace. 'What are you doing here? Does Mum know you're home? No, she can't know or she'd have been up since five this morning cleaning like a demon to calm her nerves.'

For the first time, she registered Cathy's presence. 'Cathy! It's so good to see you.'

Betty had been in the year below Richie and Cathy at school, so they'd all hung out together at the ice rink at the weekends.

Betty leaned down to embrace her, but Cathy saw her flinch at the exact moment she realised there was a baby-shaped bulge in the front of Cathy's stomach. Her maths calculation was obviously rapid and she processed that it wasn't her brother's bump. Her tact and diplomacy kicked in just as quickly.

'Congratulations on the baby, Cath.' The gaze, as it always did, went to the wedding finger. 'And on getting married too. I hadn't heard or I'd have sent you a card.'

'That's okay, Betty. It was a wee while ago. Just a quiet wedding.' Cathy had no intention of sharing her personal business in a West End café in the middle of the day.

'Well, I'm pleased for you. You deserve to be happy.'

The tears shot back up to her bottom lids and Cathy coughed to clear them.

Richie stepped in with a diversion. 'Listen, don't tell Mum you saw me. I'll be home in a while, but I just wanted to see Cath first.'

'She won't hear it from me, I promise. Just as long as when you do come home, you don't tell her you saw me. I'm here for an interview, but she's got her heart set on me going to work with her at the factory.' Richie's mum worked at the thread mill down in Anniesland. It was hard on her back and tough on her feet, but it was a job for life, and she often said that the camaraderie with the other women who worked there got her through even the hardest of times, so it made sense she'd want that for her daughter too. Unfortunately, Betty didn't seem to share her enthusiasm, but seeing her brother had definitely put a smile on her face.

Richie hugged her again. 'Deal. And good luck with the job.' He turned to the lady who had served them their lunch.

'Excuse me, my wife and I just want to let you know that we recommend this girl here. We've met her before and she's the best waitress we've ever had.'

Her teary emotional pendulum swung the opposite way, and Cathy wasn't sure whether she or Betty was trying hardest not to laugh at his cheeky lie.

Richie reached down and took her hand. In a purely friendly way. 'Come on. I think we'd better get out of here before we ruin her chances.'

Giggling, and throwing a 'Merry Christmas' out to the café owner, the two of them made their escape.

Outside, the cold had thawed a little and Cathy was glad of the fresh air.

'Do you need to go home or can we go for a walk?' Richie asked.

She thought about saying she should get back, but for what?

Loretta wouldn't be home for another couple of hours, and Duncan was going to deliver presents to his parents after work in Edinburgh and was getting a late train home.

'I can stay out a little longer. Where do you want to go?'

He thought about it for a few moments. 'I know somewhere. This way...'

Richie started off down Byres Road, walking slowly so she could keep up with him as they crossed over and cut down through the curved terraces just behind the busy road. Cathy stopped trying to guess where they were or where they were going, for at least ten minutes or so, until they rounded a corner and the sight in front of her took her breath away.

It was a tiny park. More of an extra-large garden, really. It was surrounded on all four sides by the grand old properties of bygone years, the kind of houses she'd dreamt of living in when she was a child. Fairy-tale homes with huge, twinkly Christmas trees in the windows, and people inside who had no cares at all. People who got to look out of those windows and see a million tiny lights on the trees of the garden in front of them.

Cathy had never seen anything like it. It was magical. Like an enchanted forest where you could make a wish and it might just come true.

The only thing was, she just didn't know what, or who, she wanted to wish for.

4 P.M. – 6 P.M.

13

EVE

Christmas Eve 2023

'Well, would you look at you two gorgeous specimens of womanhood,' Loretta roared down the phone, making Eve smile with her gregarious greeting and contagious enthusiasm. After her gran, her Aunt Loretta was probably her favourite person on the planet. Not that she'd tell her mother that, of course. Or Gabby or Sonny either. But she had a feeling that even if she did, they'd probably feel the same, because if there was a prize for injecting joy and laughter into every scenario and sentence, Loretta would win it.

'Aunt Loretta, we miss you! How are the fine gentlemen of Benidorm coping with your presence. Bet they're falling at your feet.'

'The pavements are littered with the bodies of my many admirers,' Loretta joked right back. 'It looks like a zombie apocalypse has befallen us.'

Eve's laughter made the phone shake, and she adjusted it again so both her and her gran were in the view of the FaceTime camera.

Loretta's face filled the rest of the screen and Eve thought, as always, how beautiful her aunt was. At seventy-one, she could pass for a woman at least ten years younger and she swore that it was down to 'good laughs, great sex, a positive attitude and spending no time with anyone who didn't bring you joy'. Which pretty much summed up why she'd been through four husbands and was currently auditioning for her fifth. It was also why music fans over the last five decades had a place in their heart for her.

The much-told story of her discovery was the stuff of legend. She'd been a teenage orphan, cared for by her older sister, who'd made it clear she expected Loretta to stick at school and get some good qualifications. However, young Loretta had defied her sister's wishes and was working part-time in a hairdressing salon. It was there, one Christmas Eve in the latter years of the swinging sixties, when the batteries on the radio had died and she'd volunteered to take over the musical entertainment in the salon. She'd been belting out 'She Loves Me', while giving a male client a blow-dry after a blonde dye job, when the gent had asked her to stop, given her his business card, and told her he was a music producer who'd like her to audition for a band. A month later, sixteen-year-old Loretta McLean was the lead singer of the Lilac Waves (everyone thought it was some clever psychedelic reference, but it was actually inspired by all the little old dears who came in for their purple toner and their shampoo and set every week) and they were in a studio recording their first album.

They'd been huge in the seventies, billed as the British version of Fleetwood Mac, and they'd ridden that bus all the way to new romantic, eighties obscurity. Since then, after a ten-year stint as a square on *Blankety Blank*, Loretta had been a fan favourite on the pub and club touring circuit, and she'd spread her wings to warmer climates when her arthritis had started bothering her knees.

'Well, you'd better get the street sweepers out for that then,' Cathy quipped back, before going with the practicalities. 'Where are you? Have you got a show tonight?'

Loretta nodded. 'I sure have. I'm just in the car on the way there now. It's a guest appearance at a big new hotel in Alicante. Apparently, it's owned by an eighty year old billionaire Greek shipping tycoon. If you never hear from me again, I'm sucking grapes off his chest in a palace in Corfu.'

'Just be sure to send your sister and your niece a plane ticket and an invitation to the wedding. I've still got the bridesmaid dress from last time. It'll do another turn.'

The two sisters dissolved into cackles of hilarity that made Eve's arm shake again. She adored these two. Someone should work out a way to bottle their attitudes to life. Loretta was single at seventy-one and her gran was recently bereaved, and yet they still sought every chance to laugh and be happy.

'How's the new house, Cathy?'

'I love it already. Wait until you see it, Loretta. It's just perfect. I can't quite believe I'm here. I mean, there's still stuff to unpack and I haven't located the box with ma knickers and ma tights yet, but apart from that it's perfect.'

'I'm happy for you, darling. You deserve it. You always have. Listen, I have to go in a minute because we're just about to pull up at the hotel.'

'No worries, Aunt Loretta,' Eve answered first. 'We have to go too. Gran is about to tell me some dark, mysterious secret about a love from her past.'

'She was asking me about the loves of my life,' her gran interjected, and that seemed to carry some kind of subliminal explanation, because, to her surprise, Loretta gave her sister a look that oozed compassion and love.

'Och, Cathy. Good luck with that, pet,' she said, in a voice that had the affection quota of a long, supportive hug.

Her gran's voice cracked as she replied with a heartfelt, 'Thanks, ma love.'

Bloody hell, this story must really be something. The tenderness it seemed to evoke in both of them made this the most touching exchange Eve had ever seen them have. They usually communicated on a firm basis of cheek, teasing, and gossipy hilarity.

'Right, well, Cathy, I'll give you a ring in the morning to wish you all a merry Christmas. Will Helena be with you?'

When Eve had reached adulthood, her traditions with her gran and grandad hadn't changed, but Helena had negotiated down to joining them late morning for brunch and then spending the rest of Christmas day with them. Earlier, Eve had tried to persuade her mum to stay overnight with them tonight, but Helena had been vague in her answer, saying she'd be working late, so Eve had little hope that she'd make it.

'Yes,' Eve answered, trying to keep a lid on her exasperation with her mother. There was no point in being irritated. Helena had always been emotionally closed off, detached and distracted by work, and that was never going to change. Eve had realised a long time ago that letting it bother her only detracted from her own happiness, so she'd let it go and focused on the love, security and positivity she received from her gran, grandad and great-aunt instead. 'She's coming for brunch as usual and we'll be eating, drinking and watching movies all day. We might venture out for a wee walk in the afternoon, so our bodies don't go into shock from over-consumption of Quality Street and After Eights, but apart from that, we'll all be here.'

'Throw in a karaoke machine and that's my perfect day,' Loretta chuckled. 'I'm glad Helena will be there – means I'll get to wish her a happy birthday too. Eve, look after your gran for me. I love you, pet.'

'Love you back, Aunt Loretta.'

With a cheery wave, and goodbyes from gran, her aunt was off and then the screen went black.

Almost immediately, it lit up and began to ring again. Gabby.

Eve answered with a smile. 'Am I required for the airport pick-up?' she asked, really hoping that she wasn't. She had enough on her plate today and she couldn't bear the thought of leaving her gran right now.

'Nope, the package has been collected and is now sitting with me in my dressing room waiting to immerse himself in the profound theatrics of yet another Christmas pantomime. Don't you dare say "Oh no, he isn't."'

'Argh, but it's so tempting. Hey, Nick,' Eve waved as Gabby's brother came into view. He was over six feet tall, his jet black hair cropped tight to his head, his deep brown eyes almost the same shade as the scarf that was wrapped tightly around his neck. Teasing him about being a California guy who wasn't cut out for the cold Scottish winters had always been one of her favourite pastimes, although they both accepted it was born of jealousy that he surfed every morning before work, while Eve spent her first half hour trying to defrost her feet.

'Hi, Eve. Tell me, am I in a safe space? Is this performance going to change my life?'

Eve had always loved his quirky sense of humour, especially surprising because he had a pretty serious job doing something technical in IT that Eve definitely didn't understand. 'Almost definitely. It'll be the most moving thing you've ever seen in a theatre.

Apart from the time Gabby played Peter Pan, broke the zipline and was left dangling over the orchestra pit.'

Beside her, her gran cackled at the memory. They'd both been at that show and after the initial shock, and then the realisation that it wasn't a high-risk situation, Cathy had tears of laughter streaming down her face as two mortified stage hands got a ladder and helped Gabby down.

Gabby took the phone back. 'I'm still planning to sue over that. There are bits of me that have never been the same since. Anyway, how's the move going? Are we still invited for brunch tomorrow morning?'

'You sure are. Around ten o'clock. Or just come whenever you get up.'

Nick gave her a thumbs up and her gran reciprocated with the same. 'Looking forward to it. I've practised my Scottish words, so I'm good to go.'

The year before, she'd bought him a dictionary of Scottish slang and his attempts to speak the lingo had her in stiches until he'd left on January the second.

'Excellent – I'll be giving you a test. Have a great time at the panto. Gabby, break a leg!'

'That's what they said before they put me in that harness,' Gabby retorted, laughing as she hung up, and setting Cathy off on another tide of infectious laughter, before she busied herself dusting down three Archangels for the fireplace. Cathy could never remember their names, so she called them Huey, Dewey and Louie.

Before Eve put her phone down, she noticed a text from Sonny.

Hey, friend with benefits.
Just heading to the pub with the rest of the office now. Will call you

later. Still curious to know if I'm getting a proper girlfriend for Christmas. 😄. Xx

She couldn't help the smile that lifted her cheeks as she replied.

Lol – are you sure you don't just want a big telly and a case of beer? Much lower on maintenance. Speak later or if the cocktails get the worst of you, buzz me in the morning. xx

Job done, all communications completed, Eve slipped her phone back into her pocket. His joke reminded her that she still hadn't addressed one of the items on her list – buy Sonny a Christmas present. If all else failed, she could re-purpose the bottle of tequila she'd spotted in Gran's alcohol stash earlier. Before she could decide if the omission was a subliminal message, orders came from her esteemed elder.

'Right, pet, let's get this place Christmas-ified!' her gran commanded, opening another box. The words, 'CHRISTMAS TAT' written on the side should have been a give-away. She pulled out two halves of a pre-lit fibre-optic tree, half a dozen red and gold candles, a door wreath, a herd of battery-operated flashing reindeer that came with suction pads so they could be adhered to the windows, two strings of fairy lights, a box of mince pies and a bottle of mulled wine.

'Hang on, hang on. I've got pals for the reindeer.' Eve sprinted to her car and returned with the penguins.

Cathy threw her hands up in jubilation. 'Are those the ones that sing?'

Eve flicked their 'on' switch. 'Sure are. Gabby and I were wondering if you'd like to adopt them.'

'Yesssssss! I've been trying to work out how to steal them from your kitchen for years! Come to Granny, boys. This is where you belong.'

Her outstretched arms immediately set them off and they burst into their one-song repertoire of 'We Wish You A Merry Christmas'. Cathy had a wee dance with them before putting them in pride of place on the mantle.

Eve surreptitiously placed a candle in front of their motion sensor so that they could get all the other Christmas stuff in place without their musical input.

The tree looked perfect by the window, under the herd of flashing reindeer. Eve wasn't sure the neighbours in this relatively posh street would appreciate their fabulousness, but she didn't care. Her gran was happy, the room was gorgeous, and, in the words of a non-penguin musical number, it was beginning to feel a lot like Christmas.

They finished just as Harry came in the living-room door.

'I'm afraid I let you down, Cathy.'

'You've stolen the box with ma tights?'

The shock on this tank of a man's face made Eve chortle.

'No,' he countered, then pointed at his watch. 'I was just going to say that we finished fifteen minutes behind schedule. Your tights are in a box in your bedroom. Next to your furry slippers and your hula hoop. Not a sentence I ever thought I'd say. Do you want to come and have a look at what's been done?'

Eve and Cathy both followed him into the spare room, which already had everything in place, and the bedding sitting neatly on top of the mattress. The main bedroom was the same, and then in the kitchen, the dining table was set up and ready to use, and the microwave, toaster, pots and pans had been unpacked and placed next to the kettle, the biscuit tin and the fully stocked wine rack. It was all perfect, like one of those house transformation shows where a whole team swarms the place and completely transforms it and makes it liveable in just a few hours. Another day of Cathy and Eve unpacking the small stuff, and the whole house would look like it had been lived in for years.

'It's marvellous, Harry. I can't thank you enough. You've all done an amazing job, especially on Christmas Eve. Hang on a wee minute.'

Her gran disappeared back into the living room and returned ten seconds later, carrying a sealed envelope, which she handed over to Harry.

'Here's a wee bonus for you and your team. Get yourselves a beer, and Merry Christmas.'

The giant of a man almost had to bend double to hug her. 'Thanks, Cathy, that's kind of you. I was happy to help out today as a favour to the boss, but I'll give this to the lads. And if you need anything at all, just get me on the blower.'

'Just a lottery win and Liam Neeson,' she shot back, making him roar with laughter.

'I'll see what I can do. Have a good night, ladies – been a pleasure working with you.'

'You too, Harry,' Eve replied with a wave, then watched as he followed the rest of the team out of the door.

'I reckon he could take Liam Neeson if he tried you know,' was her gran's verdict on the situation. 'Anyway, fancy a wee glass of wine? And by 'wee', I mean huge.'

Eve nodded. The extra perk of staying over for Christmas was that her car could be abandoned until Boxing Day. 'I sure do.'

Eve searched the nearby boxes for wine glasses and found them on the second attempt, while her gran opened the fridge and pulled out a bottle of Prosecco.

'That Harry's a gem. He's left a corkscrew right here for us. Must have read our minds.'

She opened the bottle, poured their drinks, and grabbed a packet of HobNobs from the biscuit barrel.

'Ready to spill all your secrets then, Gran? Where shall we sit? Here or in the living room?'

Her gran thought for a moment, then went to the back window, on the opposite side of the building from the entrance, and pulled up the blinds.

'Come and look at this.'

It struck Eve that she'd never even thought to check the view from the back of the flat. On the one visit they'd made here before moving, the window had been all blocked off with sheets and scaffolding.

From where she was standing, Eve could see that it was already dark outside, but as she got closer, it got weirdly brighter and brighter until she saw the reason for the glow. Thousands of fairy lights twinkling about twenty yards across the road.

'Oh my God, Gran, it's your garden!' Two fat tears slid down Eve's grinning face. Their secret place. The one they'd visited every Christmas Eve since she was a child.

'That's why you were so insistent that we had to be moved in before Christmas. And it's why you were so sure you wanted to move here!' Eve felt like the detective in every cop show, who uncovered all the secrets at the end of the episode and suddenly everything made sense.

Cathy grinned, but there was a look in her eyes that Eve didn't recognise. Not sadness, but maybe wistfulness?

Or maybe she was just tired after a crazy day.

'You're right on both counts, ma love. But maybe not for all the reasons that you think. Grab your coat. If I'm going to tell you everything, let's do it out there.'

14

HELENA

Christmas Eve 1993

Helena pushed her key into the door of her apartment with the kind of force that was only normally used in a SWAT team dawn raid.

As soon as she was inside, she dropped her bag, kicked off her boots, tossed her jacket onto the shoe bench by the door, stood still for two seconds and then raised her head and screamed, 'Fuu-uuuuckkkkkkkkkk!' to the ceiling.

She could barely remember the geography of the walk home, because she had been so stuck in her own mind, every step of trudging through the grey slushy snow taking her to a different emotional place. First, there was the fury. The absolute raging anger that Bruce Quinn, the man she thought she'd been in a happy, committed relationship with for the last six months, had been shagging someone else the whole time. And not just anyone. Oh no. Just to shove that dagger deeper into her gut, he'd been shagging one of the few other people in the world that she actually admired, cared about, respected. Friends had never really been top of her priority list, but Helena thought that, as she began to climb the ladder of success and became Bree's professional equal, their relationship could transition from close work colleagues and casual friendship to a bond of sisterhood that would carry them through their careers. Well, Bruce Quinn had just screwed that idea.

And, worse, now there was the grim fucking reality that his proposal was actually nothing more than a professional move, a token act to get his arse further up the career ladder. Did he really want her? Or just the kudos that being married to Duncan McLean's daughter would give him and the doors that would open for him?

As she'd marched on and the slush had begun to permeate the suede of her gorgeous but highly impractical boots, she'd slid across the emotional spectrum to devastation. This morning... Damn, was it only a few hours ago? This morning, she'd been so elated when her mother had announced Bruce was going to propose. That, right then, had been one of the happiest moments of her life. She'd made it. Got the prize. She'd found someone she was utterly in love with and she'd seen her whole life roll out in front of her. Mrs Helena McLean Quinn, an eminent solicitor who would go on to become just as respected and as powerful as her husband. Fearless. A crusader for justice. A brilliant criminal mind with a wonderful lifestyle in the upper echelons of society. Fabulous holidays. A gorgeous home. Together, the two of them could create a spectacular life. Maybe kids at some point too.

Nope, scratch that. She'd never had any desire for children and she couldn't see how they would fit into her life. Nor would she want them to. She'd seen too many female solicitors' careers crash and burn after childbirth because they could no longer give the job the 100 per cent focus it required to rise to the top in a predominantly male environment. The old-boy atmosphere of her chosen profession made her want to buy a crane and crash it right through that glass fucking ceiling, but she had less chance of that happening if she was covered in puke and rushing home early to pick a child up from a babysitter.

No. No kids. Just a career. Brilliant husband. Incredible life. And Bruce Quinn had just screwed that idea too.

She hadn't given a toss what any bystanders thought of the young woman storming through the streets with tears of fury streaming down her face, because by then she'd made another stop on the Bruce Quinn Fucked My Life highway. Humiliation.

Her parents already knew that he intended to propose, and her mother had seen her reaction to that scenario this morning. Admitting what had happened, that she'd been stupid enough to allow herself to be cheated on, lied to, manipulated, to be used for a career opportunity, would be more embarrassment than she could bear. And lying about it wasn't an option, because her mother had the scrutiny and interrogation skills of an undercover CIA operative. She'd suspect something was amiss, she'd dig, and she'd find it. And her dad... he was one of the very few people in life whose opinion she cared about. He was brilliant. Accomplished. He adored her and she couldn't bear to show vulnerability or poor judgement to someone who thought she could do no wrong.

Yet again, yep, bullseye – Bruce Quinn had screwed with that idea as well. And that had spun her right back round the circle of human emotions to rage.

Now, standing in her hall, she realised that screaming at the heavens hadn't made her feel a single bit better.

'Helena?' The voice from the doorway to her kitchen made her scream again as she jumped. 'Are you okay, sweetheart?'

Male. Older. Oozing Concern.

'Dad?'

The door opened wider and Duncan McLean took a few steps forward, until they were in each other's full field of vision, staring at one another, waiting for the other one to offer even a smidge of explanation as to how they'd both found themselves standing in her hall.

He went first, gesturing to the bottle of champagne in his hand. 'Your mum sent me over to put this in your fridge. Actually, this and flowers and three other bags of groceries. She said she wanted to make sure that you woke up to a wonderful Christmas and birthday breakfast tomorrow morning, but I think she got a bit carried away, so if you get snowed in for the next month, you won't starve.'

Helena sighed on the inside. Her mother's interference drove her nuts. If she wanted champagne and flowers and eggs bloody benedict, she could organise it herself. Yes, even she was aware deep down inside that that was a selfish, ungrateful bitch of a thought, but if she was going to have a moment of indulging her inner cow, this was it.

Her dad fell silent, and she knew he was waiting for her to speak. That was her dad's way. He wasn't one to demand answers, or to whip anything up into a drama. He preferred understated calm and logic. Helena was so much more comfortable with that than her mother's gregarious, overblown affection.

'Thank you,' she said, forcing a smile. 'And I'm sorry about the shouting. Bad day at work. My case got postponed. I got shackled with a whole ton of paperwork. Then I had to take care of a colleague who was having a frankly pathetic emotional breakdown. I spent money that I now thoroughly regret to try to make her feel better and then I had to trudge home in the bloody snow and my feet are soaking.'

She hadn't grown up with Cathy McLean without learning how to create a bit of a drama and today it was required for diversionary tactics. For a second, Helena wasn't sure if it worked, but then her dad's concerned expression morphed into a wide smile of sympathy.

'Well, you're home now, tomorrow is your birthday and tonight we're going out to celebrate that and... erm, celebrate... Christmas.'

It was an uncharacteristic fluff of his lines, but Helena immediately realised it was because he'd never lied to her, so this was unfamiliar territory.

She made a split-second decision to put him out of his misery. 'Dad, Mum told me Bruce asked for permission to propose tonight.'

His body language instantly changed, and she watched his shoulders relax as he let out an warm chuckle. 'That woman couldn't keep a secret if her life depended on it.'

Helena forced the smile back on her face again as she walked down the hall towards him. 'You're right. I don't know why anyone needs a television for news when they could just hire Mum. Much cheaper and you don't need a TV licence.'

Her dad backed up into the kitchen, and as she passed him, Helena took the bottle of champagne from his hand and began to unwrap the foil.

'Sod the celebrations, Dad. Let's you and I have some of this now. It'll defrost my feet.'

If he was surprised, he didn't show it, although he almost put her off the idea when he laughed. 'That's exactly what your mother would do. Sometimes I think there's a little bit of her in you after all.'

Helena didn't reply, just grabbed some glasses, poured and

pulled out a chair next to where her dad was now sitting at the breakfast bar.

'Mum said you told Bruce you'd give us your blessing, but only if I wanted to marry him.'

'Of course. Helena, I'd never be so bold or so stupid as to make decisions for you or to influence your thoughts. You're more than capable of making a brilliant life for yourself, sweetheart. You don't need me to approve your choices.'

'But do you? Approve?' This kind of conversation was uncharted waters for them. They usually stuck to work, career, or their common interests, like hill walking or politics or current affairs.

'I don't know him well enough. I've heard he's highly competent and blazing a trail of professional success, but that doesn't mean he's a good person or the kind of man who deserves to be with my daughter. I've met more than a few unscrupulous or arrogant arses in our profession over the years. However, I trust your judgement. I always have. You've been seeing him for six months and he tells me you love him, so that's good enough for me.'

The humiliation from earlier came right back again with a ferocious flush on her face. Hopefully, Dad would put that down to the champagne. The point was made though. If it got out that Bruce had manipulated her, then the world, and more importantly, her father, would think she was an idiot and she couldn't bear that.

Aaaaargh. On the outside, she was drinking champagne and having an uncharacteristically personal chat with her dad, but on the inside, she was screaming profanities at the ceiling again.

Her father took another sip of champagne, and then put his glass down on the table. 'Anyway, sweetheart, I'd better shoot off home. Your mother needs me to deliver Christmas Eve meals to all the elderly people in our street. I know better than to question it or be late. Why don't you and Bruce come over about 6.30 and we'll all head to the hotel together? I'm so looking forward to it.'

Tell him. Go on. Tell him what Bruce has done. It's his fault, not yours.

Yet, even as she was telling herself that, something inside didn't believe it or support it. She needed more time to vent. To rage. To come up with a story as to why they wouldn't be there tonight.

'Will do, Dad,' she agreed, as they both got up from the table.

He was almost outside, when something occurred to him and he stopped.

'I almost forgot one of the things that I'd come to tell you. I spoke to my partners about Bruce, and I told them that you regarded him highly. Whether you accept his proposal tonight or not, they've agreed to take him on board. We sent out the official offer an hour ago.'

It took every bit of strength she had to act pleased about that decision. 'Thank you, Dad, that's wonderful.' Afraid he'd see through her reaction, she leaned over and hugged him tight. Unlike her mum, her dad had never been the most tactile of parents, but if he was shocked, he didn't show it. In fact, he patted her back and when he pulled away, he looked almost bashfully pleased.

'You're welcome, sweetheart. I'll see you tonight and, Helena, I really am so proud of you. Not for the engagement, but just for being you.'

With that, he was gone. She closed the door behind him, then slid down the wall and put her head in her hands.

Shit. Bugger. Damn.

What the hell was happening to her life? And what was she going to do about it?

She needed time to think and she wasn't going to have that if she was in a posh hotel celebrating dinner with her parents and a cheating bastard who had just bagged a fantastic new job and was about to propose to her. Bailing out wasn't an option, because her mother would be round here in a flash demanding to know what was going on. If she took that route, she'd have to give Bruce an explanation too and that would mean revealing that she knew about Bree and had found out he was manipulating her for a job.

She needed a plan. A duplicitous one that would cover all bases. A fabrication that would even pass the Cathy McLean test. A brain that was more commonly used for complicated legal strategies and comprehensive research came up with the answer.

Reaching up to the top of the console table next to her, she grabbed the phone that lived there and dialled a number she knew off by heart.

Bruce answered on the third ring.

'Hi,' she croaked, her throat constricted by the anger that just hearing his voice had evoked inside her.

'Darling, you sound awful. Are you okay? Is something wrong?'

For the first time today, life had conspired to help her out.

'Actually, that's why I was calling you,' she carried on, forcing out the words in an altered voice. 'I'm so sorry, but I'm afraid I'm going to have to cancel tonight. I feel awful. Just terrible. I've been throwing up for the last two hours.'

'Nooooo,' he groaned, sympathetically. 'Darling, we had such a wonderful evening planned with your parents.'

It clicked that he had no idea that she knew he was going to propose, and she played on that.

'I know, but my mother will drive me crazy all night anyway, so it's no big deal. At least we'll escape the birthday conga that she always makes me do at midnight. I really couldn't bear it tonight. It must have been something I had at lunch that's turned my stomach. I should sue.'

Not far from the truth.

'Well, I tell you what, why don't I come over...'

Panic. Then her strategic brain kicked in again and she fired back, 'Oh please don't, darling. I'd never forgive myself if this is a bug and I pass it on to you. Christmas would be miserable. Look, I tell you what, if I'm feeling better later tonight, I'll call you.'

She wouldn't.

'Perhaps even come over.'

She definitely wouldn't.

Before he could comment or object, she cut him off.

'Oh Bruce, I'm sorry, but I have to go. Something is making me feel nauseous again.'

She hung up, slammed the phone handset onto the base, and leaned her head back against the wall. Problem number one solved. She didn't have to see his face again, until she'd had time to process everything that had happened and act accordingly.

Now problem number two. She couldn't use the same excuse to get out of dinner, because her dad had just seen her and she was perfectly well. And her mum would be round here with a basin and anti-nausea medication within the hour. No, the only way out of this was to go. It wasn't the worst thing in the world. Her dad had booked the table at a fabulous, very exclusive new hotel because she'd been desperate to try it out and dropping hints for months. Why shouldn't she go, spend time with her parents and enjoy it? Why should Bruce Quinn ruin anything else for her today?

Decision made, she clambered to her feet.

She was going out, and she was going to forget every shit thing that had happened today.

Screw Bruce Quinn. She was going to make this the most memorable bloody birthday conga ever.

15
_____

CATHY

Christmas Eve 1968

'I've never seen anything like this in my life.' Cathy was awestruck, gazing in wonder at the twinkling beauty all around her. Trees. Dozens of them. In a square. Every single branch covered in tiny lights. 'What is this place? And how did you find it?'

Richie took her hand, gently tugging her across the path towards the iron fence that surrounded the trees. 'It's the communal garden for all the big houses around this square. When we were at school and I used to help my Uncle Ted out with his gardening in the summers, we cut the grass here. The December before I left, he asked me to deliver some Christmas trees to these houses and I saw it all lit up like this.'

A memory jogged Cathy's mind. 'I remember you saying that you'd seen a gorgeous little park but... I couldn't come and see it then.'

She didn't need to explain. That Christmas had been the first one after her parents died, and they both remembered how distraught she'd been, how hard she'd been working to hold everything together and take care of Loretta. Back then, every single thing, whether really good or really bad, made her miss her mum and dad, so she'd locked down, gone through the motions, made everything as happy as she could make it for her sister, just concentrating on keeping her feelings on an even keel so that she didn't fall apart. Richie had told her about this place, promised he'd bring her here the following Christmas, but by that time he was gone.

Richie guided her towards a gate that was almost hidden by the foliage. He slipped his hand through the iron posts and unclicked something on the other side, making the heavy, creaking gate swing open.

Even in the cold, Cathy could feel her body warming with the excitement of it.

'Watch your feet in case there are any fallen branches and hold on to my arm because we won't be able to see any holes in the path,' Richie murmured, holding out his elbow.

'Are you sure you're not just saying that to get a free cuddle?' Cathy teased him, and for a second she didn't care if that were true. She wasn't doing anything wrong, she told herself. Duncan would understand that she'd just spent a few hours with a friend who'd been away for a while and who'd been so important to her growing up. She'd just explain to him that they'd had a bit of lunch and then gone for a walk afterwards and that nothing untoward had happened. He was a reasonable man and he'd be completely fine with it when she told him the facts.

Even as she was thinking that, she knew that there were a couple of facts she might miss out. That touching Richie's hand made her chest hurt because she found it hard to breathe. That her heart was burning so badly, it felt like her insides were on fire.

That her stomach hadn't stopped clenching for the last hour, just because he was with her and she was terrified of her feelings, of what she might do. The truth was that this was the first time since she'd said goodbye to Richie that she'd felt like herself. Felt like she could laugh, and relax and not need to be thinking about anything else other than the moment she was in.

'There's a bench over there,' he said, gesturing to a little clearing, where a narrow path wrapped its way around the trees. When they got there, he used his sleeve to clear the thin layer of snow off it before they sat down.

'It's like being in the stars,' Cathy said softly, as she looked upwards at a million twinkly lights in front of her, behind her, only feet above her head. 'After my mum and dad died, I used to tell Loretta that they were in a star, and that we could see them at night. When she went to bed, we'd look out of the window and she'd ask me which one it was and I'd always say, "The brightest one." I don't know if she still believes that, but I do because I need to.'

Richie squeezed her hand and then pulled it into his pocket to keep it warm.

Her head fell down onto his shoulder and they both sat in silence for a few minutes, her heart still burning.

'I'll never stop being sorry I left you, Cath,' he whispered, into her hair.

'I know. I'll never stop being sorry that I told you to go. But it's done, Richie. Nothing we can do about it.'

'Isn't there?'

She lifted her head from his shoulder. 'Richie, don't. You promised. None of that kind of talk. I'm married now and I can't change that.'

'Cath, I'll come home, I'll find a job, a good one because I've got more experience now. I'll work so hard, I swear to you that I'll buy one of these houses one day.'

'And I'm going to be Elizabeth Taylor and have a drawer full of diamonds,' Cathy blurted, realising she sounded harsh, but she couldn't help it. 'Richie, those are dreams. That's all. Just bloody dreams. They don't pay my rent, or feed us, or give me what I need to take care of this baby. Duncan is a good man, and this is his child. He will provide for us and he'll care of us and he'll never walk away. He gives us stability and security and that's what we need. I don't want dreams. I've had enough of them, and they don't come true.'

A sob caught in her throat and her baby gave her a swift kick in the side of her belly. Even the little one knew that she was right. The truth was that she loved Duncan. Not in the way she'd loved Richie, but that didn't matter. Duncan was this baby's father and that was what counted.

'Bollocks, I hate this,' Richie murmured. 'I hate it even more that I understand and that it's my own bloody fault and...'

He pushed himself up slightly and the change of position moved Helena's hand in his pocket. At first, the tips of her fingers barely registered what they were feeling, but then...

Don't ask. Don't ask. Don't ask.

'Richie, what's that?'

She asked.

'What?' He played innocent, but even in the dim light of the sea of tiny bulbs, she could see his face fall.

She moved her hand again, checked she was right. Her fingers were in the outside pocket of his parka, but the way he was sitting now, she could feel through the lining to the inside pocket, to where there was an object – a small, square, box-shaped object.

Slowly, he unzipped his jacket with his other hand, then slipped it inside and pulled out a tiny box. Cathy held her breath as he flipped it open and then peered closer to see what she already knew would be there.

A ring.

A beautiful, silver solitaire ring, with one little blue stone in the centre.

'I was going to ask you to marry me,' he said, so quietly she could barely hear him. 'I was going to surprise you at the house this morning, and in my mind, it was all going to work out so different. You'd be so happy to see me, and you'd cry, and I'd cry and then I'd pull this out and explain to you that I'd need to stay away a bit longer to get more money together, and more experience, but that I just needed you to know that I'd be back for you because I wanted to be with you forever.'

Her chest was tightening even further with every word, until there was no breath left in her lungs. She couldn't say a word, and he must have taken that as a sign to carry on speaking.

'I had a plan, you see. I was going to work on the ships for two more years, until I had my trade and then I'd be earning more money that I could ever have made in the yards here. Then we'd get married, and I'd get a job, but a good one because I'd be a qualified marine engineer. By then, Loretta would be away to college like your mum always said, and you could come with me and live somewhere by the sea, where I'd work and you could just be happy and have the best of everything. Or I could find a job in Glasgow and stay here and we could have a family and I'd maybe go back to night school and get more qualifications so I could get a job training the boys up at the Nautical College in the city centre.'

He paused. Took a breath. His head down now so that she couldn't see his eyes as he went on, 'That was it. That was my speech.'

Cathy struggled to force the words out. 'It was a really good speech.'

His voice was softer than the sprinkles of snow that had begun falling around them. 'I meant every word of it, Cath. I've had so much time to think while I've been away, and I've seen the kind of life I can have. I know I can do well for myself because I'll work my arse off. I meant what I said earlier. One day, I'll have a house just like these ones.' His head was back up now and he was pointing at the big mansions that could be seen through the trees around the park. 'Thing is, I just thought you'd be in it with me. And our kids. And Loretta too, if she's not in jail.'

His joke made them both smile and broke the crackling, terrifying tension. Cathy felt something inside her beginning to relax, a release in her gut.

'Can I ask you something?' he went on, facing her now, so that their eyes were locked, their faces only inches apart. A ferocious wave of longing overtook her as she remembered what it was like to kiss him, how it felt when he held her, how incredible it had been when they'd slept together before he left. She loved him. That was it. The truth of it. He was Richie Clark and she'd loved him for years.

'Sure,' she whispered, lost in him, hurting so much it felt like physical pain.

'If things were different, if you'd still been single and I'd come home this morning and told you all that and asked you to marry me, would you have said yes?'

She heard the words, processed what they meant, wanted to answer him, but she couldn't bear to hear herself say it. She should go. Get out of here, before she had to look at Richie Clark's face one more time. Before her willpower crumbled and she kissed him.

There was another sharp tug in her gut, then a startling sensation swiftly followed by a wave of horror, and she suddenly realised that her answer didn't matter.

'Richie, I need to go.'

'Shit. Is it because of what I said? I'm sorry, Cath. You don't need to answer. I shouldn't have pressured you. I'll bin the ring. I won't say another word about us, I promise.'

She put up a hand to stop him speaking, then, mortified, gasped for breath as she tried not to look at the steady trickle of water that was rolling off the bench next to her leg, and making tiny holes as it dripped onto the newly fallen snow beneath it.

She gripped his hand even tighter, petrified of what was about to happen.

'It's not you. I need to go because... because... Richie, I need to get to the hospital because I think I'm about to have this baby.'

6 P.M. – 8 P.M.

16

EVE

Christmas Eve 2023

'This place never changes, does it?' Gran mused, as they strolled into the park arm in arm. 'All these years and it's still exactly the same.'

Eve squeezed her gran's arm and pulled her in even tighter, their closeness throwing up a million memories of bygone years. Ever since she was a child, they'd come here every year on Christmas Eve, and they'd made wishes and sung carols and songs about reindeer and bells under the blanket of fairy lights in the trees that surrounded them. Eve had once gushed that it was like a swarm of fireflies, but her gran had always said that, to her, it was a galaxy of stars.

It had been their special place, somewhere that made Gran's eyes go soft and her smile grow wider. Her gran's swift and assertive decision to buy this apartment made perfect sense now, as did her urgency in moving in this week. Cathy McLean had always refused to waste a minute of her life, and there was no way she'd want to miss the opportunity to spend a whole Christmas with this on her doorstep.

They walked to their usual bench, the one that her gran had chosen the very first time they came here, even though they had to bypass several others to get to it. Eve had never thought to question why, but now it seemed significant. Like a whole lot of other things she'd never paid attention to, just taking them for granted. Since she'd got the results of the DNA test, it felt like she was staring at everything in her life through a different lens.

They sat down, both still holding glasses of Prosecco with their free hands. When Eve was a child, it had been hot chocolate, kept warm in flasks that her gran would pull out of her bag, followed by huge packets of marshmallows for dipping in it. Later, when Eve was a teenager, there had been Babycham and a thick, yellow liqueur called advocaat, that her gran would dilute for her with loads of lemonade and warn her not to tell her mother. When she'd reached adulthood, Eve had taken over the drink supply, and there had been mini bottles of champagne, or potent, warming brandy on the colder nights.

Gran dug into her Tardis of a shoulder bag once again, and this time pulled out a folded blanket, which she unfurled and placed over their knees.

'Gran, I'm so happy for you. Having this on your doorstep is so perfect.'

'In every way,' her gran replied wistfully.

Eve playfully nudged her shoulder with her own. 'But don't think the gorgeousness of this spot is going to get you out of telling me about the bombshell you dropped. Come on, Gran, spill the details.'

Her gran put her bubbly down and pulled another flask out of her bag. 'Brandy,' she explained. 'I'm afraid wine won't cut it for this story.'

'I hope you realise that you're really ramping up my expectations here,' Eve teased. This was exactly what she needed today. A bit of wonderment and excitement to take her mind off the other bombshell that had been dropped in her life. She shook that one off, her breath coming out in a cloud of cold crystals as she exhaled.

'I'll do my best not to disappoint,' her gran shot back, opening the top of her flask and taking a sip, before going on, 'Have you ever wondered why we've been coming here for all these years?'

The question took Eve by surprise. 'Not even once. But now I'm thinking I probably should have pondered it.' The reality of that sank in. More than twenty years of coming to the same place, at the same time every single year and she'd never thought to question why.

Her gran nodded, staring straight ahead, and began to recount her story. 'When I was a teenager, maybe thirteen or fourteen, I started seeing a lad I was in school with. Richie Clark was his name and oh, ma love, when I tell you that this boy was handsome, I mean it. You can keep your Leonardo DiCaprio...'

'We're off him now, Gran. He got middle-aged and he only dates women younger than that brandy.'

Her gran let out a hoot of amusement. 'Maybe a bad example there, but you get the picture when I say he was the best-looking lad I'd ever clapped eyes on. And for some mad reason, the boy loved me too. I mean, understandable really,' she joked. 'I had a beehive so big you could hide yer cigarettes in it. And yer lighter. Anyway, for years we dated, but then, of course you know that your great-gran and great-grandad were killed, and it was just me and Loretta left behind. That's when everything changed.'

Eve felt a tug of sadness as she listened to her gran skip over the devastation and the hardships they'd faced. Cathy McLean never dwelled on the bad stuff, and sometimes Eve wondered if that was because it was just too damn painful.

She got back to the story, telling her how she'd loved her job in the salon but he'd hated his back-breaking toil in the shipyards. How his mother knocked on her door one day...

Eve just listened, taking in every word, loving the way Gran brought the sixties back to life in the story. A love story. A tale of innocence. Until...

'Wait a minute!' she gasped, sitting bolt upright and turning to face Cathy. 'Hang on. His mother begged you to persuade him to leave you when you'd only lost your parents just over a year before? Bloody hell, Gran, that's brutal. Who would do that?'

Her gran shook her head. 'No, love, you don't understand. In those days, there weren't the jobs, there wasn't the money that you folks have now. There were no credit cards or bank loans for the likes of us, so in our world, you were almost always confined to the life you were born to. If you were a lad, you did the jobs that your dad and your grandad did before you, and if you were a woman... well, if you weren't married and already knocked up or carrying toddlers by the time you were twenty, it was a near miracle. I was one of the lucky ones because at least I had a job that got us by.'

'Fine. Still think she's a cow, though,' Eve muttered as she settled back down and let her gran continue the story.

She even managed not to splutter when Gran got to the part where he left, mostly because she could see how it would make sense in an unfair world where people had fewer choices. But it still hurt her heart when she thought of the young Cathy, alone, deserted, left with the responsibility for her sister. This was the worst festive anecdote ever.

'Gran, I'm just going to tell you straight up that I'm hating this story now. I thought I was getting scandal and frivolous romps.

This is like one of those TV shows that make me ugly cry. If there's a lost dog or a graveyard coming up, I'm going to need sedation.'

'Hang on, love, I'm getting to the good bit. This is where your grandad steps in.'

Her grandad. The loveliest man that there ever was. And what Gran told her next didn't change that opinion. Her grandad had swooped in and loved her gran back to happiness. He'd helped take care of Aunt Loretta too, and even though Gran had become pregnant soon after, he'd stuck by her, promised to love his baby and give them all a fantastic life. It was exactly what Eve would have expected of that absolute gem of a man.

'Okay, so wasn't that the happy ever after?'

'Aye, pet, it was... Until Richie Clark appeared at ma door on Christmas Eve that year.'

Eve reached over and borrowed the flask of brandy and knocked back a generous slug. 'Dear God, Gran, my nerves are shattered. Right. I'm feeling mildly inebriated and equipped for what comes next.'

Over the next half hour, her gran told her how Richie had brought her here, how he'd had a ring in his pocket, and he'd asked her to choose.

'Before I could do that, my waters broke, right here on the bench...'

Eve couldn't help but look down at the wooden slats and wonder if they'd been replaced since then.

'And I went into labour with yer mother. That night. In this very spot. But yes, I chose your grandad. And I'll always be glad I did, because we had a lovely life together. It was the right thing to do, and I've never regretted it for a second.'

'So why come here then, Gran? Why come to the place that reminded you of Richie? Of saying goodbye to someone so special to you?' Eve barely got the words out past the lump in her throat.

'Because the love I had with your grandad was wonderful, but it wasn't the same kind of love that I'd had with Richie Clark. That first love. I don't know how I can explain it. I adored your grandad, loved the bones of him, but Richie made me feel something I never felt again. When I came here, it wasn't because I wanted to be reminded of Richie. Although, I always was, in a way. It was because I wanted to remind myself that I'd felt that incredible once-in-a-lifetime love. When you and I sat in this park, I could close my eyes and just for a moment it would all come back, and I'd feel it again. And that was good enough for me.'

Tears pooled on Eve's bottom lids, grief for the young Cathy, who had lived through that, who'd had to make an impossible choice and who'd spent a lifetime with a tiny piece of her heart missing.

Somehow, despite woolly gloves, a flask of brandy and a thick coat with ribbed elastic around the cuffs, her gran still managed to free her trusty hanky from her sleeve and blow her nose. When she tucked it back in, she finished her story.

'That's why I moved here. Now, I'll be able to come sit here whenever I want, and be grateful that I had that love, and that I was lucky enough to spend my life with two magnificent men.'

They sat in silence for a few minutes, letting it all sink in.

Eve found her voice first.

'In case I don't tell you enough, I think you're fricking sensational, Gran. I really do.'

'Och, that's mutual, my love.' It was a perfect, poignant, unforgettable moment, until her gran added, 'And that might be the last thing I ever say to you, because I'm fairly sure this chill is getting right under my coat and the hypothermia could strike me dead any minute. Let's get back inside and get heated up before I croak.'

Laughing, Eve stood up, pulled her gran up off the bench, and they left the park the way they'd come in – arm in arm and cuddled tight for warmth.

They'd just gone through the gate, when Eve realised she had another question.

'I forgot to ask, did you ever see Richie again?'

Her gran gave her a slow, sad smile, as if remembering something that mattered, and then she slowly nodded.

'I did, my love. I met him one more time.'

17

HELENA

Christmas Eve 1993

Helena was wondering which option would be preferable – going to dinner with her parents after discovering her potential fiancé was a cheating prick, or poking her eyes out with the star on the top of the wonky Christmas tree in her mother's front porch. They'd had that ancient old tree for Helena's entire life-time and despite being well able to afford a new one, her mother insisted on dragging it out every year and putting it in full view of the neighbours. 'I don't give a damn what anyone thinks,' Cathy would chirp every year when Helena tried to persuade her to bin it. Problem was, teenage Helena had always minded, and she'd had no idea why her mother insisted on embarrassing them.

She let herself in her mum and dad's front door with her own key, just as her dad was coming down the stairs. 'Ah, sweetheart. You look beautiful, Helena,' he greeted her with a kiss on each cheek. 'You'll be the most spectacular woman in the room. Just don't tell your mother I said that.'

'I heard it fine myself, Duncan McLean,' her mum shot back, with mock disdain as she teetered down the hallway, before opening her arms to greet Helena with a hug. 'Hello, my love. Oh, my word, that frock is a cracker. You've definitely got our Loretta's legs.'

Helena didn't reply, but inside she congratulated herself on her choice of outfit. This was the kind of dress she'd never normally dream of wearing. It was a bright red, baby-doll-style mini, that barely covered her bum and had a deep V at the front of the halter-style top. It had been an impulse buy in a boutique on Ingram Street last summer, because it had reminded her of a photograph she'd seen in *Harper's Bazaar* a couple of years ago of Linda Evangelista, Cindy Crawford, Naomi Campbell and Christy Turlington at the 1991 Versace runway show. As soon as she'd got home, she'd snapped back to her senses and decided to take it back, but never quite got round to it. It had caught her eye tonight when she'd been flicking through her wardrobe and she'd thought, sod it. Why shouldn't she wear it? Walk on the wild side. Be a little daring. After all, playing by the rules wasn't bloody working for her at the moment, was it?

'Where's Bruce? Is he meeting us there?' her mum asked breezily, fixing her dad's bow tie while she chatted.

Her mum and dad were like a synchronised dance before they went out, both of them instinctively working round each other, without prior planning or discussion. He zipped up her dress and then she would turn to fix his bow tie. He would then lift her bag and take her coat from the chair, while she would ruffle her fingers through his hair and tell him he was handsome. They had been married for over twenty-five years and they were still a perfect match, despite having not a damn thing in common.

Yet tonight, they looked beautiful together. Her dad, pushing fifty now, was in his favourite black tuxedo, his patent leather shoes polished until they shone. His curly hair was longer than usual, swept back, and his natural sandy shade had mostly been replaced by grey. He was distinguished. Sharp but understated.

Whereas, there was absolutely nothing understated about her mother. Cathy had been a hairdresser for almost thirty years, and she now owned her own salon on Dumbarton Road, catering for the fine ladies of Kelvinside and the punk-loving students of Partick, so, as expected, she knew how to work the latest fashion. Helena might have Linda Evangelista's frock, but Cathy had her hair, a chin-length platinum bob, that was tucked behind her ear on one side and fell in a carefully crafted wave that framed her face on the other. She was wearing bright red lipstick, smoky eyes and a stunning off-the-shoulder black gown with a corset bodice that melted into a pencil skirt that reached her calves. Helena had never seen her look more beautiful than she did right now and it stung. Her mother was forty-five years old and she could still outshine the twenty-five-year-old in Linda Evangelista's bloody dress.

She realised her mum was still waiting for a reply and she switched straight into solicitor mode, knowing that her answer had to be absolutely pitch perfect to throw Cathy off the scent of trouble.

'You're never going to believe it – poor Bruce went out for lunch today and he thinks he must have eaten something that didn't agree with him. He's sick as a dog and throwing up constantly. I was going to go over to his place and take care of him, but he insisted I come with you, because he didn't want to spoil our Christmas Eve. He's so thoughtful like that.'

Helena finished with a smile, while trying to suss out if her mum had bought the story. The woman had absolutely no legal training, but she could spot a lie at a hundred paces. Their eyes met, Helena maintained her stare, brazened it out, didn't look away first.

After a moment's hesitation, Cathy's expression switched to concern. 'Ah, that's such a shame, especially tonight of all nights.' Everyone in the room knew what she meant, but her mum obviously didn't want to exacerbate Helena's disappointment by coming right out with 'especially tonight when he was supposed to be asking you to marry him and presenting you with a bloody great rock for your finger.'

The sound of a car beeping its horn came from outside the front door, spurring her dad into action and he pulled on his coat. 'That must be the taxi. Right then, shall we go? How lucky am I, getting to take you two beautiful ladies out tonight.'

Her mum kissed him on the cheek. 'Yeah, well milk it while you can because this kind of natural beauty doesn't last very long. In about three hours' time, my dress will be stretching at the seams, my hair will have flopped, my make-up will have sweated off and I'll be asking for my slippers because my feet will be killing me. I'll be begging you to bring me home and make me a cup of tea to go with the Curly Wurly out of my selection box.' The way they looked at each other made Helena wince on the inside. This morning, she'd thought she had that kind of loving relationship, but now she knew she was wrong. She hadn't had it at all. Maybe she never would. God, she just wanted to get to the hotel and have a large, strong drink.

The taxi smelled faintly of chips and beer when they climbed in. Not hugely surprising for Christmas Eve, even at this time of the day. Most of the offices and factories in the city would have closed at lunchtime, and a fair swathe of the workers would have headed straight to bars, restaurants, or anywhere else that they could eat, drink and be merry.

They were about ten minutes into the journey, when Helena spotted from her mother's puzzled expression that something was amiss.

Before Helena could ask, her mum spoke up. 'Duncan, I thought we were going to the Grosvenor? I think we're going the wrong way. You need to ask the driver to turn—'

'It's not the Grosvenor, darling. I changed the reservation weeks ago to the new hotel that's opened just off Great Western Road because Helena was desperate to try it. I thought I'd told you?'

This wasn't a huge shock. Her dad would get so caught up in his cases at work, that he regularly forgot to pass on information on the domestic front.

'Oh, that's exciting. I love to try new places,' Cathy chirped. 'Wait till the girls in the salon hear about it.'

Her mum sounded genuinely pleased, and if she minded that her daughter and her husband had made this decision without her, she definitely didn't show it. That was her mother. As long as everyone had a smile on their face, she was happy.

Helena was well aware that wasn't a trait she'd inherited. She continued to stare out of the window at the packed streets, the crowds of fired-up, half-pissed students partying outside bars in sub-zero temperatures, the loved-up couples walking along hand in hand and snogging in doorways, the single revellers keeping their eye out for the catch of the night. She was none of those things. Tomorrow, she would be twenty-five years old and she was just a workaholic solicitor whose boyfriend couldn't even love her without a stunt double and an ulterior motive.

The car took a sharp right turn into one of the curved Georgian streets that were prevalent in this part of the city, then a left turn and then another left onto a breathtaking square that Helena recognised.

'Mum, isn't that your garden?' Helena already knew the answer as she pointed out the wooded area in the middle of the square, every tree covered in fairy lights that twinkled under the night sky. Her mum had taken her there a few times as a kid, always late afternoon on Christmas Eve, whenever Dad was held up at work and Aunt Loretta wasn't around to babysit.

'Your park?' her dad asked, curious.

Her mum brushed away his question and Helena thought for a second that she saw something else in her mum's expression. Sadness? Irritation? Maybe she was annoyed about them changing the plans without consulting her after all. Whatever it was, she covered it up with a shrug.

'Och, it's just a park that we used to go to when we were kids and it's always done up like this at Christmas. Sometimes I still pop down on Christmas Eve, just to put me in the festive spirit.'

Her dad was even more curious now. 'How come I don't know this?'

Her mum leaned over and kissed his cheek. 'Because you're always at the office, my lovely, work-obsessed husband.'

Again, Helena had a strange feeling that her mother was deflecting something, but she brushed it off. Cathy didn't do deflection – she did brutal honesty and unbridled candour.

Helena still needed a drink, and she wouldn't have long to wait, because the car drew to a halt outside a stunning sandstone mansion that looked like something out of a Hollywood movie.

A red carpet snaked up the beige steps to an imposing art deco glass door, flanked on each side by magnificent stone columns, and spotlights in the corners bathed the entire three-storey building in golden light.

For once, her mother was speechless as they climbed out of the taxi and up the stairs, to doormen in top hats who greeted them with a reverential bow. This was definitely a step up from the places that they usually frequented and before she could stop it, Helena's treacherous mind had the thought that she wished Bruce were here. Tonight should have been so different. She should have walked up these stairs arm in arm with her handsome boyfriend, to a glittering celebration that ended with the happiest moment of her life.

* * *

'Good evening and welcome to The Kentigern On The Green. The cloakroom is just to the left of the foyer.'

Inside, her dad took charge when he saw the queue. 'I'll take your coats and you two can have a wander around the lobby.'

Helena shrugged off her coat and handed it over, then her mum did the same. While her dad went off to check them in, Helena followed her mum as she walked slowly across the lobby, taking in the grandeur of the high ceilings, the gold embossed wallpaper, the dark parquet floors and the huge chandelier that dropped from the ceiling. No tacky decorations here. There was just a massive white Christmas tree in the corner of the lobby, decorated with baubles in metallic tones of gold, silver and bronze. It was truly dazzling.

Helena realised her mother hadn't said anything for almost five minutes.

'Mum, are you okay? You've gone really quiet.'

'I'm fine, love. I just... When I was a lass, I used to sit in the park outside here and I'd look at these buildings when they were houses, and I never thought I'd actually ever be in one. I didn't realise this had been converted into a hotel. And one as gorgeous as...'

She stopped, froze, and there was a look of utter shock on her face that Helena had never seen before.

'Mum, are you having some kind of medical episode? Are you okay?'

No answer. Instead, a male voice cut into the conversation.

'Cath?'

Helena turned to see a man who appeared to be just as shocked as her mum. He was tall, well over six foot, mid-forties like her mum, with light brown hair and the most piercing blue eyes. He reminded her of the actor, Rob Lowe, just a few years older and minus the American accent and the sordid sex tape.

'Richie.' Her mother looked like she'd been slapped. 'What are you doing here?'

He threw back a grin that, if possible, made him even more handsome, although there seemed to be an edge of nervousness to it. 'Having dinner with... my family.' His eyes darted to the side, and Helena followed them to a raven-haired, pretty woman in a red velvet, off-the-shoulder dress, who was deep in conversation with a younger female doppelganger who had to be her daughter, and a tall, suited guy who bore a close enough resemblance to this man to be related.

'Me too,' her mother managed to croak out, then the strangest thing happened. The two of them just stood, eyes laser focused on each other, saying nothing for what felt like a minute and a half. Helena's gaze went from one to the other, searching for clues as to what was going on. It was as if they were having some kind of silent, psychic conversation and she didn't have the frequency.

Eventually, he broke the silence and the gaze. 'I'd better get back. It was good to see you, Cath.'

'You too,' her mum whispered.

They both watched him go, but before Helena could ask the obvious question, her dad re-joined them. 'It's all bells and whis-tles, but they might want to put another pair of hands in the cloakroom. The poor girl in there is rushed off her feet. Did I see you speaking to someone there, Cathy?'

Her mum slowly nodded, then, as if she'd been jumpstarted like a car battery, snapped back to normality. 'It was just someone I used to know from school. No one important.'

'Really? I only got a glimpse, but I thought there was something familiar about him. Are you sure he's not on the TV? Maybe one of those celebrity chefs.'

'Positive. Like I said, he's just someone I used to know. Shall we go in? I'm ravenous.'

Helena's bullshit detector tingled. Ooooh, second deflection of the night. Well, well, well. Wasn't this a turnaround that she didn't expect? Cathy McLean was acting like she barely knew this man. And Helena was 100 per cent sure that her mother was lying through her pearly white teeth.

However, disinterest soon cancelled out the curiosity as they moved through to the restaurant and were shown to their table, ice bucket waiting with a bottle of cold champagne. Helena asked for it to be opened straight away and was on her second glass within fifteen minutes, doing little to join in her parents' conversation. If they noticed, they didn't say anything, probably putting her lack of enthusiasm and chat down to disappointment over Bruce's no-show on the night of his planned proposal. That suited Helena just fine.

Their starters had just been cleared away, when Helena got the sensation that someone was staring at her. Never a good thing for a solicitor in public because there was a fair chance that it was a former client that they'd defended for anything from car theft to shop-lifting shellsuits. Although, maybe not in this crowd.

Like a periscope, she slowly turned her view until she locked on the target. Sitting a few tables away. Handsome. Smart. Smiling.

at her. Seated next to the man who had shocked the life out of her mother earlier. So maybe his son after all.

Helena suppressed a sigh, refusing to return his smile.

What the hell was she doing here? This was a mistake. She should be home, in her pyjamas, contemplating how to salvage the absolute disaster that had become her life.

Everyone else was laughing, eating, drinking, having a good time and all Helena wanted to do was go home and sob. Or perhaps take a contract out on Bruce.

She glanced around her, taking in the joy, the revelry, the celebration of it all. Why couldn't she be like everyone else? Why couldn't she just loosen up, have a great time and live in the moment for once?

Just as that very thought struck her, she saw the guy who had been smiling at her get up, lift a packet of cigarettes from the table and make his way to the door, his gaze on her as he walked, extending what she was fairly sure was an invitation.

It was an obvious decision. Stay here and chat to her mum and dad, or go and have a harmless flirtation with a drop-dead handsome stranger? She already knew what the answer would be. Stay here. Do the right thing. Be well behaved. Have decorum. Show nothing but class. Like always.

Well, for once in her life, fuck that.

Helena got up, lifted her bag, smoothed down the chiffon of her baby doll dress.

'I think I've just spotted someone from my office and I'm just going to go and say hello.'

And with that, she flicked her hair off her face, pulled back her shoulders and swayed her hips as she followed in the footsteps of the undeniably sexy stranger who had just left the room.

18

CATHY

Christmas Eve 1968

The car turned the corner so violently, Cathy thought the weight of her could push the door right open and she'd go flying out into the street.

'Hang on, hen. Hang on,' the panicked taxi driver begged her. 'I've got a fare to Rutherglen after this one and I canny do it if yer having that wean in the back of ma car.' He blew out his cheeks. 'I knew I should have finished at lunchtime, but ma missus would have had me up the shops and I'd have been skint by dinnertime.'

Cathy was barely listening, too busy trying to breathe and stop what felt like a blade in her lower back from twisting. 'Richie, I can't... I can't do this.'

The first pain had ambushed her right as they'd got to the park gate, buckled her over with the fierceness of it, and she'd had to cling to Richie's arm to steady herself. She wasn't naïve. She'd seen this before when a woman went into labour in the salon last summer and they'd had to clear the place and use every towel in the storeroom to make her comfortable. The baby had been born before the ambulance came and its cries had been the most amazing thing Cathy had ever heard. The woman had been so grateful for the help she'd brought them all in vanilla slices from the bakers two doors along every Friday for the next month. Cathy wished now that she'd paid more attention to the birth bit. Jesus, was it meant to hurt this much? Was this normal? It couldn't be, otherwise half the women she knew wouldn't be on their fourth or fifth kid.

Just as she'd started to think she was going to have the baby right at the park gate, the pain had faded, eased off and then disappeared as if it had never been there in the first place.

'Okay, okay... I'm going to go bang on one of those doors and ask them to call an ambulance, but I'll be back...' She could tell Richie had been trying to stay calm, but the panic in his voice was unmistakable.

She had hung on to his arm with a vice grip that ten men couldn't have broken. 'No, don't leave me. It's okay, I can walk, I can...'

They'd made it to the other side of the road, then she'd reluctantly let him go so that he could run up the stairs to the closest house, just as, by an absolute miracle, a black hackney had turned into the square and stopped at one of the doors further along. A man and woman had climbed out and the orange light above the front window of the taxi had lit up. Richie had belted along, stopped the cab from driving away and then had come back for Cathy and helped her walk the twenty yards down the cobbled street.

By the time they had reached the car door, the driver had whipped out a towel and put it on the seat. 'Nae offence, hen, but I'll be off the rest of the night if I've got soggy seats.' As soon as they'd climbed in, he'd switched to action stations. 'No need to say it, son, I'll get you to The Queen Mother's pronto,' he'd promised, taking off like a racing driver.

Cathy had stared straight ahead, concentrating, bracing herself for the next pain. Why was this happening now? She wasn't due for two more weeks. Was this her fault? Was the baby okay? She'd grabbed Richie's hand again, 'I want my mum, Richie. I just want my mum with me,' she'd cried.

In the dim light of the back of the taxi, he'd taken both her hands in his, 'I know, Cath, and I'm so sorry, but I'm here. Hold on to me, just squeeze my hands as hard as you need. I'm sorry. I'm sorry. I should never have taken you there, and asked you those things, and got you upset and—'

His words had been cut off by another pain, just as bad as the first one, and she'd squeezed his fingers until they were close to breaking before it passed.

The traffic had been heavy, the West End roads packed with cars and people, but they'd edged along Great Western Road, crawled down Byres Road and then across Dumbarton Road, finally speeding up as they neared The Queen Mother's, the new maternity hospital that had been built right next door to the children's hospital at Yorkhill.

As they'd started the climb up the winding hill that led to the front door, Richie had still been holding her hands, his face so close to hers she could feel his breath on her face. 'We're almost there, Cath, just two more minutes.'

That's when the taxi driver had pleaded with her to hold on, just as the third pain came tearing through her and she screamed. The cab careered around that last corner and up the final stretch to the doors of the emergency department.

At the hospital, the driver leapt out and dashed back to wrench open Cathy's door. 'There you go, hen,' he said, reaching in to support her and then wittering away anxiously as she slowly clambered out. 'Don't worry about the fare, just get yerself in there and f the wean is a boy, you can name it after me. Roger. I know. I don't look like a Roger, but my maw had delusions of grandeur.'

Cathy was so grateful she could have hugged him, but she didn't want to waste another second out there in case another pain came. Richie was round beside him now, taking her arm in one hand, the other hand round her shoulder as the relieved driver waved them off, with a shout of, 'And congratulations, pal. No' every day you get to be a dad.'

The emergency room was packed with bodies, with anxious men, stressed-out women, crying kids, but Richie cut right across to the desk. 'She's in labour. She's having a baby. Right now. I think it's coming right now.'

A nurse in a white cap immediately broke off from her conversation with an older man who was demanding to see someone about his gout and refusing to accept that this was a maternity hospital. She whipped a wheelchair out from behind the desk. Within minutes, while the nurse multi-tasked by walking, gathering details, and noting them on a pad, Cathy had been pushed through the double doors, down a dozen corridors and into a stark, white-walled room where another weary-looking nurse jumped up and grabbed a clipboard, muttering, 'In the name of the Virgin Mary, they just keep coming today. I only just got this room straightened up after the last one. Right, pet, let's get you sorted. Climb up on to this bed for me and—'

She didn't finish because Cathy let out another groan, trying to fight the pain that was building, building, building until she was gripping the arms of the wheelchair, making a sound that she didn't recognise, through gritted teeth.

'Cathy, I've got you. I'm here. I love you.' Even through her pain, Cathy heard the words and she had to stop herself from blurting them back to him. No. She couldn't. Even if it were true. She'd love Richie Clark until the end of time. But she loved Duncan too. How could it be possible to love two men with her whole heart?

She kept her mouth clamped shut, breathing in through her nose, out through her mouth and didn't reply, which was just as well, because the nurse clearly had no time for pleasantries. She almost body-slammed Richie out of the way as she took over rubbing Cathy's back, saying soothing words that she couldn't hear over the noise of the thunder in her head. When it finally passed, the nurse took charge. 'Right,' she snapped Richie to attention, 'you take that side, and I'll take this side and we'll get her into this bed. What's your name, pet?'

Cathy took a moment to answer, too busy trying to focus on manoeuvring her body round.

Richie jumped in for her. 'Cathy. Cathy Farmer.'

'No,' Cathy mumbled, glancing up and watching as his expression changed to confusion and then to realisation and then to something that looked like hurt. 'It's Cathy McLean. I'm married now.'

The nurse was already pulling the pillow up behind her head to make her more comfortable. 'Either you're not her husband or you're easily confused, son.'

'He's not my husband. My husband is Duncan. He's on his way home. From Edinburgh. On the train. Richie, you need to find Loretta, tell her to get him. Tell her where I am.'

The enormity of all that was happening was breaking through the panic now that she was here and she felt safer. She was going to have her baby. Soon. She was going to be a mum and how could that even be right, when every single day she still prayed for her own mother to come back. But she could do this. She could. Her baby needed her to. She was going to be the mum now. She just needed to get everything sorted.

'Right, let's get you ready, Cathy. And you...?' The nurse nodded over to the man that Cathy had been in love with for years, the one whom she'd always thought would be by her side when she had her first child. Just not like this.

'Richie,' he said, answering the unasked question.

'Okay, Richie. Well done on getting this lass here, but you need to let us do our work now. Best thing you can do to help here is to go track down Cathy's husband and tell him that his baby is on the way.'

'Is that what you want, Cath? Do you want me to go?'

The pain in Richie's eyes was so raw, all Cathy could do was look away.

8 P.M. – 10 P.M.

19

EVE

Christmas Eve 2023

It took at least twenty minutes for Eve to defrost when they got back into the flat, but she barely noticed the heat returning to her body because she was so engrossed in Gran's story about meeting Richie Clark again in a hotel twenty-five years after she'd last seen him in a hospital labour ward. She described every detail. How her grandad looked so handsome in his tuxedo. How her mum wore a shocking red mini-dress. Eve took a minute to digest that one, because Helena in a scarlet mini-dress was so out of character. Her mum didn't do red. She didn't do flouncy. And she definitely didn't do legs. However, after Eve absorbed that shocker, she could picture her gran, in her beautiful evening gown, glammed up to the nines, meeting the love that she'd said goodbye to.

A realisation came to her, making her gasp. 'So, wait – the hotel is in this square?'

Her gran gestured to her to follow her over to the kitchen

window again and they peered out, this time their focus not on the blanket of fairy lights in the little park, but the gorgeous building Gran was pointing to on the street that ran alongside the end gate.

'I think it's been turned into flats now too,' Gran said. ' remember looking at them when they came up for sale, but you grandad was still alive then and well... this place wouldn't have been for him. He loved our home and he'd never have wanted to move.'

Eve sat back down at the kitchen table, nursing her second brandy, the one that Gran had poured for her when they got back right after she'd put an Elvis Christmas album on the record player in the lounge. Mr Presley was now crooning about a blue Christmas. 'Do you think he ever knew? About Richie, I mean. About that night. About how you felt?'

Her gran shook her head. 'No, he never did, and I had no mind to tell him.'

'Do you regret it, Gran? Do you wish you'd chosen Richie?' Eve could barely bring herself to ask the question because she could barely bring herself to hear the answer.

Her gran, who made it a life mission to blurt out exactly what she thought as soon as it came into her head, took her time with the answer. 'No, love, I don't regret it. Your grandad was a great man and we had over fifty years of happiness together. I don't know what way the other path would have taken me, and back then, it wasn't something I was prepared to take a chance on because I had responsibilities to other people. Loretta. And your mum. How could I have taken that wee one away from her father knowing that he was a good man who would support her and love her more than anything all his days? So no, I've never regretted my decision because it was the right thing to do.'

Oh, the absolute heartbreak of that choice, and what a history to carry around for a lifetime. 'I think you did the right thing

Gran. Grandad was a rock star. I mean, a rock star who wore a suit and carried a briefcase and had a brain the size of a space hopper because he was so smart, but still a rock star.'

A million memories of her grandad came flooding back. Eve had never been as close to him as she'd been to her gran, simply because he wasn't there as often and when he was, he was usually in his study, surrounded by piles of books or in deep discussion with her mum. When they were over visiting, Mum would go in there sometimes and they'd get lost in conversation for hours about legal cases and... Actually, Eve had no idea what they talked about, because as soon as they disappeared, her gran would say, 'Och, they'll be in there the rest of the night. Come on, ma love, what'll we do to amuse ourselves?' and that would invariably lead to baking cakes, or singing along with the record player or dancing in the living room to her gran's favourite Temptations song, or snuggling up on the couch under a blanket watching *Friends* and eating ice cream. Would they have had that relationship if her gran and grandad had spent every night in each other's company, their lives more intertwined?

'You know, however it happened, I really think it all turned out the way it was supposed to, Gran.' Eve let the profound sweetness and wisdom of that settle, before adding, 'Because I'd have been buggered for someone to talk to if you'd been all loved up and obsessed with some big hunk.'

Her gran let out a cackle of laughter. 'Aye, it would have got boring after a while. I mean all that romantic slushy stuff is fine when you're twenty, but at forty you'd rather have a good book, a foot spa and blether with your pals. Unless you're yer mother. She still hasn't used that foot bath I got her last Christmas. It was a fancy one with infrared lights and jets and everything.' Her gran pursed her lips, then unpursed them again straight away so that she could have another sip of brandy.

The conversation was interrupted by a buzz from Eve's phone. She checked the screen. A text from Sonny.

Drunk. And gegging dratted to a club. Might note make it ovr tomight. Takk tomottow?

She immediately replied.

Lol. No worries. Buzz me when the hangover eases and you recover full power in your thumbs. Have a good night. Xx

She didn't mind in the least. In fact, she was relieved to put that conversation off a little longer. Or a lot longer. She didn't have a chance to ponder what that said about their relationship, because her gran was nudging her.

'Anyway, I'm over talking about me. When are you going to tell me what's going on with you?'

Eve went for her best innocent face. 'Nothing is going on with me. I mean, apart from the stuff I told you this morning about Sonny wanting to change our relationship. Everything else is tickety-boo.'

She was rewarded with a look of cynicism, before her gran leaned forward, hands clasped on the table. 'Eve Quinn, that's the exact same look you gave me when you used your pocket money to buy two hamsters and hid them under your bed.'

'I loved those hamsters.'

'I didn't love them quite as much when they bred and we had dozens of the buggers.'

Eve giggled at the memory. They'd escaped and overtaken Gran's house and she'd only realised it when she'd opened the breadbin and one of them was sitting there quite happily chowing down on a Hovis loaf. 'That wasn't my fault. The guy in the pet shop told me they were both male.'

'And he was telling porkies just like you are now, Eve Quinn. So go on. Don't make me guess, because I've been watching serial killer documentaries all week and my mind can go to scary places.'

It was like being cornered by a crack squad of snipers. The only way out was to surrender with her hands up.

'Fine. But I warn you now, Gran, this has to be between me and you. I'm not raising it with my mother yet, because I need to do it when I'm ready.'

'Okay.'

'Promise?'

'I promise. But I've got my fingers crossed, so it might not count.'

Eve shook her head, well aware that she was dealing with a master in the ways of both gossip and crisis management. The thing was, she was desperate to share this. And now that she realised her gran wasn't traumatised by the move, or losing herself in sadness because she'd closed a chapter of her life, there was no one else she wanted to tell more.

'Okay, but it's shocking, so I don't want you keel over when you hear, and then it'll be on my conscience for ever.'

'Right then, I'll brace myself. Shoot.'

There was only one way to rip the plaster off. 'Bruce Quinn isn't my dad.'

Eve saw that her gran was still staring at her, waiting for the punchline, so she felt the need to back up that statement.

'That's it. I did one of those DNA tests. It's a long story. Angus was doing one because he's studying genetics at university, and we thought it would be interesting to compare, and also, I thought it would be cool to learn if I had any other close relatives. We're such a small family on our side. Thought maybe I'd find some cousins I didn't know about. Anyway, it all backfired, because the thing I discovered was that Bruce isn't my dad. There's no connection to him, his family or my brothers in my DNA whatsoever.'

Her gran, for possibly the first time in Eve's living memory, was struck speechless. 'I warned you,' Eve added.

'Hang on, I'm just... what is it you young ones say now? Processing. That's it. I'm processing.' Another pause. 'Okay, I've processed it and that must be a load of bollocks, ma love, because Bruce is many things – mainly a smarmy tosser who is way too fond of himself – but he's definitely your dad. The test must be wrong, Eve.'

'It isn't, Gran, because your side of the family showed up. It's just the paternal line that wasn't what I expected. There's no doubt about it. It's not Bruce.'

Flabbergasted, her gran exhaled and slumped back in her chair. 'Bloody hell. So did it tell you who your dad was?'

'No. The only close relative on that side was a woman who lives here in Glasgow called Bethany Muldoon. Does that mean anything to you? She owns a café just off Byres Road.'

Eve crossed her fingers, made a wish, said a prayer, but...

'No,' her gran answered, brow furrowed, 'Nothing at all. Sorry, love, I know that doesn't help.'

'I only found out about her this morning and I was thinking about going to see her today, but we had enough going on. I'll track her down after Christmas and hopefully learn more.'

Her gran was still open-jawed and staring at her in shock.

'I can't believe this. I really can't. But...' A visible realisation dawned. 'That's why you were asking her all those questions this morning about her love life. It was putting me right off my pancakes, I have to tell you.'

'Guilty. And it was totally confusing when you said that Bruce asked Grandad if he could propose to her on the Christmas Eve before I was born. That means they were definitely together then and that's roughly when I must have been conceived. I don't get it. None of it makes sense. My mum isn't the type to have an affair, so I don't think she'd cheat.'

'Jesus, no. She's my lassie and I love her dearly, but she's not one for frivolous hedonism or making bad decisions. I used to joke with her that I was affronted because she hadn't done a single thing wrong since the day she was born. I don't think that's changed.'

Her gran fell silent again, deep in contemplation, sipping her brandy, and Eve wondered for a second if her mind had gone somewhere else, somewhere dark. There was no escaping the thought, and Eve had nudged it away a couple of times since the results had dropped into her inbox – what if Mum had sex with someone against her will? Had she been attacked? Assaulted? Raped? This could be a whole horror story and Eve suddenly wasn't sure she wanted to hear how it unfolded.

'Hang on a minute,' Gran said suddenly, sitting forward, eyes glinting like someone on *Antiques Roadshow* who'd just been told that their great-auntie's ancient vase was worth more than a Ferrari.

'She didn't get engaged on Christmas Eve...'

'But this morning you said—'

'No, he was supposed to propose that night, but he didn't, because he was sick and didn't show up. They got engaged a month later. And Helena lied to us that night... I knew it at the time, of course, but I didn't say anything. Figured that they'd had a fight about something and he just hadn't shown up. Besides, that was the same night I was telling you about, when I bumped into Richie Clark and his family and it's fair to say that distracted me and put me off my game. I couldn't wait to get out of there.'

Eve was putting this together at the same time as her gran, but repeated a couple of facts to make sure she had it right. 'So hang on, the night you were in the swanky hotel here and Mum was flashing her legs – that was when Bruce was meant to propose. And he didn't show up because they had an argument? So do you think the fight was because he found out Mum was cheating on him?' Eve asked, trying to follow the train of thought. Maybe there was something in that.

'I can't say for sure why he wasn't there. That was a bit of guess work on my part. But I know who can set us straight on it all.'

Gran picked up her mobile phone and dialled a number. 'Helena, it's me. Listen, love, I just want to check if you're going to pop in tonight.'

A pause while Gran listened to the voice on the other end, and Eve's stomach flipped over. Bugger. Gran wasn't going to let this go. Eve should have known that her gran wouldn't take the subtle non-confrontational approach and she chided herself for bringing this up. If Christmas was ruined it would be all her fault. Actually, technically it would be the fault of her mother's younger self, but that was just semantics. Meanwhile, as usual, her gran wasn't letting any kind of resistance get in the way of what she wanted. Her tone was firmer as she countered whatever argument her mother was putting up on the other end of the line.

'Yes, I know you'll be tired. But it would mean such a lot to me if you still came.'

Another pause. There were clearly objections coming back the way.

'Well, Helena, at my age I might not be here tomorrow.'

Eve had to suppress a giggle at her gran's shameless hustle. Another pause.

'Yes, she's still here. And we'd love you to come back over and have a special moment at midnight to celebrate your birthday.'

A pause.

'Well, like I said, I'm seventy-five. It's my job to milk every celebration like it's my last.'

Pause.

'Okay, well that's smashing. We'll see you soon.'

Her gran hung up the phone, victorious. Oh shit. Shit. Shit. Shit. This was happening. Cathy The Bull was in the china shop, and she wasn't leaving until she'd wrecked the joint.

'She's still at the office, but she's going to stop in on her way home. I can't give you any answers, but yer mother won't be leaving here until we know exactly how this all happened.'

20

HELENA

Christmas Eve 1993

Helena caught his eye again and her face flushed the same colour as her dress. For the last two hours, they'd been playing an intoxicating game of seduction, and she'd never felt anything even close to the thrill of it.

The first time she'd gone outside, he'd been standing against the stone balustrade that bordered the front wall on each side of the main doors, creating a narrow terrace on the top step of the entrance, smoking a cigarette. She'd walked past the doormen and casually approached him, not sure if she felt sick, stupid, or both.

'Can I steal one of those cigarettes off you?' she'd asked, trying to sound more friendly than 'sexy spy in a honeytrap'.

He'd given her a casual shrug/grin combination that was, she had to admit, pretty sexy and spy-like. If Timothy Dalton gave up being James Bond, this bloke could definitely fill his tuxedo. 'Steal away.'

Helena had reached over and taken one, then let him light it for her, all the while thinking this was crazy. Not her at all. She didn't approach strangers in the street. She didn't flirt. She rarely smoked. She should put this cigarette out right now and go back inside before she froze to death in this stupid bloody baby-doll dress. She was going to burn the fucking thing when she got home.

'That dress might be the most gorgeous thing I've seen tonight,' he'd said.

Okay, maybe she wouldn't burn it.

She hadn't been sure where to go after that. How did this casual flirting thing work? Other people did it. She'd seen plenty of hook-ups at work parties. That was how she'd first got together with Bruce, but their flirting that night consisted mostly of double entendres, legal jargon and complimenting each other on their work, their cases, their ambitions... The very thought of work reminded her of Bree Halston. Bree and Bruce probably had a brilliant flirt every time they saw each other. Clearly, they'd been flirting their way in and out of each other's beds for bloody months. The thought emboldened her and wiped out any notion she had of abandoning this guy who was drop-dead gorgeous, impeccably dressed and paying her compliments.

'Thank you.' *Okay, flirt. Flirt. Say something.* Nope, she had nothing. Put her in a courtroom or a boardroom and she could talk her way in and out of anything, but this was a whole different playground.

'Are you cold? I'm happy to give you my jacket. As long as you don't steal it,' he'd teased. 'I'll never get another one that's a perfect match for these trousers.'

For the first time, Helena had smiled. Okay, so he was light-hearted. Funny. It wasn't normally her lane, but her mother had spent her whole life wisecracking, so Helena had learnt from the best and could pull off wit and guile when she needed to. 'I promise I won't steal it. I mean, under normal circumstances I definitely would, but I can't run in these shoes.'

His grin was back, wider this time. 'Good to know. Maybe I should take your name, just in case.'

He'd waited expectantly for her to answer and Helena had got a case of the jitters. She didn't want him to know her name. Or what she did. Or who she was. Because none of this was her. This wasn't how she behaved. Tonight, she just wanted to be reckless and be anyone else other than the fool who had let her boyfriend use her. And she wanted to do all that with no comeback or worry of potential consequences.

'Definitely not,' she'd purred, in a voice she didn't even recognise. 'I don't give out my name on the first cigarette. Or the second.'

'Okay,' he'd laughed. 'So how about the third?'

'I think you'll just have to wait and see.'

With that, she'd stamped out the cigarette, and gone back inside, feeling his eyes on her every step of the way. Damn, it felt good. Sexy. Powerful. A complete contrast to the foolishness and helplessness she'd been feeling all day.

That had been the first time. The second time he'd caught her eye and made a subtle 'let's go outside' gesture, she'd made her excuses and followed him, and they'd flirted up a storm. Helena had well and truly found her provocative, seductive groove, yet she could barely remember a single thing they'd talked about. All she remembered was how it felt. Intoxicating. Sexy. Freeing.

The third time, emboldened by a couple of glasses of champagne, and merry on the festive atmosphere of joy and celebration in the lavish restaurant, she'd initiated the move and he'd responded. Outside, he hadn't even asked this time, just slipped off his jacket and put it around her shoulders to protect her from the dropping temperature.

'I never usually do this,' she'd said, his thoughtfulness suddenly giving her an urge to explain.

'Do what? Smoke a stranger's cigarettes instead of buying your own?'

'Yep, definitely that. But the rest of it too. I don't generally speak to people I don't know, I don't flirt with strangers and I definitely don't wear their jacket and stand this close to them.' She took a step forward, so that she was almost touching him, their faces close enough that she could feel the heat of his breath.

'So why are you doing that now then?' He'd regarded her thoughtfully, and she'd wondered if she'd ever seen eyes as piercing or a face that made her want to reach out and touch it so badly.

'Because I've had a really, really bad day and I was feeling really, really awful. And now I'm not feeling anything other than happy and warm in this jacket that I've changed my mind about stealing.'

'This jacket?' he'd asked, placing his free hand on one of the lapels and gently pulling her just an inch more towards him, until their bodies were touching, and she felt every part of her respond to him in a way that she couldn't ever remember experiencing, not even with Bruce.

She hadn't answered his question. Instead, driven by an unfamiliar urge to throw caution to the wind, she had raised her face to his and kissed him, softly at first and then harder, more insistent, until her heart was thudding and her senses were flooding with desire for more. She'd had to wrench herself away before her body stopped answering to her brain and went even further over the line she'd already crossed.

Now she was back in the ballroom and the waiting staff were

bringing the after-dinner liqueurs. The fifties-style big band wa
belting out an instrumental version of 'Last Christmas' and peopl
were already on the dance floor. It struck Helena that this was lik
a scene from a Christmas movie, one of those ones that showed
picture of perfection, where the whole world was a glittering kalei
doscope of happiness.

Although, that didn't seem to extend to her parents for som
reason. Her mother had barely spoken all night and seeme
agitated and distracted. Her dad had asked a couple of times wha
was wrong, but she'd just claimed tiredness. 'It's been such a bus
week at the salon, Duncan. Why people leave it to the last minut
to get their roots done, I'll never know.'

Laughing, her dad had slipped his hand over her mum's, an
kissed her on the cheek, which just seemed to make her even mor
jumpy. Helena had no idea what was going on there.

'Are you alright, Helena?' Her mother cut right through tha
thought. 'Only you're looking a bit flushed, and you've been to th
loo an inordinate amount of times.'

For a horrible moment, she wondered if her mother was goin
to ask her if she was doing coke in the bathroom, but she shoul
have known that her mum's mind worked in a different way.

'The amount of urine infections doing the rounds just now i
unbelievable. Sandra at work has been off three times this month
with them, although she did seem to get all her Christmas shop
ping done early, so it could have been a well-planned skive
Anyway, pet, leave yourself plenty of time if you need to go to th
loo because the queues in the ladies are like ten o'clock at th
bakers, when they bring out the fresh pies. Last time I went ou
there,' she gestured to the foyer, 'my dignity was only saved by tha
wee lassie in the cloakroom who gave me a tip that there was
powder room up on the mezzanine. Just one. Private. It has posl
dispensers with soap and hand lotion and thick towels. None o

your paper stuff. And there's a separate little area with a beautiful velvet chair and one of those marble dressers for you to fix your make-up. If they could have brought my pudding up there, I'd still be sitting on that seat with my feet up, enjoying the luxury.'

If it was any consolation, at least when Mum was ranting on, it made her dad smile. It never failed to baffle Helena how a man so brilliant could happily listen to her mother telling stories and joking from morning until night and still look at her in the utterly adoring way he was watching her now.

'I'm fine, Mum, but I might just heed your warning and head to the loo again before it's urgent.' Her mum had unwittingly just given her the perfect excuse to leave the table again, as she'd been desperate to do from the second she'd sat back down.

As she rose from her seat, she caught his eye again and that slow, sexy smile told her he understood.

She sensed him following her out of the restaurant and she put on just a hint of extra sway, her whole body already responding to the prospect of touching him again.

This time, she didn't even make it outside. When she reached the foyer, she waited for him to come through the doors, then immediately took his hand and guided him upstairs to the mezzanine bar, where a few guests were relaxing with brandies and coffees.

Helena wasn't interested in joining them for a beverage. Instead, she stopped in the corner, outside a heavy wooden door, out of sight of the other guests and staff.

He got the message immediately, turning his body to hers, his hand softly cupping her neck as he leaned down and kissed her again, with an urgency that shot every sense on to high.

'You are the most intoxicating woman I've ever met,' he whispered, then grinned again, 'And the craziest too.'

She kissed him again. 'You forgot sexy,' she murmured.

'Definitely sexy,' he agreed, before his lips came down hard on hers this time.

In the distance, in a place in her mind that was getting further away with every thud of her heart, she could hear a voice asking what the hell she was doing, reminding her that she wasn't this person, this wasn't her style. She didn't pick up strangers in bars and kiss men she didn't know in hotels she didn't frequent. She was Helena McLean. She thought things through. Played it safe. Strategised every move and predicted ten steps ahead. She definitely didn't...

The voice in her head got so far away she couldn't even hear it any more.

'Have you ever done something so wild and crazy that you didn't even recognise yourself?' she found herself asking.

'No,' he replied, his hand on the small of her back now, caressing her.

She broke off their kiss, opened her eyes, met his gaze with the flare of her own.

'Want to start?'

Slowly, achingly slowly, he nodded almost indiscernibly.

It was all that this reckless and spontaneous version of Helena McLean needed to press her body back against the door she'd been leaning on, and pull a complete stranger into the bathroom with the marble dresser and the velvet chair.

21

CATHY

Christmas Eve 1968

The contractions had settled into a steady rhythm now, but one that was speeding up through a cycle of pain, gradual relief, momentary calm, anticipation, fear and then bam! Straight back into pain again.

Cathy had never been more terrified in her life. She didn't want to do this on her own. What if she did it wrong? What if she made a mistake that would harm her baby?

She rubbed her stomach, whispering to the little one inside it.

'Please hang in there, baby. Don't move. Not yet.'

The nurse who'd been with her until a few moments ago, came back into the room with a nightdress. 'Here you go, lass. We keep a stock of these for emergencies. They're not the best, but they cover the important bits and give you a bit of dignity. It's probably going to be the last you get for a while.'

Cathy had no idea what she meant by that, but she thanked her anyway.

'Right then, let me check you out again. The doctor is on his way, but I'm not sure when he'll get here because there's a rush on tonight. Seems like every wumman and their granny wants to give birth on Christmas Eve this year. Never seen anything like it.'

Cathy let her talk, comforted by the cheery, confident sound of her voice. Her mum had always been one for chatting, although Cathy hadn't realised at the time. She'd only noticed it after Mum was gone, and the house was silent. That would always be the thing that she remembered most. Singing and dancing and blethering up a storm equalled happiness. No good things happened in the quiet.

The nurse helped her change into the nightdress, then she put a big cuff thing around her arm, blew it up and did something with a stethoscope, listening for something Cathy didn't understand. Nurse seemed satisfied with the results though, because she moved on to taking her pulse, chattering away again.

'Any guesses on whether it's a boy or a girl? I would offer my thoughts, but I only get it right about one in every ten times, so I don't think I'm best placed. Some of the lassies have taken to asking me what I think their patients are having, and then they bet the opposite way. They're lucky I don't take offence easy,' she declared with a hearty laugh.

Cathy put her hand on her belly again, wondering if the baby could hear. 'I don't know. I think my husband would like a boy, and I've already got a sister in my house, so yes, a boy would be nice. But then I think it would be lovely to have a girl. They say that girls always stick by their mums when they're older, and they become more like friends, don't they? It would be nice to have that to look forward to.'

'Aye, that would be lovely. My girls take me up to Goldbergs in he town for a wee bit of shopping and lunch every Saturday. I wouldn't be without it.'

Cathy didn't dwell on that picture. Not now. Not when she couldn't have that with her mum. Instead, she concentrated on practical things.

'How long is it going to be before the next pain comes? Only I want to be ready this time.'

The nurse checked a watch that was pinned to her white uniform. 'Another five minutes or so. You're speeding up nicely. I don't think this baby is going to be long in getting here.'

The wave of anxiety was almost as strong as the contractions. Duncan had to get here. He just had to. When Richie had left, she had been clear about what she needed him to do.

'Is that what you want, Cath? Do you want me to go?'

She'd choked back a sob as she'd nodded, then thought about her baby and what it needed her to do, and switched straight to practicalities. She'd been swallowing pain and getting on with it for years. She was an expert.

'Yes. Please, Richie. Go to the house. Get Loretta. Tell her to leave a note for Duncan, so that when he gets home, he'll know to come straight here. His train should be getting in about half past nine, so if he gets a taxi home, he could maybe get here about half past ten.' Richie had squeezed her hand when she'd paused.

'And Richie,' she'd whispered, so that the nurse couldn't overhear. The woman's mind must be racing already. 'Today...' She'd paused, unable to say it, but it didn't matter because he knew.

'Today didn't happen,' he'd murmured, with a smile so sad her heart almost cracked open. 'I'm leaving day after tomorrow, so I won't see you again. I'm sorry, Cath. I wish it were different. I love you.'

'I love you.' She'd said it so quietly she wasn't sure he'd even heard as he'd bolted out of the door, away to find the people she needed to be with her right now. They weren't here yet, but hopefully they'd make it in time.

'Will my husband be allowed to come in when he gets here? mean, are men allowed in while, you know...' Why hadn't she asked these questions before tonight? She'd only had one appointment with her doctor after she found out she was pregnant and all he did was confirm it and tell her roughly when she'd be due. He'd even got that bloody wrong, because he'd told her it would be well into January before her baby made an appearance.

'Yes, lass, we let him in while you're in labour, but when it gets closer to the time, he'll need to wait outside. Is your man going to be one of those ones that paces up and down that corridor out there or will he go to the pub across the road? That place must be packed out tonight with the number of women we've got on this ward right now.'

Cathy wasn't sure of the answer to that, but she didn't even get a chance to ponder it. There was no warning when the pain came this time, just straight from nothing to everything, taking the wind right out of her. She buckled forward and gasped for air to get through it, while the nurse rubbed her back and said soothing words that Cathy could barely hear.

She was right in the midst of it when the door flew open and Loretta burst in, then stopped dead in her tracks. Even in the fire of the pain, Cathy registered the fear and terror on her sister's face and immediately realised why. Loretta had never seen this before. She had no idea. It was one thing telling her what this was going to be like, but that didn't prepare her young sister for the reality of it. The only time Loretta had seen someone she loved screaming, it was their mother, and it was in the nightmares she'd had for months after the crash, when she imagined she was in the car with Mum and Dad, and the other car was coming straight at them, and then smashing into them with a bang that woke Loretta screaming every night.

When Cathy could breathe again, talk again, she tried to reassure her. 'It's okay, Loretta, this is normal. It's fine. This is just what happens. Every ten or fifteen minutes, the pain comes just like it's meant to, so don't give me that look or run out of the room because I'll never let you live it down,' she joked, trying to reassure her.

It was only at that moment that Cathy registered that her sister's blonde hair had somehow been transformed to a vivid tangerine. Loretta spotted her looking and jumped in with, 'Don't ask and don't say a word! Sally wanted me to try out this colour. Said I'd look like Lulu.'

Her sister came right by the bed now, and took her hand, then abandoned it and gave her a ferocious hug instead. 'Sorry, Cathy, but that was terrifying. I can't believe it hurts so badly. If I ever say I want kids, just shoot me.'

Cathy felt the relief of normality returning and her sister's usual personality kicking back in.

All she needed now was for Duncan to get here so she could see him. Hold his hand. Feel that safety and security that always warmed her when she was with him.

Today, with Richie... that hadn't been real life. This was reality. Christmas Eve. This hospital. Her sister. Her baby. Her husband. Everything else was just memories, ones that she would probably think about forever, but that she'd keep all to herself.

'I'll be back again in a couple of minutes, love. Don't be shooting that baby out without me.' The nurse warned her. Cathy knew it was a joke, but it still sent a lump of panic to her throat.

'Sit here on the bed and distract me,' she told Loretta. 'Tell me about work. Was it mobbed?'

'Insane! Honestly, Cath, I've never seen it so busy, but I had the best day ever.'

'Because you made a fortune in tips?'

'No. Well, yes that too. I'm loaded. But it wasn't just that...'

She paused to gather her words and Cathy couldn't help getting caught up in Loretta's enthusiasm. Before she knew it, she was beaming from ear to ear and she didn't know why.

'Okay,' Loretta exclaimed. 'Do you want the bad news, the good news or the great news?'

Cathy made an instant decision. 'I don't know if I'm prepared for bad news, but give me that first and let me get it over with.'

'Okay. But don't be mad.'

'Even if I was mad, I'm hardly in a position to chase you round the room with my slipper.'

Loretta seemed pleased with that answer. 'You're right. Okay. Here it is. I'm definitely not going back to school after the summer. I just don't want to do it. In fact, I don't even want to go back after Christmas.'

'Oh, Loretta,' Cathy groaned. All she could think was that her mum would be so disappointed. She wasn't going to tell Loretta that right now though, because this wasn't the time or the place for an in-depth career discussion. Not that Loretta gave her a chance to object before she carried on.

'But the good news, for you, is that I'm not going to be a hairdresser either, so you don't need to worry about me working my knackers off for low pay.'

Cathy didn't understand. 'So what are you going to do?'

Loretta paused to build up to the moment. 'I'm going to be a singer. It's a long story and I'll tell you about it when... you know... there isn't a baby waiting to drop out of you. But a music producer heard me singing today and he gave me his card and wants me to come see him. He said I could be the next Lulu. That's what gave me and Sally the idea for this hair.'

'Bloody hell, Loretta. If I wasn't already in labour, I would be now. I'm happy for you, honey, I really am. Although I wish he'd said the next Dusty Springfield and you could have kept your own colour.'

She wanted to laugh, but she was scared it would set off another contraction. Truth was, she didn't think for a second that the singing thing would happen. He was probably some con man that used that line to pick up girls, but she wasn't going to say that right now. Let Loretta have her moment and she'd get Duncan to look into it later. That was the kind of thing solicitors could sort out no bother.

That thought led straight to another one.

'Loretta, did you remember to leave a note at the house for Duncan?'

'What note? I didn't write one.'

Cathy groaned. 'Richie was supposed to ask you to leave it, so Duncan knew to come here.'

'Oh no. Cathy, that's not how it happened. Richie came to the house, and he told me to come straight here and bring the bag you'd packed with your hospital things, but he didn't say anything about a note.'

She felt the panic rising again. 'So how's Duncan going to know that the baby is coming?'

'Cath, I think I might be about to give you another bit of bad news. Richie says he's going to the train station to find Duncan and tell him himself.'

10 P.M. – MIDNIGHT

22

EVE

Christmas Eve 2023

If a meteorite had crashed to earth and landed on her head, while she was holding a winning lottery ticket and having sex with Channing Tatum, Eve wouldn't have been more shocked than she was right now, after listening to the story her mother had been sharing for the last hour.

It wasn't an overstatement to say that her mum was in shock too. Completely stunned. At first when Eve had broken the news, Helena had gone deathly pale, then, like watching a computer whir into action, she'd obviously run through the entire sequence of events in her mind and made sense of it, before uttering the words Eve would never have believed would come out of her mother's mouth. 'Eve, I'm so sorry you've had to go through this. The thing is, if I'm being completely honest, and I don't see that there's much choice here...' She'd paused, and for the first time in her life, Eve had seen her mum stutter. 'There was one... *indiscretion.*'

That had sent her gran straight back for the brandy, and it was needed as the full story came out.

At first, Helena had been hesitant to share the details, but when she realised there was no choice, she'd spilled like a bad witness for the defence.

The truth was... drum roll and clutch those pearls... Her father had been a one-night stand, a revenge shag for catching Bruce cheating with their colleague on the day he was supposed to propose. Eve had been conceived in a hotel just across the park from where they sat right now.

'I bloody knew something was going on that night!' her gran had blurted. 'You'd never had a urine infection in your life, yet you were back and forward to the loo all night.'

Now, her shell-shocked mum was sitting at the kitchen table, in grey yoga pants and a sweat top that came down over her fingers, holding the large glass of brandy that her gran had topped up twice.

'But, Mum, how could you not have known that I wasn't Bruce's child? Did you never even think that could be a possibility?'

'No. I honestly didn't. Obviously it was a spur-of-the-moment thing and I'm not proud that we didn't use protection, but Bruce and I had been sleeping together for months before it, and months afterwards too, and we'd had a couple of...' Helena hesitated and Eve could see it was killing her mother to share such personal secrets. 'contraception lapses, so I just assumed... Oh God, Eve. For a smart woman I can be incredibly thick sometimes. I was so shocked when I found out I was pregnant and, to be honest, Bruce was livid, because it wasn't planned. I never questioned the paternity because order worked for me and Bruce being your father was the only scenario my mind would consider.' Eve watched as her mum's whole body deflated. 'I'm so sorry. I can't believe it. Bruce will have a bloody field day with this one. He'll have me in court and demand years of child support back.'

Eve spluttered, outraged, 'Mum, I don't really think that's the point here. Can you stay focused on the daughter who's just found out she was conceived when her mum shagged some anonymous bloke. So what, did you get a room after the party?'

'No, we... erm... there was a private powder room.'

Eve wondered if she was about to pass out with the relentless shocks. Helena. Having sex. In a toilet. It was the most un-Helena thing she could ever have imagined.

'That's right! I remember that toilet as well. Beautiful it was. A velvet chair and gold taps.'

For once, it was Gran who was on the receiving end of Eve's daggers. 'Can we all just come back to the point here?' She needed to take this all in. Get it all straight in her mind. 'So it was a hotel toilet, across the road, on the night Bruce was going to propose, but didn't because you secretly discovered he was seeing someone else. Oh, and it was on Christmas E... Oh no. Mum. Is that why you called me Eve? Do you think you really did know on some level?'

A red rash of embarrassment began to climb up her mother's neck. 'No. I called you that as a reminder that in my way I'd got some kind of payback. It was my secret. My little nugget of satisfaction. No matter what, Bruce would never know that I'd exacted my revenge for him screwing our colleague.'

'I need another drink for this,' her gran muttered, getting up and taking her glass back over to the bottle of brandy on the kitchen sink, throwing Eve a murmur of, 'It's a bloody miracle you're normal, pet.'

Eve was back in the midst of a full-scale rant. 'Holy shit, you couldn't make this up. Mother, don't you ever judge me again. Not ever. I don't want to see a snotty expression or hear a single word…'

Eve didn't get the rest of the sentence out because all of a sudden there was a crash and the sound of a bottle smashing on the tile floor. She leapt to her feet and instinctively grabbed her gran, who was holding on to the edge of the worktop, her face a deathly pallor, her eyes wide with shock.

'Gran! Gran! Oh no. Mum, call an ambulance! Right now! Hurry up! I think she's having a—'

Her mum leapt up and rushed into the living room to get her phone.

'No!' It was barely above a whimper. The tiniest sound. Then, a second later, a breathless, 'I don't need an ambulance.'

Eve's heart was pounding out of her chest. Fuck! How could she have been so stupid, so insensitive, to land all this on her gran today. The woman was seventy-five and this was probably the most taxing, stressful, emotional day of her life and now Eve had piled all this other stuff on and it had all been too much. If this… She choked back a sob. If this killed her gran, she'd never forgive herself.

'Gran, please. Come and sit down.' She tried to steer her away from the counter, but her gran was holding on like a vice.

Her words came out in a staccato whisper. 'Eve, look. Down at the lights. In the park.'

Oh, for Christ's sake, she was garbling now. Hallucinating. Eve added that to the list of symptoms for the paramedics.

But her gran wasn't giving up. Her voice got stronger as she demanded,

'Eve, look! Out the window!'

'Gran, I…' Eve was seriously panicking on the inside now, but her gran was so insistent, and she seemed a little steadier on her

eet, so Eve took her eyes off her for just a second, so that she
ould see whatever Gran was so fixated on and then get her back
o a seat. Her gaze had barely shifted when she saw him. An
lderly man. Sitting on their bench in the fairy-lit park. It seemed
hat he was staring up at this window, but maybe he was just
aving a funny turn too. Shit, what was happening tonight?

'Gran, what is it? Who is he? In fact, who cares. Gran, all that
natters is that we get you to a doctor—'

'Eve...' There was a heated stubbornness in her tone that made
ve stop.

'Eve Quinn, you listen to me right now. That man down there...
hat man is Richie Clark.'

Eve's jaw dropped, stopping her from forming words. Not that
he could think of a single one to say at that moment.

'Now I know this is an important time for you, but I need you
o indulge me because I'm seventy-five and I don't know long I've
ot left...'

Eve's whole body sagged with relief. Her gran was doling out
er usual trusty tool of manipulation. If she had an extra day for
very time she mentioned her age and said she didn't know how
ong she had left, she'd live to a hundred. She was fine. Totally
ormal. Medical emergency averted.

'Sorry! I couldn't find my bloody phone,' her mum gasped as
he stormed back into the room. 'I've got it now. They're asking
vhat the address is.'

Eve was still in a state of astonishment, her gaze going like a
endulum between her gran and the man outside and back
gain. Thankfully, however, she'd managed to regain her power
f speech. 'It's okay, Mum. She's fine. We don't need an
mbulance.'

'Oh, thank God,' her mum blurted, before retreating to advise
he emergency service that they could stand down.

'Eve!' her gran chided her, snapping her out of her gobs macked stupor.

'Sorry, Gran! Okay. Tell me what you need.'

'I need you to get my lipstick. And then I need you to go down there and bring Richie Clark up here.'

Eve glanced down again. He was definitely staring up here, but just to be sure, she waved and... yes, he waved back. Now he was smiling and she was gesturing that he should come up. He gave her a thumbs up and got up from the bench.

She watched him walk towards the gate nearest to their building.

'I don't think I need to, Gran. I think he's on the way here.'

Her gran wasn't listening, too busy delving into her bag. She brought out her hairbrush and her red lippy, then applied it perfectly without a mirror.

What. The. Hell. Was. Going. On? Eve continued to peer out of the window, and saw him cross the street towards their building.

Two minutes later, she started to worry that he was lost. Their intercom buzzer hadn't gone, so had he got in the front door downstairs? And even if he'd somehow managed that, how would he know what flat to come to? Would he just guess? Was that poor man out there knocking on every door on this floor?

Eve was about to go and find him when the doorbell rang. Lipstick on and hair brushed, her gran sat ready.

'Mum, can you get the door?' Eve shouted, into a vacuum of no reply.

Bugger. She must be in the loo.

'Right, Gran, you're gorgeous, I love you and I'll be back in a minute.'

Eve's heart was bursting as she answered the door to see a man who was well over six feet tall. He was clearly in his seventies but wearing well, still broad-shouldered, with a full head of grey hair that was swept back off his handsome face. If this was what Richie Clark looked like now, she couldn't even begin to imagine how attractive he'd been in the sixties.

She stuck out her hand. 'I'm Eve. I think you're looking for my gran.'

The twinkle in his eye was as clear as the warmth of his smile.

'I think I am. And I have to say, that's been the story of my life.'

The chuckle took her by surprise, and the urge to throw her arms around him and give him a hug shocked her even more, but she didn't care and he didn't seem to mind in the least.

'It's a pleasure to meet you, Mr Clark. I've heard all about you.'

She decided not to add that she'd only heard about him today. It seemed like an irrelevant detail.

'Come right in,' Eve beckoned, as she took a couple of steps back into the hallway, then opened the living-room door. 'Gran is just through in the k—'

'I'm here.' Cathy McLean was standing, all five foot two inches tall, in the middle of the living room, her face beaming with happiness, matching the look on Richie Clark's face as he rushed towards her, then suddenly stopped, their faces just inches apart, taking in the sight of each other.

Her gran was the first to break the spell, reaching up, touching his face, as if to make sure it was real. Then Richie took her hand from his face and kissed it. Eve realised she'd stopped breathing as time stood still for one second, two, three… Before, suddenly, both of their faces cracked into smiles of absolute amazement and wonder, and Richie threw his arms around her gran, picked her up and swung her round.

Eve gasped aloud at the sheer loveliness of the reunion playing out in front of her. It was the last scene of *Dirty Dancing*. Of *An Officer and a Gentleman*. Of *Pretty Woman*. Of all those old romcoms she used to watch with her gran on a rainy Sunday afternoon.

Although, granted, this one came with the risk of an elderly muscle strain and the presumption of a bus pass.

'What the hell...?'

Eve turned to see Helena come out of the bathroom, her red-rimmed eyes wide with confusion.

'It's Gran's old boyfriend. The other love of her life. I'm not sure how it happened, but he's here.' Eve could hardly believe the words she was saying, or the tears that were streaming down her face.

She wiped them away with her sleeve, then watched as he eventually put her gran down. Gran stared up at his face, then caught her breath and turned to her mum.

'Helena, this is Richie Clark.'

This time, it was her mum who looked at him, took in his face, reeled back in shock and then gasped.

'Oh, holy shit. I remember you. That night in the hotel, you were there.'

23

HELENA

Christmas Eve 1993

Helena joined her dad in his study, where they'd often sit and talk about work, or the law, or anything else that she had on her mind, in the two armchairs in front of the coal fire. They'd been back from the lavish Christmas Eve party at The Kentigern On The Green for twenty minutes or so. Her mother had excused herself and gone to bed the minute they'd got home, but Helena hadn't paid attention, too wrapped up in what had happened back at the hotel. The sex with the stranger had been incredible. Thrilling. Like nothing she'd ever felt. But as soon as it was over, she'd straightened herself out, said she had to go, given him one more long, sexy, heart-thudding kiss.

'Can I see you again?' he'd murmured into her hair.

She'd shaken her head. 'No.' It was regretful, but in a weird way, somehow grateful and empowering and a whole load of other emotions she couldn't quite identify. She didn't need to.

They'd held their gaze for a moment, both of them under-standing, and then she'd walked out of the door. When she'd got back downstairs, her parents were already making moves to leave, because her mum had a migraine coming on.

In the taxi home, she'd noticed a missed call from Bruce and checked her voicemail. 'Hi darling, I know you're probably sleeping, but I was just checking in to see how you were. This is wretched not being with you tonight. Call me when you can. I love you.'

Helena had pressed delete.

When the taxi had stopped at her parents' house, she'd thought about staying in the cab and going back to her flat, then decided against spending the night in an empty house, sitting alone as the clock struck midnight, Christmas Eve became Christmas Day and she turned another year older.

Her bedroom here at her childhood home was exactly as she'd left it, so she'd had a long, cleansing shower, pulled on an old pair of pyjamas from her chest of drawers, and gone down to where she knew she'd find her dad.

Now that she'd joined him, he poured her a drink – a balloon glass with a shot of creamy Baileys – and they talked about nothing in particular before he got to the point. He always did. Her dad could read her better than anyone, even her mum.

'Something on your mind, darling?' he asked.

Helena thought about bluffing, but, for once, she didn't have the strength for it. She needed advice. Relationships. Love. Motivations. She needed to get his thoughts, but she still couldn't bring herself to tell him what Bruce had done to her, couldn't reveal the shame she felt about not seeing it coming.

'I think I'm just having second thoughts as to whether I'll accept Bruce's proposal. It's a big decision.'

'The biggest,' he agreed, then fell silent again, waiting for her ɔ speak. Unlike her mother, he never rushed her, never tried to ɔrce his opinions or jump to fix whatever was wrong.

'Can I ask you something? Did you only marry Mum because he was pregnant?'

A flinch of consternation crossed his face and she immediately aw that the question had disappointed him. It had never been a ecret that her mum was pregnant when they married – the hotos of their wedding day told that story – but it just had never een discussed.

'Why would you ask that?'

Helena thought about it, answered truthfully, 'Because, you're ɔ different...'

'Helena, you've got it round the wrong way. I was so thrilled hat she got pregnant because it allowed me to marry her. Back in hose days, let's just say that judgements were harsh and the repre- ensible stigmas were difficult to shake. As a single mother... well, our mum had enough challenges back then without trying to ring you up on her own. And it happened so soon after we met hat there was no other option, really. To be honest, I'm not sure he'd have stuck with me otherwise. She certainly wasn't in love vith me at that point.'

The Bailey's caught in her throat as a realisation dropped in. So, wait a minute, are you saying that you wanted to marry Mum nyway, pregnant or not, and that you don't think she'd have narried you otherwise? Why would you go along with that? Why vould you marry someone who didn't love you?'

Her dad smiled, shrugged. 'Because I adored her from the first noment I met her. She was so different from me in every way – nd God knows, my parents definitely didn't approve – but she was ntoxicating. The most caring, most selfless person I'd ever ncountered. And she made me laugh every day, made me feel like could do anything with her by my side. So when she told me she

was pregnant, I offered to marry her, because I knew that if w
could make it work, we'd have the most wonderful life togethe
For once, and maybe the only time ever, I took a gamble. I wen
into our marriage hoping she'd fall in love with me and she did. S
all I'll say is that you and Bruce already have so much in commo
and you're already in love, so if you believe, just as I did, that you'
have a wonderful life together, then I think the odds are definitel
stacked in your favour.'

They sat in silence for a few more minutes, watching th
flames of the fire crackle in the hearth, while Helena's min
processed, analysed, thought everything through from all angle
Eventually, she put her empty glass on the side table betwee
them and unfurled her legs from under her before getting up an
kissing her dad on the cheek.

'Thanks, Dad,' she said softly.

'For what?'

'For making me see things more clearly. I don't think I'll sta
here tonight after all. I'm going to go over to see Bruce and chec
on how he's doing.'

At the door, she threw her coat on over her pyjamas, pulled o
the only warm pair of boots she could see – pink furry ones tha
obviously belonged to her mother – and grabbed her bag. She ra
down the drive, along the street and out onto the main road. Eve
at this time of night, late on Christmas Eve, it was still busy an
she searched left and right looking for a vehicle with an ambe
light. A few minutes later, she saw one, whistled, hailed it dow
and jumped in. She gave the driver Bruce's address and prayed h
wasn't the chatty type. He wasn't.

For fifteen minutes, they drove through West End street
thronging with revellers, then into the more serene, beautifu
streets of Park Circus. When they drew up outside Bruce's apart
ment, she paid him an exorbitant amount and didn't even listen a

he mumbled something about double fare due to the occasion. Instead, she climbed out, banged the door shut, and trudged wet furry boots to the entrance of Bruce's building.

For a horrible moment, Helena thought he wasn't going to answer his buzzer. Maybe he'd gone out. Maybe he was sleeping. Maybe – oh, hell no... maybe he was with Bree Fucking Halston or had her up there in his bed.

'Hello?'

He answered. He was there.

'It's me.'

The door catch buzzed open immediately and she ran inside, ignoring the lift and racing up the stairs. He barely had the door open when she got there to see him standing in his pyjama bottoms, no top, every muscle of his torso defined thanks to a gym schedule that he never missed, hair messy as if he'd been asleep.

'Darling! Are you feeling better? Come on in.' He stood to the side to let her by and then carried on, 'I must have dozed off on the sofa, but I'm so glad you're here. We can celebrate your birthday together now.'

He followed her into his grey and black glossy kitchen, where she spun around, eyes blazing.

'I know you were going to propose to me tonight...'

His charming grin was instant, and she knew that on any other night it would make her melt. 'I was. I should have known your parents would tell you. Oh well, secret's out. Darling, I think we could be so happy...'

'Shut up.'

His head jerked back, shocked, 'Helena, what the hell...?'

It struck her that she'd rather do this in one of Bree Halston's Valentino suits, but here she was, in her eighteen-year-old self's pyjamas, and her mother's pink furry boots.

'I also know you've been fucking Bree Halston for the last year, and you dumped her today.'

He didn't even have the balls to reply, so she stormed on.

'Do you love her?'

'No. I don't.'

'Do you love me?'

'Yes.'

Helena waited for her bullshit detector to go off, but weirdly it was just a faint hum in the background. Okay, the next question would determine if she was losing her touch.

'Why were you going to propose to me? Why today? Why now? And don't fucking lie to me.'

'Because I love you and I think we'd be incredible together...'

Her sharp intake of breath told him that he was on the wrong track.

'Try again,' she warned, with lethal fury.

'Helena, that's true, I swear. But, look, we'd be kidding ourselves if we both didn't see what we bring to the party here. You want the status that will come from being with me. I want the connections that being married to Duncan McLean's daughter will give me. There's a position going at his firm, Head of Corporate—'

'I know. You got the job. They've posted the offer to you.'

He didn't even try to hide the rush that news gave him. And she couldn't deny the rush that his words gave her. He was right. She wanted to be the woman who was married to Bruce Quinn, the man widely regarded as the most promising, ruthless, brilliant young solicitor in the city.

'So here it is. Moment of truth. You got the job. You don't have to marry me now. So is that it? We're done.'

He shook his head, seemingly incredulous. 'Helena, that's not even the start of it. I love you. I meant that. You're the most brilliant, sexiest woman I've ever known and you're going to be a star in our world. Everyone sees it.'

'If I'm so incredible, why the fuck have you been shagging Bree Halston for the last year?'

'Because it was... easy. That's the truth. A habit. It was just sex. I was already seeing her when we got together and just never fully cut it off. It's nothing like what we have. I've tried to end it a dozen times, and then she turns up on my door and... I swear that's all it was. Sex. I know I should have stopped it, but I'm sorry. That's all I can say. It was a fuck-up and I'd give anything to go back and change it, because from the minute I met you, in my mind, you've been the only one. I love you.'

Even if it was bullshit, there was a tiny part of her that wanted to record that. Bree was the other woman. It was Helena he was in love with.

'The truth is I want to marry you because we'd make an unstoppable team. That's it. That's what I'm offering. Us. Love. Great sex. And a life that will be everything you could ever want.'

She couldn't deny, even to herself, that she was finding him so incredibly sexy right now. 'What about kids?'

'Never been on my wish list,' he shrugged.

Better and better. They had never been on her wish list either.

She put her bag down, lifted a packet of cigarettes and a chrome lighter from his granite worktop and lit one. She only ever smoked socially, just one or two at parties, and this was her third or fourth of the night. And yes, she had a tiny thrill when it gave her a flashback to two hours ago, when she was in a hotel with a stranger, and they were...

'Okay, here are my terms,' she said, exhaling. The defence litigator in her saw the danger here. Her world was full of repeat offenders. The whole, 'leopards don't change their spots' thing.

But some leopards could be tamed and if Helena had to bet on anyone taming Bruce Quinn, she'd bet on herself.

'You never touch Bree Halston again. She told me all about the boyfriend who ditched her today, but she didn't identify him, so she has no idea I know it was you. You never tell her I knew about you and her seeing each other. I'll play dumb and I'm pretty sure she won't have the balls to tell me. She won't want to lose face, and if she does, I'll deal with that. I have a hunch she'll move to another firm, and if she doesn't, then I'll take my rising star elsewhere. Either way, in a month's time you propose to me and declare your undying love in front of the whole damn world. You tell Bree Halston that you realised you were in love with me all along. If you ever so much as brush against another woman, we're done. 100 per cent monogamy. And don't dare test that theory because I'll divorce you in a heartbeat and I'll make sure that your position at my father's company comes to an abrupt end. Those are my terms. That's the deal.'

His hands were on his hips now, and he was walking towards her.

'You know, this, right here, is why I want to marry you. I might not have mentioned this before, but we are the same. I accept the terms. I take the deal. Now come over here and let me show you how I feel about that.'

All hesitation was gone, replaced by nothing but an attraction that she didn't even want to try to resist.

As she walked towards Bruce Quinn, Helena knew that she was making a deal with the devil.

She knew that she could get burned.

She knew that this man could wreck her.

And she knew that was a risk she was willing to take.

24

CATHY

Christmas Eve 1968

The baby was almost ready to arrive. The contractions were getting closer together and Cathy knew that it was going to come soon. And Duncan still wasn't here.

The lovely nurse was back, and she checked her out down below and then came up to her end of the bed.

'Lass, you don't have long left to go. I've let the doctor know and he will be here soon.'

'No. Not yet. I need Duncan here. I don't want to do this without him. Even if he's outside. I just want him here.'

Loretta replied before the nurse. 'Cath, I'm here. I'll stay with you, don't worry. I won't leave you.'

Cathy could feel her breaths coming thick and fast and knew another contraction was on the way. Loretta didn't understand and Cathy didn't want to explain it. If something went wrong, if anything happened that she couldn't control, then she needed him to be here to take care of it. Her parents had gone out that night and they hadn't come home. Cathy knew things could happen and if the worst happened to her tonight, she needed to know that he was here, to take care of Loretta, of the baby, of the life she would leave behind. But she couldn't say any of that to her sister because it would terrify her, and she couldn't put a single new scar on Loretta's soul.

'I'm. Waiting. For. Duncan. I'm. Waiting. Until. He. Gets. Here.' She panted.

The nurse was losing patience with her stubbornness. 'You might be waiting, lass, but this bairn is getting a shoogle on.'

The door began to open. 'That'll be Doctor...'

It wasn't. Every single aching bone in Cathy's body screamed with relief when Duncan charged in looking like a man possessed, then flew to her side.

'Well, hallelujah,' the nurse cheered, with just a hint of sarcasm amongst the jubilation.

'Cathy, I'm so sorry. I got here as soon as I could. Are you okay? Is the baby...?'

'We're both fine. Especially now that you're here.'

He was holding her hand so tightly, his gaze fixed on hers. 'I should have been here all day with you. I shouldn't have left you today. I should have skipped work, stayed with you. I should have brought you here...'

'It's okay. I got a taxi.'

A look passed between her and the nurse, an unspoken agreement. The kind professional wouldn't say anything. And of course Loretta wouldn't either. They all knew there was nothing to be gained from upsetting Duncan when he was about to become a father.

'Anyway, you weren't to know,' Cathy reassured him. 'The baby isn't due for two more weeks. It just decided to get a move on.'

Cathy didn't even want to contemplate how different today would have turned out if he'd stayed off work. He would have opened the door to Richie Clark, and every single moment of today, the good and the bad, would have been lost. When today was over, she knew she would think about that, but right now, all she cared about was delivering her baby, making her family, giving Duncan his child.

'All that matters is that you're here,' she told him, her words oozing gratitude.

'Aye, she was going to send the police out to look for you,' Loretta joked and Cathy watched as Duncan gave her the biggest smile. He'd always been good to Loretta too, taking her on as if she was his own.

'That's okay, I got the search party that she sent. No need to call the police.'

The contraction was building again, so Cathy almost missed what he said. Almost. Loretta's comment came straight back to her. Richie was going to find Duncan. Had he told him where she'd been when she went into labour? That they'd been together? Did Duncan know that the man she'd loved before him had begged her to be his again today? That he'd brought her a ring. That he wanted her back. Was Duncan only here out of duty, because he'd got her pregnant, and now that she'd lied to him about how she'd got here, would he decide she couldn't be trusted and leave her?

'What search party was that?' It was Loretta that asked the question, with a worried glance to Cathy.

'The man at the station. Said he worked here at the hospital. He was holding up a sign with my name on it when I got off the train. Told me you were here, and the baby was on the way. Nice chap. I'll need to track him down and thank him properly.'

If the nurse's eyebrows raised any further, they'd be in her hairline. Cathy knew that this would be retold in the staffroom a hundred times today. The young lass that came in with one man, clearly more than friends, and then sent him to find her husband. Cathy met her gaze, and the nurse understood.

'Aye, that was our porter,' she declared breezily. 'I'll thank him for you, no worries at all. It was on his way home anyway.'

Cathy shot her a glance of gratitude, just as a door burst open again and in marched a doctor in a white coat, stethoscope around his neck, clearly on a mission with no time for idle chit chat.

'Okay then, Mrs...'

'McLean,' the nurse finished the sentence.

'Right. Mrs Mclean.' Cathy could feel her cheeks burn as he had a good old stare down below too. Oh, the mortification if it. 'It looks like this baby is about to make an appearance.'

Mr McLean?' he addressed Duncan, in a pointed way that her husband clearly didn't comprehend.

'Yes?' Duncan replied, as the nurse coughed and nodded to the door.

'If you'd like to wait outside...' the doctor continued.

'I'm not leaving,' Duncan replied, his grip tight on her hand.

'Mr McLean,' the nurse took over. 'There are seats right outside...'

'I'm not leaving,' Duncan repeated.

'I don't think we're going to have time to argue about it,' the doctor commented calmly, just as another contraction buckled Cathy's body. It lasted so long, her teeth hurt from clenching, and her throat hurt from the low, pained howl that was coming out of her chest. She gripped Duncan's hand so tightly she was sure she must be crunching his fingers, but he didn't even flinch. This was what she needed. Duncan. Here. His reassuring presence was the only thing stopping the panic that kept threatening to rise. The morbid thoughts came rushing back. Her mum. Her dad. But now there was a comfort. If anything happened to her, if anything went wrong, Duncan was here to take care of her sister and her child. And his face would be the last thing she saw before…

'Mrs McLean, on the next contraction I'm going to ask you to push.'

He didn't need to say it again. She barely had time to breathe before the next one came and she pushed with all her might, again and again, time after time, pain ripping through her until she felt the unmistakable sensation of her baby leaving her body, followed by the cry of a newborn.

'I'm never doing that,' Loretta mumbled as the nurse quickly stepped in, clearing the baby's airway, then cutting the cord and wrapping the crying child in a blanket before finally handing it over to its sobbing parents.

'Baby McLean, born at one minute past midnight on Christmas morning,' she announced. 'Congratulations Mr and Mrs McLean – you have a baby girl.'

MIDNIGHT – 2 A.M.

25

EVE

Christmas Eve 2023

The clock that Gran had put on the mantle earlier struck midnight with a loud chime. The vibrations must have set off the penguins, because they were now singing 'We Wish You A Merry Christmas', and that wasn't even the strangest thing that was happening in the room right now. Eve had absolutely no idea what was going on.

It was Christmas Day. And her mum's birthday.

Yet instead of popping open champagne, her mother was standing in the living room staring at Richie Clark, and her outburst had just shaken Eve to the core.

'I remember you!' she'd gasped, and now Richie and her gran were wearing the same astonished faces that she was pretty sure she would see if she looked in the mirror.

'That night in the hotel. You were there.' Her mum went on, just blurting out words. 'Christmas Eve. The party. Across the street.'

Oh no. Oh no. Oh no. All sorts of Netflix documentary thoughts of horror were going through Eve's mind. If this was the guy that her mother had trotted off to the loo with...

'You were with him. I saw you. At the beginning of the night.'

Oh sweet, blessed relief. This wasn't the guy she'd be buying Father's Day cards for. Her gran looked pretty thankful about that too.

'What night?' Richie asked, obviously as confused as everyone else in the room.

Eve couldn't bear it and felt compelled to step in before her gran had another funny turn.

'Mr Clark, if you wouldn't mind having a seat, I think I can fill in some of the blanks. Do you want the pamphlet edition or the encyclopaedia version of the story?'

'Whatever one comes with a brandy,' her gran interjected. 'Richie, come on into the kitchen and I'll pour you a drink. And I'm going to apologise in advance.'

'What for?' The poor man was mystified.

'Every single thing that's about to come out of that lassie's mouth. Believe it or not, finding you again isn't the most shocking thing to happen in this house tonight.'

To her surprise, Gran's old flame laughed. 'I can't wait for this. You always were full of surprises, Cath.'

Eve checked to see if there was any hint of a dig in his words, but his face said otherwise – there was just pure joy in his smile.

In the kitchen, Gran opened a new bottle of brandy to replace the one she'd dropped earlier, poured a drink for Richie and slid her own back in front of her as she took a seat at the kitchen table.

'Mum, can I get you something?' Eve asked Helena. 'You look like you need it.'

'Wine. Brandy. Anything,' her mum replied, still staring at Richie, who was sitting at the table, gazing at Gran like he still couldn't quite believe she was there. Eve tuned into their conversation while she was pouring her mum's drink.

'I keep thinking this isn't real, Cath,' Richie said.

Eve never heard anyone except her Aunt Loretta call her gran that. To everyone else, she was Cathy.

'I know.' Her gran had her hand on his, and Eve just wanted to capture this moment. And maybe have a cry. It was so romantic. So perfect. So... 'But what were you doing out there at this time of night, you daft bugger? You could have had pneumonia before the night was out.' So... Gran.

'Sitting on our bench, looking up at the window to see if I could see you. I know how pathetic that sounds,' he pointed out with a low, warm laugh. 'I mean, it's not even really our bench, is it? We only sat on it once.'

'I've gone there every Christmas Eve since that night,' her gran admitted, bashfully.

'And I would wander through there every year too. Same night. I can't believe we never met.'

'You two are killing me,' Eve teased, and her gran flushed red for the first time ever, then turned back to Richie.

'But how did you know I was here? That I'd bought this flat?' Her gran's brow furrowed as she tried to work it out. 'The only way you could know is if...' A pause, then a realisation, then she raised her eyebrows in question. 'You bought the building?' He nodded, setting Gran off on a train of amusement. 'Oh, Richie Clark, you did. You bought the bloody building.'

Eve could count on one hand the number of times she seen her gran shed a quiet tear, or sometimes a noisy sniff, but never in her life had she witnessed Cathy McLean with a full-blown river running down her cheeks, laughing and crying at the same time.

'He bought the building,' she sobbed, relaying the information to Eve in case she was one of the only people in the street that hadn't heard her saying it already.

'I gathered. But, Gran, you're going to have to help me out more on that,' she said, as she returned to the table and passed her mum's drink to her. Helena was sitting perfectly still, staring at their visitor.

It was Richie that opened the explanation. 'When we were twenty, we sat in the park out there, and I had nothing. Not a penny to my name. But I promised your gran that one day I'd make something of myself and I'd buy one of these buildings.'

'Don't say it, Gran,' Eve warned, holding up her hand to stop her gran repeating her exclamation yet again. 'So, I gather you bought it. When was that?'

Richie thought about it. 'Maybe twenty-five years ago. It was offices for a long time and then I decided to turn it into these retirement flats when my wife passed away a few years ago.' Eve saw a shadow of loss cross his face and she felt for him. 'It took a while to get all the permissions, but we started construction last year. It was always meant to be an investment, but I also hoped...' His words trailed off.

'How did you know I'd find them? That I'd move here?' her gran asked.

'I didn't. I suppose I just hoped that you would still live nearby, and that maybe you'd pass them, see the signs. It felt like a pipe dream though. I didn't know it had come true until my solicitors sent me the names of the buyers and I saw it there. I think it was one of the best moments of my life. And I'm sorry about Duncan, Cath. I saw on the paperwork that you were widowed.'

Her gran nodded. 'That was what made me think about moving.'

They were just gazing at each other again and then it was as if

er gran suddenly remembered her mother's outburst in the living
oom.

'Richie, the reason our Helena's sitting there staring at you like
1e's a fart in a trance,' Eve felt the motion of her gran kicking her
1other under the table, 'is that we've only just discovered tonight
1at she met a fella in the big hotel on the corner over there nearly
1irty years ago.'

Eve lost the ability to breathe, the links pulling together and
locking her brain from normal function. Her gran must have
een feeling the same, because she'd stopped speaking and she
nd Richie were just staring at each other again, lost to the world.

'Hello?' her mum interrupted, losing patience and gaining
ritation.

'Sorry!' her gran pulled it together. 'Anyway, the pure beamer
1ere...' Gran gestured to Helena, 'and this bloke had a one-night
and – and if you knew how out of character that is, you'd under-
and our shock. I'm not judging and, in fact, I'm delighted
ecause the result was our lovely Eve here. I remember the night
1e's talking about and she's right, you were there. It was the last
me I saw you.'

'I remember every minute of it,' he said, with a look of such
:nderness that Eve knew he'd replayed that moment time and
me again over the years.

Eve decided she'd be happy to abandon the search for her
ither and just sit here and watch these two all night. Their
onnection was almost tangible. Like a cord going directly from
ne to the other, one that was woven from joy and familiarity and
:lief that they were together. It was one of those situations that
1ould have been awkward, yet it was the opposite. This felt
:rangely comfortable.

'I'm so sorry about the outburst.' Her mother finally found her
>ice. 'It's been a bit of an emotional night. The man I'm referring

to...' Her mum had slipped into solicitor speak, so she must b starting to feel better. 'He was with you.'

'What was his name?'

Her mum blushed the same colour as the scarfs around th penguin's necks. 'I didn't ask. It was a rather... *spontaneous* situa tion. But he was sitting at your table. Back then, I thought h might be...'

'My son.'

Eve's millionth shock of the day got the better of her. 'You son? Your son might be my dad?' The first time it was a reactiv outburst, the second time it was a profound realisation. 'Your so might be my dad.'

'And that would make you... my granddaughter. Oh, blood hell, lass.'

Eve held her breath as he absorbed that and waited for h response. If he got up and left here right now, she'd never forgiv herself for spoiling her gran's happiness.

He started to speak again. 'That's... that's.... The best thin that's happened to me in the ten minutes since the last incredibl thing happened to me. A granddaughter!'

Her gran had her hankies out of both sleeves and was doubl dabbing at her face. 'I can't believe this. I just... can't. But I do. An I know that doesn't make sense but... Oh, my goodness, it woul be wonderful if it were true. I'd be delighted.'

All the strain, the stress, the pain Eve had felt since the resul was being squashed by a lovely elderly gent who was alread someone special to her gran, but maybe to Eve now too.

'As would I,' Eve answered honestly, trying desperately not t get her hopes up in case they had this all wrong.

'Our Eve.' Smile beaming, Richie said that as if he were tryin it out, then turned back to her gran, his voice thick with emotio 'Our granddaughter. You and me. Imagine that, Cath.'

Her gran replied with another double dab, then pulled a third hanky out of her sleeve and handed it to him.

Eve was definitely imagining it, but she needed to know for sure. It would take time though. Another test. Maybe Richie would give his DNA. Unless...

The obvious question came to her. 'I think I know how we can be more definite right now. Mr Clark, do you know someone called Bethany Muldoon? Owns a café called—'

'Café Croissant. She's my niece.' Richie turned to her gran. 'That's our Betty's daughter.'

'Betty! Oh I loved that girl. Is she... is she... still with us?'

Richie laughed, clearly getting the inference in Gran's hesitation. 'Aye, she's still here. She lives across the corridor. Flat 6.'

Her gran shrieked with delight. 'Oh, this day! Please tell me Tom Jones is in the next room too, because he's the only thing that's missing now.' Her gran's joyful smile was still on her face when she pulled herself back to the other important stuff. 'Sorry, Eve, got carried away again there. Is that the right answer? All this DNA stuff is impossible to follow. What does the Muldoon lady being Richie's niece mean then, pet?'

Eve's gaze went to her mum again, who appeared to be incapable of conversation at the moment. Eve understood – all this emotion and shock was the polar opposite of the way her mum lived her very organised, very disciplined life. She must feel like she was in a tumble dryer, getting tossed around in every direction.

And Eve felt exactly the same right now. 'I think... I think it confirms that I'm Mr Clark's granddaughter.'

Richie got back up to his feet, tears unashamedly running down over his cheeks, arms outstretched. This was her grandad. Her actual grandad. And going by everything she'd seen and heard, he was just as kind and decent and loving as the grandfather she'd lost. This was like being struck with grandpa lightening twice.

Eve got up to hug him and he held her until she pulled back, suddenly desperate to stare at his face, to see if there was some familiarity, a hint of what her father would look like.

'Your son is my dad, Mr Clark. Your son in my dad!' Now she was the one stuck on a repetitive loop, as if repeating it would make it sink in more. 'Can you tell me where he is? How do I meet him?'

'I think you already have,' he said. 'He's the project manager here, but your estate agent told me that none of the removal companies would work on Christmas Eve, so I sent him over with some of the lads from my other business to help you out today. I've got a removal company too. He was an extra pair of hands and a bit of muscle.'

Eve couldn't keep up. This wasn't making sense.

Her gran was obviously feeling the same. 'You sent him to help me? At my house?'

'I did, Cath. You wouldn't have missed him. Our Harry is always down at the gym and he's the size of a tank these days.'

'Noooooooo.' Eve spotted Richie's alarm at her words, and immediately corrected herself. 'I mean, yessssss. Harry. Oh wow, it's Harry? But Mum, didn't you recognise him?'

'No. Who's Harry?' Helena appeared truly perplexed.

'He was there this morning at my house and then here this afternoon,' Gran piped up. 'Lovely man. He found my box of tights.'

Eve saw that her mother didn't find that little nugget to be either useful or pertinent.

'I didn't meet anyone in your house today,' her mum countered. 'I left straight after breakfast.'

Eve replayed flashbacks to this morning in her mind and

realised her mum was right. She had already left by the time Harry came in.

Wow. Just wow. Harry was her real dad. And although she didn't know him, he'd left the impression this morning that he was nice. And kind. And now she knew he helped her gran and Richie out of the goodness of his heart, she figured that made him a decent person. She just hoped that also meant he'd be open to speaking to her. Or was it too much to expect someone to welcome a twenty-nine year old daughter that he didn't even know existed? If it was, at least some of her questions had been answered and that would have to do for now.

'Do you think that maybe tomorrow...' Eve chided herself. 'Sorry, I shouldn't have suggested that. It's Christmas Day. Maybe some time next week, he might be open to meeting me again?'

'I don't think so...' Richie began, and Eve's heart sank. That was that, then.

Eve barely registered that Richie was still talking. 'I think he'd rather meet you tonight. I live on the top floor here and he's up in my apartment. He always stays with me on Christmas Eve, ever since my wife passed.'

He fished a phone out of his pocket, hit a few buttons, then spoke. 'Harry, it's me. Aye, I know my name flashes up. Anyway, I'm down in Cath's apartment. Yes, Cathy McLean. Downstairs. You helped her move in today. I'm here because... It's a long story, son.'

It didn't escape Eve's notice that Richie obviously hadn't told his son the full story about her gran. It was almost more romantic that they'd been each other's secret their whole lives.

'Can you just pop down? There's someone I want you to meet.'

26

HELENA

Christmas Eve 2023

Helena wasn't ready for this. Tonight had been the most excruciating, most terrifying, most mortifying evening of her life. Her mother now knew she'd once had a one-night stand and that her relationship with Bruce had been built on a lie. Her daughter had discovered that... She could barely bring herself to admit it. Eve had discovered that Bruce wasn't her father and that Helena had barely known the man she'd hooked up with.

Damn, she'd been a mess that night, and now she was a mess again tonight. The two most traumatic evenings of her life, both on the same night of the year, twenty-nine years apart. Her cheeks burned. Somehow, the fact that she'd been the epitome of class, organisation, dignity and order on every other day of her adult life didn't matter right now. And who the hell was Harry? Was that really him? From back then? Helena wasn't even sure she wanted find out. Sometimes, contrary to what she said every day in ourt, the truth was over-rated.

Bruce had certainly thought so. They'd made it work for a few ears, but he'd never truly got over the shock of becoming a father, omething he'd neither wanted or been happy about. If she were uthful, she hadn't wanted it either, but she'd had no choice. By ne time she'd realised she was pregnant, he'd already proposed nd she'd somehow managed to convince herself that she could ill have it all. The amazing husband. The fabulous career. The erfect family. Bruce was too caught up in his new job, making big noney while basking in the glow of her father's delight that he as going to be a grandad, to do anything but go along with it. e'd even kept up the pretence for a few years, but Helena knew. ate nights at the office. Long lunches at Rogano. Zero sexual nterest in her before the baby was born. Even worse, no interest of ny kind in Helena or their daughter after Eve had arrived.

Four years later, her father had found out Bruce was shacked p in a suite at One Devonshire Gardens, an iconic Glasgow hotel, ith a colleague, Annabel Maxed. Apparently half the solicitors in ne city knew about them, so they'd both been fired on the spot for ringing their company into disrepute.

Some women might have confronted him, but not Helena. he'd simply packed his clothes, and had them delivered to him ith their divorce petition. Over. Done. She'd gone into it with her yes wide open and she'd still been played. Maybe some day she'd orgive herself for that, but it would be around the same time that ell froze over.

Their divorce had of course caused a blaze of controversy, a ery public scandal that had only dissipated when he'd married nnabel and had the twins, leaving Helena both professionally nd personally humiliated, but satisfied when she'd found out

that the twins were unplanned and Bruce was furious when he
discovered Annabel was pregnant. Once bitten, twice... well, wha
a tit.

After that, she had chosen to focus on the parts of her life tha
she could control, that required no emotional risk or short-terr
reward for long-term pain. For Helena, that had always been in th
courtroom.

Of course, there was a price for that, and she had the sel
awareness to know that was paid by her child. It was a cop out, bu
she was a big believer that people should play to their strength
and for Helena that was never going to be motherhood. She'
been happy to abdicate the majority of that to a woman wh
specialised in fun, in caring for others, and in loving the peopl
that mattered to her. Her mother had never once complained, an
that reassured Helena she was doing the right thing. She'd eve
learned to ignore the occasional stab of pain and guilt that cam
when she was reminded that her daughter was closer to her gra
than to her own mother. Helena McLean (formerly Quinn) knew
was no more than she deserved.

'Mum, do you want to go and freshen up before he gets here
Eve asked her, eyes full of worry and concern and fear. She too
zero credit for how this young woman had turned out, and muc
as she found it impossible to show, she was proud of her. Ev
would have every right to take this out on Helena, yet she was sti
being kind. That was the Cathy Farmer genes in action. They'
skipped a generation, but they were here, stronger than ever.

With a grateful smile, Helena took her daughter up on th
suggestion, grabbing her bag and taking it to her mother's ne
bathroom. In the mirror she barely recognised the red eyes, th
pinched cheeks, the dry lips. It took a good ten minutes to pu
herself back together again, at least on the outside. The inside wa
still an anxious mess when she left the bathroom and made he

way back to the kitchen. She was almost there when she heard the new voice, and she stopped, just outside the door, but close enough to watch the introduction of the man who had his back to her. He was tall, so the height was right. But this guy was much wider in the shoulders, and bald, so she immediately ruled him out and decided it couldn't be him.

'Okay, son,' Richie Clark was saying. Helena hadn't seen that one coming. She'd always thought her dad was the only man her mum had ever had a relationship with, but she didn't begrudge this because she knew her dad would want her mum to be happy, even after he was gone. Helena hadn't seen Cathy's face beam like this for a long, long time. Even now she was staring at him in wonderment as he spoke. 'This is going to come as a bit of a shock, but I need to ask you a few questions.'

'If this is a pub quiz, I'm all in,' the other man replied. Helena wished she could see his face, but she wasn't ready to dive into yet another whirlpool of drama and emotion just yet. Or maybe ever. Running was a definite possibility right now.

'Not quite, son.'

'Didn't think so. Right, Cathy, what have you lost and I'll try to remember where we put it.'

Did she recognise the voice? Maybe. But not enough to place it.

'No, it's not that,' Eve interjected, and Helena could hear the tremor in her voice. What had she done to this poor girl? Saddled her with Bruce Quinn all her life, and now this. If Eve ever forgave her, it would be a miracle. 'Harry, we're just trying to put together the pieces of a story. Bear with me, but I'm just going to go with this... Do you remember being in a hotel across the green with your family, at a Christmas Eve party a million years ago? Actually, thirty years, to hit that nail right on the head.'

There was a pause, then Helena saw his head nodding. 'Yeah, actually, I remember it well. It was quite a night.'

She could be imagining it, but the back of his neck seemed to be slightly pinker when he said that.

Eve carried on. 'Is that because you met someone? A woman?'

'Can I plead the fifth?' he asked.

'Not tonight, son,' his dad answered.

Her mother snapped, desperate to get to the point. 'I can't stand this suspense. I'm seventy-five and I don't know how long I've got left, so I can't be doing with dragging this out. Harry, I apologise for the massive invasion of your privacy, but trust me, I wouldn't be asking if it wasn't important. Did you by any chance, meet a beautiful young woman that night, and have a brief but very close encounter with her in a posh loo, only for her to disappear like some panto Cinderella never to be seen again?'

The back of his neck was definitely redder now.

'I did.'

Helena gasped, but everyone was too caught up to notice her there. She should step in now. Take over the explanations. Deal with this in a cool, professional way. But for the first time ever, her voice wouldn't work and her feet were welded to the floor.

'Ok, so the thing is, that woman was my mum,' Eve explained, her hands now visibly shaking as much as her voice. 'And that was actually twenty-nine years and nine and a half months ago. And I've just done a DNA test that shows that I have a cousin called Bethany Muldoon. Who is your cousin too.' Helena half expected him to run now, but he stayed put.

'So that means...' his voice was an astonished croak.

'That putting it all together, I think there's a very good, almost definite possibility that you're my dad. I'm so sorry. I know that must be a shock.'

Nobody spoke for a week and a half. At least, that's how long it felt. Every eye on the room was on the bloke in the centre of it, and if they all felt the way she did, then every heart was waiting to beat until there was a conclusive reply.

'Please don't apologise. I mean... I don't know what to say...'

Helena was starting to feel lightheaded and Eve looked like she was about to pass out.

'But...' he was speaking again. 'I think that...'

What? What did he think?

'I think that I really hope that's true, and if it is, then...' His voice cracked and he cleared his throat. 'Then this might be the most brilliant thing that's ever happened to me.'

'Really?' Eve's face had crumpled and Helena couldn't work out if she was laughing or crying or both. Her mother had the hankies out of her sleeves and Richie was dabbing at his eyes too.

The guy – Harry – responded to Eve's tentative announcement by wrapping his arms around his newfound daughter and the two of them stood there, hugging each other, until their shoulders stopped shaking. That was when Eve opened her eyes and spotted Helena in the doorway.

She stepped out of the embrace and beckoned her forward. 'Mum... meet my dad.'

At that, the guy turned around and clichéd as it was, their eyes met. Helena could see the recognition there. It was the same one she was feeling right now too.

It was him. Much had changed, but he had the same eyes, the same face, the same smile.

'Red dress,' he said, almost teasingly.

Helena nodded. 'Black jacket. I almost stole it.' She knew no-one else in the room would understand, but it was enough that it made him laugh.

'I don't believe we were properly introduced last time. I'm Harry,' he said, sticking his hand out, definitely teasing her now.

For maybe the first time in twenty-nine years and nine and a half months, she decided she quite liked that.

'Helena. And I think this time I should maybe stay and talk.'

27

CATHY

Christmas Eve 2023

was two o'clock in the morning, and Cathy knew she should be
xhausted, but she couldn't ever remember feeling so awake or
ive.

Eve, Helena and Harry were through in the living room, where
ey'd been talking for the last hour. Cathy had taken them
rough a bottle of champagne, to celebrate Helena's birthday, to
lebrate them all finding each other and to celebrate the fact that
er wonderful granddaughter now almost certainly had a father
ho was so much better than the idiot who'd had the job for the
st twenty-nine years. It was even more incredible that he was
chie Clark's son. Richie had told her fifty-five years ago that he
anted to have a family with her. They'd come a convoluted road,
it maybe they'd finally got there after all.

Richie thought so too. Even without all the other evidence,

now they could see that there was definitely a similarity betwee
Eve and Harry that they'd all missed this morning because the
hadn't been looking for it. The same eyes. The same easy gri
They get it all sorted officially in the New Year, but Cathy was 1c
per cent convinced.

Just as she was 100 per cent convinced that her love for th
man hadn't diminished since the day he walked out of the hospit
room. It was all so familiar; his voice, his words, his touch, as I
held her hand across the table, and the sheer force of her need
be with him. She was, as she often reminded everyone, sevent
five years old, yet she felt all the same feelings that she'd had as
young woman, desperately in love.

'Do you want to go out for a walk?' she blurted out of nowhere

'Didn't you tell me I'd get pneumonia out there?' Richie she
back, playing with her.

'At my age, I'm allowed to change the facts on a whim. It's th
law.'

'Then I can't possibly object,' Richie conceded, standing an
holding his hand out to her. 'Not that I would, anyway. If we coul
withstand the temperatures at the ice rink every weekend, I reckc
we've got 2 a.m. in December nailed. Even if we're ancient now.'

The memory of those early dates made Cathy smile. As did h
willingness to go along with her spontaneous and possibly dea
defying impulses now.

When they passed through the lounge and told the young
ones what they were doing, she saw Helena open her mouth
object, but Eve immediately jumped in with a gentle, 'Let them b
Mum. They're happy.' If only her daughter could embrace th
concept of only living once and making the most of it, she'd be
lot bloody happier too. Maybe this whole situation would hel
Cathy lived in hope.

In the hallway, Cathy grabbed her thickest coat and pushed her feet into her warmest boots, then wrapped a thick scarf around Richie's neck and gave him gloves that might just stretch enough to fit his hands.

It seemed so perfectly natural to slip her arm through his when they got into the lift, and even more comfortable to drop her head onto his shoulder, and then feel the contact as he kissed the top of the woolly hat on her head.

When the lift opened, they didn't even have to communicate where they were going, as they made their way into the little park and down the path to their bench.

Just like the last time, Richie's arm went around her and her hand went into his pocket for extra heat, as they sat in the glow of a million fairy lights above them.

'I can't believe today,' Cathy said softly. 'It's been one of the most incredible of my life. We found each other again, Richie. How amazing is that?'

He exhaled, making clouds in the cold air. 'You've no idea how many times I've imagined this happening and never once did it come even close to feeling as great as this does now. I want to tell you I still love you. I still feel exactly the same as I did when we were little more than kids. Is that crazy?'

'Absolutely. But say it anyway.'

'Cathy Farmer...' It felt churlish to correct him with the married name she'd had for over half a century, so she didn't. 'I love you.'

'Richie Clark, I love...'

She didn't get the rest of the sentence out because she was startled by a familiar sensation. Her hand. In his pocket. Touching something square and small. That had only happened to her once before in her life.

'I kept the ring,' he said, answering her unasked question. He gently slipped his hand in next to hers, then pulled out a tiny box, fifty-five years after he'd done it last time.

He opened it and there was the same ring, a tiny silver band with a blue stone.

'I found it when I moved out of my house and into the flat in my building. It's been in my pocket ever since. I know this will sound like I'm losing the plot, but I felt that somehow it might help find you.'

'I guess it worked. Well, that and the bloody great big billboard that was outside your building last year.'

His laugh was pure joy and this time, she raised her face when he leant down to kiss her head and their lips met. Cathy wanted to freeze time and just stay in this moment for ever. Or at least, until the pneumonia threat became a reality.

His hand stroked the side of her cheek, and she didn't even care that her face had a hundred more wrinkles and creases than the last time he'd touched it.

'Do you think that, in a while, I could give you the ring again? Maybe ask you the question I had teed up last time?'

Cathy didn't even hesitate.

'Richie, I don't need to think about it, and I don't need to wait. And to be perfectly honest, did you hear the bit about us being seventy-five? Ask me again now.'

He laughed so loudly she wouldn't be surprised if some of the folks who lived around the square phoned the police to report suspicious late night noise in the park. Thankfully, his next words were softer, and only reached her ears.

'Cathy, you were the first person I ever loved and I'd like you to be the last. Will you marry me?'

Cathy moved her hand forward and the first love of her life

slipped the ring on to her finger. It felt like some kind of wonderful omen that it still fitted. Sitting on their bench, under the twinkly lights, on a chilly December night not too different from the last one, Cathy nodded.

'I will, Richie Clark. I definitely will.'

EPILOGUE

ONE YEAR LATER

Christmas Eve 2024

The fairy lights in the park were like a sea of tiny spotlights and every one of them was shining on Loretta Farmer, the seventies icon who was belting out 'Jingle Bell Rock' on a makeshift stage of six beer crates turned upside down and covered with the top half of a picnic table.

Eve was standing in the corner of the garden, watching the performance, when she felt an arm snake around the neck of her favourite red padded coat. There was no snow this year, but it was near to freezing and she'd already come close to frostbite in this park once before.

'So have we decided if they're shagging again or not yet?' Gabby's voice drawled in her ear. This was the first year her best mate had forfeited the panto season, but her filming commitments in her new role as lead detective Shelley McDonald, a half-Scottish, half-American detective on the new cop show, *Glasgow*, gave

er no time for anything else. It did, though, give her Christmas
f to spend celebrating with them here today.

Laughing, Eve followed Gabby's gaze, until it landed on her
um and her dad - her non-fake one - sitting really close together
1 a bench over by the gate.

'Almost certainly. Last weekend, I caught Harry sneaking out of
um's flat at eight o'clock in the morning. He said he was just out
r a jog and passing by, but he was wearing odd shoes and his T-
iirt was on backwards.'

Not that she needed any other evidence of Helena's new-found
ippiness. Just one glance over at her, head thrown back in laugh-
r, was all anyone needed to see. Eve had no idea where this
elena had been for the last thirty years of her life, but she was
ippy to welcome her to the gang now. Although, it would need
reful explanation that her mother was seeing her real father and
er gran on her mum's side was dating her grandad on her dad's
de. It was like one of those riddles that popped up on TikTok. Or
the occasional court case or a documentary about cults.

There had been a dozen heart-to-hearts over the last year, and
ve had seen layers of her mother that had previously been
nothered in regret and bitterness. Eve had always thought that
er mother's refusal to embrace love or happiness in any form
me from the fact that she'd never got over Bruce's betrayal, but
ie'd learned that it came from a completely different place – self-
proachment because she'd walked into a marriage knowing that
ie was doing a deal with a master manipulator but thinking that
ie could play on his terms. Turned out she couldn't, and it had
oded every shred of trust in her own judgement, so she'd simply
iut her emotions down.

Eve would never fully understand it, and she would definitely
ot choose that life for herself, but now that she knew her mother
:tter, at least she understood where it came from. And that

single-minded focus had come in handy when her mum wa working with the family law division of her company on a defenc against Bruce Quinn's potential court case to reclaim eightee years of child support.

Her old dad had been astonished that Helena had had th audacity to sleep with someone else. Which was, by all account pretty fricking rich coming from him. Her mum had kept Eve ar her gran updated with all the developments in the case durir their newly established Saturday morning brunch commitmer Although her mum still only ate muesli and drank wheatgrass.

In the end, the case had fallen through anyway, because Bru had decided that the embarrassment of being cuckolded, eve unintentionally, wasn't worth the money he would win on th deal. Besides, he was distracted because his twenty-nine-year-o wife had buggered off and left him after having a very public affa with Bruce's partner, who was also the guy whom Bruce ha trusted to draft up their utterly ineffective prenup. Bruce was no in litigation to dissolve his company, in a fight against losing 50 p cent of his assets in a cut-throat divorce in which the validity of th prenup was being challenged, and his whole world had bee thrown into turmoil. Her gran murmured, 'Karma's a bitch,' eve time his name was mentioned.

Eve had seen him once since she'd found out he wasn't h father. He'd wished her well and shook her hand as he said goo bye. Pretty much summed up their relationship. He hadn't cared the least when she'd changed her surname from Quinn to Clar although her mum, gran and her new dad and grandad had bee thrilled.

'Are you two having a private chat or can I join in?' came voice from behind them.

Eve felt a tiny bubble of joy pop in her heart at the sound of h voice. In the last year, he'd gone from being a friend, to so much more.

'It still thoroughly disgusts me that you two are a couple,' Gabby groaned. 'I just need to try really hard to never picture you having sex.'

'My sister, ladies and gentlemen,' Nick announced, with mock ceremony. 'Come dance with me under our tree,' Nick asked Eve, taking her hand and leaning down to kiss her slowly, tenderly, but oh so sexily. Gabby made vomiting sounds and pretended not to look.

'*Their tree*' was on the other side of the park, just in front of her gran's building. Nick had found her there last Christmas Day, composing a text to Sonny, to say she just wanted to be friends and nothing more. Words her gran had said had stuck in her mind. *Don't ever settle for less than a great love.* She'd known Sonny for eight years and it had never felt like that. Deep in her heart she knew it never would, so she'd let him go.

Before the text had even reached Sonny's phone, Nick had sat down next to her and begun to chat. An hour later, the sound of music had reached them from her gran's open window and before she knew what was happening, they were dancing and then she was kissing him. Since then, she'd spent her entire holiday allowance on trips to California to see him, and he'd done the same. He'd only landed the day before, so much to Gabby's disgust, there was still a whole lot of that snogging going on. Eve wasn't quite sure if he was her one great love, but she was happy to keep dancing until she knew.

Sonny hadn't had quite the same level of patience. On New Year's Day, he'd reunited with Anouska, the ballet dancer he'd been dating right before he gave Eve the ultimatum, and they'd got married in the spring. Eve had happily lost their 'benefits' and in return had gained a new friend and client in Anouska. Eve was determined to get her on the next series of *Strictly Come Dancing*.

'Dad approaching, dad approaching,' Gabby announced. 'See, this is why I'm a detective now. Acute powers of observation.'

Harry reached Eve and held out his hand. 'Thought I might come have a swirl around the dance floor with my daughter,' he said. 'But we haven't got a dance floor so that mushy bit of grass over there is the next best thing.'

Eve giggled as she took his hand and let him twirl her around before enveloping her in a bear hug that technically became a dance because they were shuffling from side to side in time to the music.

Nick may one day qualify as one of the great loves of her life, but getting to know Harry Clark had been one of the great joys of her life. He'd had a few long-term relationships, but he'd never married and he had no children, yet he'd been delighted to embrace his newfound fatherhood. They were taking it slowly, no pressure, just a weekly dinner date and calls whenever they felt like it. She wasn't sure what having a real dad was supposed to feel like, but she was loving the friendship and the affection that grew between then with every passing day.

The song had barely ended when Cathy's voice permeated the garden. 'Hello, everyone,' she chirped, to a rousing applause, led, of course, by Richie and Loretta. The three of them had been inseparable since her great-aunt had returned from Benidorm in the summer. Gran had moved up to Richie's penthouse on the top floor, one of the most beautiful apartments Eve had ever seen. Loretta was living in Gran's apartment, although Richie was currently threatening her with eviction because Loretta and his sister, Betty, had a party last weekend that ended up with three calls to the police to complain about the noise.

Cathy was beaming, as she scanned the crowd of everyone she

loved. 'My fiancé and I...' That got a rousing round of applause. 'Would just like to thank you all for coming to our Christmas party. And we just want to pay tribute to the loved ones who aren't here to celebrate, but who made us the people that we are and gave us the wonderful lives that we've had. Richie's wife, Marsha, and my husband, Duncan, will always be with us and Richie and I will always love them dearly.

'And thank you to every one of you who are standing here in this special place, freezing your bits off, because you didn't wear appropriate footwear.'

There was a loud cheer of agreement for that one, then Richie held his hand out and beckoned to her gran to share the microphone. As she handed it over, Eve knew she'd never seen Gran looking happier than she did right now.

Suddenly, a woman Eve didn't recognise appeared behind them, but instead of being surprised, her gran and grandad took a step apart and beamed at each other as the lady took the microphone and began speak.

What was this? If it was a police raid, her mother would go into full solicitor mode and she'd sue half the city authorities.

'Ladies and gentlemen, my name is Val Murray, and I'm a humanist celebrant who has been asked to come along today by this wonderful couple, who have decided to pledge their lives to each other. However, Cathy has asked me to make it quick because apparently she's seventy-six and time is ticking.'

Eve's hand went to her mouth and she gasped, as the rest of the crowd burst into laughter.

Her mum suddenly appeared at her side, looking just as surprised as Eve felt. 'Did you know about this?'

Eve shook her head. 'No. But it's marvellous. I fricking love them.'

Helena's arm came around her daughter's shoulders as she

nodded in the direction of the happy couple. 'I do too. She's bloody fabulous.'

This was all new. The hugs. The loving words. The emotion. It was little, and it was late, but Eve was open to every bit of it.

The celebrant got right to work.

'Richie Clark, do you take this woman, Cathy McLean, to be your lawfully wedded wife. To have and to hold, for richer, for poorer, in sickness and in health, and to love with all your heart and soul for as long as you both shall live?'

Her grandad took both her gran's hands in his. 'I do.'

'And do you, Cathy McLean, take Richie Clark to be your lawfully wedded husband? For richer, for poorer, in sickness and in health, and to love with all your heart and soul for as long as you both shall live?'

'I do.'

Eve watched as her gran pulled a hanky out from up her sleeve and opened it to reveal two perfect white gold bands.

'With this ring, I thee wed,' Richie whispered, as he gently pushed the smaller band on to her gran's wedding finger.

'With this ring, I thee wed,' her gran repeated, doing the same.

The celebrant kept right on track with the speed-ceremony Gran had apparently asked for.

'Then, by the powers invested in me, I now pronounce you man and wife. You may kiss.'

And they did, as everyone around them cheered.

'Ladies and gentlemen, thank you all for being here and apologies for springing this on you.' Eve decided her grandad didn't look sorry at all. He looked positively ecstatic as he went on, 'I just want to let you know there will be food back at our apartment, and music and dancing too. It's just like every other day of the week with this one.'

Eve watched as her gran feigned outrage.

'Well, I'm sev... Oh bollocks, never mind. Richie Clark, I love you. You make me want to do all those things. Thank you for making me the happiest woman on the planet today.

Grandad only had eyes for his new wife now. He leaned down, kissed her again, before replying. 'I'll try not to keep bringing it up that it took you nearly six decades to say yes. Cath, my darling, I love you. I remember a million years ago, you used to say that we could see the people we loved and lost in the stars. I never forgot that. And I just want to tell you that in every lifetime, be it this one or the next, or the one after that, you will always be the brightest one of all.'

The only things that sparkled more than the fairy lights in their special place, were the smiles of all the people who loved the newlyweds.

Her mum stepped to the side to cheer with everyone else, clearing the way for another arm to snake around Eve's shoulders. 'What do you reckon,' Nick whispered in her ear. 'Us one day?'

'I've no idea. But if I ask you, or you ask me, I just have one condition. Make it here.'

Before he could say any more, the music started again, and there was Aunt Loretta with a microphone. As the bride and groom danced, they all joined in, singing a special song about sunshine on a cloudy day.

ACKNOWLEDGMENTS

With heartfelt, huge thanks to the incredibly talented, creative, supportive team at my publishing home, Boldwood Books.

Truly one of the greatest blessings of my career.

And to you, the wonderful readers who allow me to share my stories.

I heart you all.

Love, Shari

ABOUT THE AUTHOR

Shari Low is the #1 bestselling author of over 20 novels, including *One Day With You,* and a collection of parenthood memories called *Because Mummy Said So*. She lives near Glasgow.

Sign up to Shari Low's mailing list for news, competitions and updates on future books.

Visit Shari's website: www.sharilow.com

Follow Shari on social media:

 facebook.com/sharilowbooks

twitter.com/sharilow

instagram.com/sharilowbooks

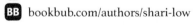 bookbub.com/authors/shari-low

ALSO BY SHARI LOW

My One Month Marriage

One Day In Summer

One Summer Sunrise

The Story of Our Secrets

One Last Day of Summer

One Day With You

One Moment in Time

One Christmas Eve

The Carly Cooper Series

What If?

What Now?

What Next?

The Hollywood Trilogy (with Ross King)

The Rise

The Catch

The Fall

Boldwood

Boldwood Books is an award-winning fiction publishing company seeking out the best stories from around the world.

Find out more at
www.boldwoodbooks.com

Join our reader community for brilliant books, competitions and offers!

Follow us
#BoldBookClub

Printed in Great Britain
by Amazon